UNDER THE MOON OF SYDNEY

MÓNICA DE LA TORRE

# UNDER THE MOON OF *Sydney*

Text copyright © 2019 by Mónica De La Torre
Translation copyright © 2021 by Emma Sheridan

Editing: Ramos de Olivo Ediciones www.ramosdeolivoediciones.com
Cover design, interior layout and formatting: Nerea Pérez Expósito
www.imagina-designs.com

All rights reserved. No part of this publication may be reproduced, distributed, or transmitted in any form or by any means, including photocopying, recording, or other electronic or mechanical methods, without the prior written permission of the publisher.

*To my family.*
*To my friends.*
*To my readers.*
*Thank you for the support you always give me.*
*You are my motivation to keep writing.*

*To the Leigh family; Jay, Mickey, Harry and Jess.*
*You are like our family in England.*
*Thanks for being there.*

# Thursday, 2nd November, 2017

Finally! After a twenty-six hours journey and two stopovers, I'm here. I'm in Sydney. I can't believe it, with all the effort and paperwork I had to do! It's not easy to come and live in Australia.

I look around, observing every corner, every detail of this new place.

I walk among people while following the signs looking for the exit.

I'm nervous and I feel a little bit scared. I have never lived far from my parents, and at this moment I feel the bewilderment of what this stage of my life is about to start.

I wait in line at the security checkpoint. I take my passport out of my rucksack and my work visa. The queue is very long. There are many counters; so many that I can't see where they end.

I take my mobile phone out of my black leather jacket pocket and look at the time. Both the current time and Spanish peninsular time appear on my mobile phone screen. There is no more than a ten hour difference.

It's still half past eleven in the morning in Madrid.

While I wait in the long queue, I take the opportunity to send a *WhatsApp* to the family group I have with my parents and siblings. I also have several messages from my friends with photos from our trips and parties, some of them with sad faces.

> *I've arrived safely. I'm in the security check queue. I'll call you when I get to the house. I love you very much.*

The answers come immediately. I try to hold back the tears, but I can't. I miss them already.

> *Daughter, I'm so glad you got there safely. Be very careful and eat well.*

My mother's words, which usually drive me crazy, now manage to bring a subtle smile to my face.

I take a picture of myself and send it to my friends.

An argument can be heard in the back of the room between a policeman and a man who is trying to get out of control. It seems that he doesn't want to show what's in his backpack.

They demand a lot of requirements to enter, and I have to sign a few documents declaring what I am carrying and what I'm not, like the rest of the passengers who want to enter Australia.

I'm on my way to the luggage pick up. There are a lot of tapes in motion. I search among the many screens to fine the tape in which mine are.

Tape number twenty-three.

There they are! They have arrived without any problem. I had been told so many things about lost luggage that I was worried I would lose them during transfers.

I carry my rucksack, my laptop on my right shoulder and a suitcase in each hand. I can't go any heavier. My whole life comes in these suitcases. Everything but him. Everything but Hugo.

I get that thought out of my head, leave the terminal and look for the taxi stand. It is close by. I get into one of the free ones.

'Good night. Eighty-five Wellington Street, please.'

'Bondi Beach NSW 2026?' he asks to confirm the address.

'Yes, thank you.'

The taxi driver starts without delay.

He is a young man, about thirty. Handsome, tall and blond, like almost all Australians. I see him looking at me through the central mirror. I pretend not to notice.

My cheeks turn red.

'You're not from around here, are you?' The taxi driver tries to make conversation with me.

'No.'

'Let me guess... from Spain, maybe? Your accent...' He's got it right.

'Yes, from Madrid. Is it that obvious?' I'm curious.

'Not too much, but I bring a lot of tourists with me every day, and I can tell the difference between accents very well.'

Of course. He seems to be an expert on the subject.

'Have you come for work or on holiday?'

'I'm here for work. I start on Monday.'

'And what do you do for a living?'

'I am a Vet. I graduated last year.' I love to boast about it. 'This last year I was doing a master's degree.'

'Ah,' he seems surprised. 'I love animals,' he adds.

I can see the city lights in the distance and some buildings in the background. It is already night. The streets are almost empty. I go down a street where you only see ground floor houses and trees on both sides decorating the landscape.

'We're getting there,' the taxi driver tells me.

I can't wait to get there and meet Carol. She is the person I contacted to rent the room. We've been talking for a month on *Skype* and she seems to be a great person. I'm sending her a *WhatsApp* to let her know I'm on my way.

> *Good night, Carol. I'm getting there.*

Her answer comes a few seconds later.

*Yes! I can't wait to see you.*

'We have arrived!' These three words come to my ears like a breath of fresh air.

'Thank you. How much is it?'

I take my wallet out of my rucksack, pay the taxi driver, who gets out of the vehicle quickly and goes to the back. He opens the boot and takes my luggage out.

'Thank you very much.'

'Thank you, Miss…' And, without letting him finish his sentence and I don't know why, I tell him my name.

'Daniela.'

'What?'

'My name is Daniela, although my friends call me Dani.'

The taxi driver hands me a card that he has taken out of his pocket. The card is white and has his name, surname, telephone number and profession printed in black capital letters.

'Here is my number in case you need it again.' He gives me a handsome smile and a wink. 'I hope you enjoy your stay in Sydney. I hope to see you again.'

'Thank you very much. I will try to do so.'

'Oh, by the way; if you need a tour guide, you can call me. I will be happy to show you the most beautiful places in this city.' He smiles at me again.

I stand there not knowing what to say. I just say yes by nodding my head, smiling uncomfortably, arching my eyebrow and waving goodbye slightly.

Charlie, that's the name of the kind and seductive taxi driver, disappears with his taxi into the darkness of the street. I'm not sure what he meant by being a tour guide. Interpreting words is not my thing.

'DANIELA! DANIELA! DANIELA!'

I can hear someone shouting my name. I take a small leap of faith. I turn and... There she is. That's her.

Carol comes to me running through the garden. She's tall, taller than she looked in the pictures. With blonde hair that goes well below her shoulders and she's thin. She's wearing a short sleeved pyjama and pink shorts with hearts.

A somewhat mocking smile comes out of her without meaning to.

We give each other a hug as if we knew each other forever. As if we were two sisters who hadn't seen for a long time. That's how it will be the day I see my family again, I guess. I don't think I'll see them for quite some time.

'How I wanted to meet you!' she says to me with a huge smile.

'Me too.' I answer.

'Let me help you with the luggage.' And without giving me time to answer, she already has one of my bags in her hand and is going straight to the house.

Wow! The house is better than I expected. The photos don't do it justice. The living room is very spacious. It has a very large chaise longue and two individual armchairs upholstered in chocolate colour. The dining table is made of glass, with six bone colour leather chairs around it. The American style kitchen is on the left, with white furniture. The floor is made of wood, in a dark tone, and it shines with the halogen lights.

'Come this way. I will show you your room. You must be very tired.'

'A little bit, yes.'

We go into a corridor between the kitchen and the living room. Carol turns on the light. There are four doors. The corridor has cream coloured walls and some very modern paintings.

'This is my room,' she says, pointing to the first door on the left, 'and this is the bathroom,' she goes on, opening the door just after her room.

She opens the first door on the right, just in front of her bedroom. That's my door. It is wide. The furniture is in white. The built in wardrobe has two sliding doors with two mirrors covering the entire length and width of it. The bed is double. It has a large window.

I can't stop smiling. I am happy. I like everything I've seen so far and Carol is very friendly.

'You can see the garden from the window. Tomorrow you will be able to enjoy it.'

'The house is very nice and my room looks nicer than in the photos.'

'Thank you' she replies flattered by my comments.

I smile.

'This is Luca's room,' she says as she points to the door which is next to mine. 'He's not here today; he'll be back on Monday.'

'Oh.'

'Well, I'll let you get settled. If you need anything, I'll be in the living room.' She closes the door, and I hear her walk away from the room.

I throw myself on the bed. I think about him. About Hugo. Again. And the smile on my face suddenly vanishes. I try to get him out of my mind, but he's tied to my thoughts like a koala to its own eucalyptus tree.

This is more difficult than it seems. Even the thousands of miles that separate us don't make it anymore bearable.

While trying to suppress that thought I take out a pair of pyjamas and a toilet bag from one of my suitcases. Luckily I had already left everything at hand. I like to keep everything tidy.

I'm going to the bathroom to take a shower. I'm sweating. It's too hot. Summer is coming here, while in Spain winter is coming. It's going to be the first time I've had a hot Christmas. It's strange.

*Family, I have arrived safely. Now I have a low battery in my mobile phone and I'm very tired. I'll call you tomorrow. I love you.*

> *Okay, sis. I'm glad that you'll get there fine. Kisses.*

I leave my mobile phone charging on the bedside table and go into the living room.

Carol is in the chaise longue with her laptop on her legs. She's wearing glasses. She looks very focused on whatever she's doing.

'Good evening' I say almost whispering. I don't want to disturb.

'Night, Daniela. Sit down and tell me how did everything go?'

'Well, I left Madrid yesterday at half past nine in the morning. I made a stopover in Barcelona. I stayed there for an hour and a half and then left for Hong Kong. A twelve hour flight.'

Carol is amazed.

'My goodness!' She exclaims.

I nod my head and continue my tour.

'At Hong Kong airport I had to wait a little more than one and a half hour, and then nine more hours by plane until I arrived in Sydney. Altogether about twenty-five and a half hours of travel. I don't believe it myself.' I sigh.

'Well, it has been a long journey. I don't know how you are here and not sleeping.'

'I slept a little during the flights. Besides, with the time change it's difficult. It's still midday in Spain.'

'Right! It's ten hours less there. I remember because it was very difficult when we were trying to get in touch to talk on *Skype*.'

'You have a good memory' I tell her. It makes us laugh.

'I'm going to try to sleep. I have to go to the clinic tomorrow to sign some documents because I start on Monday.'

'Aren't you hungry? I have prepared something, in case you arrived hungry.'

'No, thanks. I'm not.'

'There's everything in the kitchen. Take what you need without any problem. The other guy and I are used to sharing what we buy. I hope you don't mind.'

'Not at all. It makes me feel at home.'

'I'm glad to know that your first impression is good. I hope it's always like that. Luca and I spend very little time at home.'

'I hope to spend little time too, but due to work. I'm a bit nervous about meeting my future boss.'

'You'll see that everything is going to be fine with you.'

Carol's words fill me with energy and strength to face tomorrow. So far I've done well with my English. The classes at the university have been very useful and, above all, the certificate, which has helped me a lot when it comes to sending out CVs.

'I'm going to sleep too,' says Carol as she turns off her laptop and gets up from the sofa. 'I have a hard day's work ahead of me tomorrow. I'll leave you a copy of the keys on the kitchen counter. I'll be here around four o'clock in the afternoon.'

I get into bed and fall asleep faster than I expected. And he comes back to my mind. I close my eyes tightly, hoping that he will disappear, but it's impossible. I feel as if he was here, next to me.

His face...

His hair...

His smell...

## Friday, 3rd November, 2017

Where am I? I wake up startled. This is not my room. Oh, yes! I'm at Carol's house in Sydney. I look at the clock. It's seventeen past ten in the morning.

I get up; open the curtains and the windows. The sun comes in brightly. It's already hot. It smells of summer and of the sea. The back garden looks very nice. The grass is a deep green colour and there are two trees in the background. It's a big garden.

I have to sort the clothes from the suitcases in the wardrobe. I start doing do. I feel like talking to my mother, but it's still one o'clock in the morning there. I need her. I leave all the clothes in place and put the suitcases at the bottom of the wardrobe. I go to take a shower.

It is very hot now.

I look for a pair of jeans, a white sleeveless shirt and some black ballerina style shoes. I want to impress my new boss. I usually go with leggings and T-shirts, but the occasion deserves to be a little more dressed up than usual.

I do my hair. I always wake up with my hair very dishevelled. It only obeys me when I mould it with the irons. I finish and go to the kitchen. I open the fridge looking for something to eat for breakfast. Milk, fine. A good glass of milk with some toast will do me good. Now I'm starving.

I turn on the TV in the living room. I like to feel that I am accompanied by the noise it makes. I finish my breakfast and leave everything washed and tidy.

I go to my room. I take a bag, the black one, and I put the wallet, the passport, the visa, the mobile phone and the headphones. I close the window. I put on my black leather jacket and the bag on my right shoulder. I go out and close the door with a gentle knock.

Oh! Shit! I've got the keys left inside. What now? I arch an eyebrow and move my head from side to side. It's always the same for me. I snort. I try to think of a solution. Arg! I'm a mess with the keys. If I remember correctly, Carol said she'd be here around four in the afternoon. Well, no problem... I'll just have to wait for her to get here.

I put the address of the Vet clinic on my *Samsung*'s GPS and start walking. I turn right on the corner of the street and walk up O'Brien Street. The GPS indicates thirty minutes on this route.

I look for the headphones and connect them to my mobile.

A *bachata* begins to sound, *El malo*. I think about changing it for a second. It reminds me of Hugo. This song feels as if it was made with him in mind. He is in my thoughts again. It can't be. I don't want to think about him, but my subconscious betrays me.

I walk through the strange streets of Sydney that the GPS indicates to me.

Without realising it I find myself in front of the veterinary clinic. My legs are shaking. The clinic is a big two floors house made of brown bricks. The window frames are made of white PVC. A few steps separate me from the main door.

I take a deep breath and start climbing the steps one by one with a determined walk. The automatic doors open by themselves when they detect my presence. I go to the reception. The girl on the other side of the counter stands up to receive me. She has brown hair, she's about my height and she's a few pounds overweight. She has a wide smile. She seems very friendly.

'Good morning. What can I do for you?' says the friendly receptionist.

'Good morning. My name is Daniela Duarte. I start working here on Monday. I have an appointment with Mr. Darel Williams.'

'Very good, Miss Duarte. My name is Kayla Robinson. Wait for me to check my calendar. Yes!' she states. 'You have an appointment at a quarter to one. Mr. Williams will be with you shortly. You can take a seat' she says very politely while she shows me the seats to the right of the counter.

All the furniture is new. The reception desk is made of white lacquered wood and it has glass shelves in the middle with some products for animals, and with the clinic's name in bright green.

The floor is made of dark grey stoneware and the walls are white. The stairs that go up to the first floor are made of wood. There is a long corridor. "Enquiries", indicates a sign suspended with some threads from the ceiling.

From the office in front of me, a tall man with curly blond hair in his forties is coming out. He is wearing a black suit and a white shirt. He is coming towards me. My pulse and breathing are racing. I can't deny that I'm nervous.

'Good morning, Miss Duarte. I'm Darel Williams, director of this clinic.'

I knew that because we have exchanged several emails. I'm jumping to my feet. He extends his hand to me and I hurry to extend mine. He gives me a very confident and firm handshake.

'Good morning,' I answer almost without knowing what else to say. I am impressed. I didn't imagine him to be so handsome. His dark blue eyes are very intense and they stare at me.

'How was your trip? I seem to remember you arriving yesterday.'

'Yes, I arrived last night. Now I'm better, although I was exhausted when I got here.'

'If you like, I will show you all the facilities and then we'll sign the contract.'

'Perfect for me.' I nod my head.

We go into the corridor.

'This is a waiting room.'

He points to the first door near the reception. There are two people, one of them with a golden retriever, and the other one with a mongrel.

'These are the consultation rooms. They are listed. There are four, but I can't show them to you now because they are busy.'

'I understand.'

He continues with his walk as if he was a professional tourist guide. The taxi driver from yesterday comes to my mind, offering to be my tour guide.

'Here we have an operating room' he says opening the door that is there at the end of the corridor.

'Everything is new!' I say impressed.

'Yes, Miss Duarte. We've renovated everything in the past year. Come this way and I'll show you the first floor.' He makes a hand gesture for me to go in first. We go up a narrow staircase on the left side of the operating room door, where there is also a lift. 'Here we have a postoperative room and also a small room to rest when we are on duty.'

There is a full kitchen, a large sofa and even a television. All the walls and the floor are decorated the same style as on the ground floor.

We go down other different stairs; they are also made of wood. When we arrive downstairs I realise that they are the same stairs that were next to the reception. We go to his office. It is quite simple. A glass desk, a computer and some pictures on the wall with the university diploma and some more pictures.

He takes out some documents from a file.

'This is the contract. It is for one year, renewable. You will be on probation for one month. Do you agree?'

If I remember correctly, we had already discussed it in the emails.

Wow! My eyes open wide when I see the salary. Eight hundred and eighty dollars net a week. Now that's more than I expected. I do a mental calculation in a hurry. I can't believe it! About three thousand and eight hundred dollars a month.

Darel looks at me in bewilderment; his head is tilted trying to guess what my face says.

'Does it not seem much to you?' *How can he ask me that? But can it be more? Maybe he's pulling my leg. I'm in denial. I don't think he's joking.* I hear myself and I think I'm listening to an ignorant person who doesn't know what a vet can or cannot earn in this country and I really don't know. 'Are you feeling fine?'

I come out of my astonishment and manage to speak.

'Yes, no... Sorry. It's just... I was a bit confused about the salary.'

'Yes, I know. It's the basic salary in this profession, but... you know, you're just starting out. You have no previous experience...'

'Not at all! It's more than fine. My salary in Spain would be half that.' I leave him with his mouth open with what I just said.

'So, Miss Duarte, do you agree with the terms of the contract?'

I nod with my head and sign before Mr. Williams changes his mind. We shake hands in compliance.

'Thank you very much for this opportunity, Mr. Williams. I am very pleased.'

'Well, say no more. I look forward to seeing you on Monday at eight o'clock in the morning.'

We get up from the chairs and he follows me to the entrance. The automatic doors open and I say goodbye to Mr. Williams and Kayla.

I look at the clock on my mobile. It is a quarter to two. I think about what I can do until Carol arrives. Can I go to the beach? If I remember correctly, it's very close to home. I check the GPS. Thirty-eight minutes. It's not the same route as before.

I'm happy and I love the clinic. I hope there will be exotic animals to treat. I feel like seeing a koala or a kangaroo, although I think it will be impossible. I can't imagine a man arriving with a koala on a leash... I get a laugh out of it.

I go down Bondi Road. It's a two way street with two lanes in each direction, but there are cars parked on each side occupying the lanes closest to the pavement and that hinders the traffic. There are a few buildings, but most are two floors houses and many shops.

I like this city. *Pablo Alborán* and some of his songs resonate in my ears: *Solo tú*. I can't help but be sad and remember Hugo again. Damn you! Why have you gotten so deep inside me? Why don't you leave now? *'He's not leaving'*, my subconscious warns me. "Yes!" I answer and stick out my tongue. It annoys me that it's always right.

I can see the beach in the distance. It smells of the sea. This smell gives me life. In Madrid there are only buildings, traffic jams, noise and pollution, but my family is there and I need them. It's the first time I've shared a flat with someone who's not part of my family. I had once sporadically stayed at a friend's house, but it wasn't usual. The funny thing is that I never slept at Hugo's house. At first I didn't understand why. When I found out everything I just wanted to die. The humiliation was so overwhelming that I spent a month without going out or meeting my friends. My family even thought of sending me to a psychologist.

I take walks on the beach trying to kill some time until four o'clock, when Carol arrives home. There are people windsurfing, others surfing, and then there are people just sunbathing or walking around.

There are shops and many terraces full of people eating in the Bondi Pavilion. That makes my stomach ache, and that's because it's time to eat. It's almost three o'clock. While I'm eating, I take out a notebook from my bag, write down some things I have to buy and take the opportunity to send a *WhatsApp* message to my family group.

> *Hello, family. It's three o'clock here. I'm eating, and look at the view. I already signed the employment contract.*

I send the message together with a smiling emoticon, an attached photo of the beach and a big eyed emoticon as well. I have no answer. Of course, it's still five in the morning. I don't know anymore if my mother or my sister were on duty at the hospital or not. I am totally disoriented.

I'm carrying two bags from the supermarket. I needed to buy some things. I knock on the door, but nobody opens it. Carol is still not here. I look at my watch. It's ten past four. So I wait.

I sit down on the kerb of the door and take the opportunity to review my work contract. I smile when I look at the salary. It's clear that not everything in life is going to be bad and that everything has its reward and this is mine.

'What are you doing here?'

I raise my head. Carol is in front of me. She is wearing a grey skirt suit and a white shirt. She has a briefcase in her left hand and the house keys in her right one.

'I've forgotten the keys inside.' I'm shaking my head and lowering my eyebrows.

'It's not the first time this has happened to you, is it?' she says, smiling.

Does it show that much? I'm sure it does. It's the same face I always make when I forget and have to wait in the doorway of my parents' house. Unmistakable.

I place my shopping bag on the tray of the fridge and on the furniture that belongs to me. Carol is in her room. I don't know who she's talking to, but I can hear her screaming from the kitchen. She seems very angry.

'No! That's not so. I need those documents now. You told me that yesterday. What? Are you crazy? Mind the consequences. We'll talk about it.'

She's coming to the kitchen. Her face reflects frustration and anger, especially anger. She doesn't say anything. She just makes a sandwich and goes back to her room. I prefer not to ask, I don't want her to yell at me. She's scary.

I'm in the shower. The water is running warmly down my back. It relaxes me. I think of Carol and the words she said on the phone: *"Mind the consequences"*. What will it be all about? My curiosity kills me. I'm not going to ask, though. I rule out that idea. I'm in denial. I sigh. My goodness, how bad it is!

As I have time, I take advantage and dry my hair with the dryer and straighten it with the irons. It was already curling and it was very sweaty due to the heat.

I go to the living room and turn on the TV. I don't know what channel to put on and I zap until I find a channel where the series Friends is being broadcast. Great memories!

'I'm sorry.'

'What?'

Carol is leaning on the corner of the wall in the corridor. She's wearing the same pyjamas as yesterday and her hair is wet.

'The screams from before. I didn't mean to scare you.'

'Don't worry.'

'I'm on a complicated case and my assistant isn't up to it and it's getting on my nerves.'

She explains to me as if she had a reason to do so. She's at home and can scream whenever she wants. I think.

'How has your future new job been going?'

'Very well. I have already signed the contract. I start on Monday at eight.'

'I'm very happy for you. After all we've talked about during this time and what you've told me, you deserve it. We should celebrate.'

I agree with that completely.

'Of course. Besides, I'm looking forward to getting to know this city a little better.'

'That's done. Shall we go out to dinner and then dance?'

I like the plan. They are the plans I like the most.

'What do you want for dinner? We can go to an Italian I know that's really great.'

'Perfect for me. I like Italian food.'

Carol is calling. She's reserving a table for three. *Three? Carol, me and...* I raise an eyebrow. I count on my fingers. I can't figure it out. One plus one, three? Who else? I'm curious and I don't hesitate to ask.

'You've booked for three. You, me and...' I raise my shoulders.

'And my assistant.'

'Huh? Wasn't he the one you argued with before?'

'I'll tell you about it.' She winks at me and walks down the aisle laughing.

Now I really don't understand anything. A while ago she was shouting at him and now it turns out that the three of us are going to have dinner. I pass my hand over my forehead.

My phone vibrates.

> *Hi, sis. How are you? I just saw your message. Can we talk?*

Yes, of course! And before I finish reading my older sister's message, I'm already making a video call to her. I'm looking forward to seeing her.

'Little sister!' shouts Amelia from the other side of the phone.

'How are you?'

'I'm fine.'

'How's the house? Is it OK?'

'Yes. The house's very nice and my room is very big.'

'So, tell me. How are the conditions of the contract? You've made me very jealous of the views in the photo.'

'Of course,' I'm laughing. 'The contract, good.'

'And the salary?'

'About eight hundred and eighty dollars a week.'

'Wow! That's very good. Ask how much the nurses earn and I'll go with you,' she laughs, joking. Amelia is very happy with her work at the hospital.

'It's about two thousand four hundred and fifty euros a month, but it's already twice as much as I would earn working there.'

'That's for sure.'

'Working today?'

'Yes, I have an afternoon shift.'

'And mum?'

'No, mummy has the day off today.'
'You'll have to send me your work schedule. I'm very disoriented.'
'And you?'
'I start Monday at eight.'
'Nervous?' She knows me.
'Very much. Well... a lot, more like, but my future boss, he's been great, he's very nice. He showed me around the clinic.'
'So?'
'So what?'
'What's he like?'
'What a gossiper you are!' I make faces at her. 'Just normal.'
'Normal? Come on.'
'Okay. He's quite handsome, tall, with curly blonde hair. He's about forty five years old, I reckon.'
'Do you like him?'
I get angry. How can she ask me that?
'Are you crazy? No, I don't! He's got at least twenty years on me.'
'Okay. I'm sorry. It was just a question.'
'And how are Dad, mum and our little brother?' I ask.
'Good. Mum was very sad. You know how she is. Dad, you know he doesn't show his feelings and Jonny then...' Amelia sighs. My brother is in a difficult stage. 'He only thinks about video games and girls' she continues.

We laugh at the same time. We can't help it.
'Well, Amelia. I have to leave you. I'm going out to dinner and then to dance.'
'With whom?'
'With Carol, the owner of the house. She invited me.'
'Have fun!' She gives me a look with her eyes half open as if trying to warn me of something. I don't even listen to her and hang up.

I go to the bedroom and open the wardrobe looking for what to wear tonight. *This one is fine.* I take out a black tight short dress with very thin straps. It's one of my favourites. I take a pair of matching low heels.

I see myself looking at myself in the mirror in the wardrobe. I turn over and over to check that it fits. I love this dress. It doesn't look bad on me.

I plug in the hair iron and make some curls, not too marked. I have brown hair. I decided some time ago to stop dyeing it. It's too long; it's already up to my elbows.

'Are you ready?' Carol asks me from the door.

'Yes.'

'Well, let's go.'

'Let's go.'

Carol wears a silver dress that makes her an enviable shape, and very high heels. It makes me dizzy just to see her. It seems that she is going to fall with the first step she takes.

I feel like a little girl with a new toy. I feel like going out, enjoying myself, dancing and, above all, forgetting about him. It's always him.

My subconscious always betrays me. I deny with my head. *"Out,"* I shout into my mind to get him out.


We go down Ocean Street. Carol drives fast, but very safely. Far away you can see that she's a very confident woman. I wish I could feel like her, feel no doubts and go through life with my head held high.

We arrive at Pitt Street.

'The restaurant is on this street,' she says.

Carol manages to park on the first street. The restaurant is just a few steps away.

It looks like an expensive place. It has a big window in the entrance that lets you see inside. It's full. Now I understand why it was necessary to book a table.

We go in.

I look around. It smells so good that I have an immediate appetite. I look up where there is a half floor full of people. There is a lot of noise and Italian music is playing in the background. The kitchen is in sight, all made of steel. I see at least five cooks working in a hurry to get the dishes out on time and the waiters seem to be flying around the room.

One of the waiters accompanies us to our table.

There are some red upholstered sofas along the walls with tables for four diners, and there is another row of tables in the centre of the restaurant, also with four chairs. A round lamp hangs above each table. The walls are decorated with paintings from different places in Italy. They are beautiful.

Carol looks at the phone and turns it off. She knocks on the table and makes me jump.

'What happens?' I regret asking at once. I don't know how she'll answer me.

'My assistant just told me that he's not coming.'

'Ah! I don't know what to say.'

'It's not the first time that my assistant has done so. We'll talk about it on Monday.'

I'm trying to make her feel better by changing the subject. I think Monday is going to be a difficult day for that assistant. I don't know what they're about. Will it be just her assistant or will there be something else between them? I try to decipher her gaze and I think there is something more between them.

'Well, I think we'd better forget about this incident and take a look at the menu. I'm hungry.'

'Yes, that'll be better.' She is angry and doesn't hide it.

I open the menu. There is plenty of variety. I need a few minutes to decide.

'Good night. I'll be your waiter tonight. Do you know what you're having, ladies?'

The waiter is very young, maybe he is a student who works the weekends to earn some extra money. He stares at Carol with gawkiness.

'Yes,' I answer. 'Spring ravioli for me and to drink…' I think for a moment, I have doubts.

'A *rosé* wine,' Carol suddenly says.

I nod my head. I agree.

'And a seafood *risotto* for me. Thank you very much,' she adds.

We give the menus to the waiter, who leaves immediately for the kitchen.

The food is exquisite and the wine has gone to my head a little. We laugh, remembering our long *Skype* chats when we talked about our things.

Carol already has another face. She seems to have forgotten about what happened earlier.

'Would the ladies like some dessert?'

The waiter is standing in front of us and is keeping an eye on Carol, who is still ignoring him. He recites all the available desserts and I go for the *tiramisú* while Carol decides on the cheese and vanilla cake.

'What do you say we pay and go for a drink?'

'Yes. I'm looking forward to seeing what the atmosphere is like here.'

Carol waves to the waiter, who comes immediately.

'Can you bring us the bill, please?'

The waiter flies off to the bar where the cash register is and another waiter hands him a bill on a plate.

'I'm paying,' says Carol.

I don't have time to say no.

We leave the restaurant. Carol mentions that there is a restaurant very close by, in the back street, and we walk towards our next destination.

We arrive in just four minutes. At the door of the place there are two security guards and a locker where people are queuing to get in. You have to pay an entrance fee. This time I'm quicker and I pay for both tickets.

The premises have four floors. We go through each and every one of them. Different types of music are played on each floor. The place is full and we find it hard to move around in the crowd.

We arrive at the rooftop where there is a huge swimming pool. There are people bathing. We approach the bar and Carol orders two cocktails.

'You have to try this cocktail, Daniela. It's really good.' I take a sip. It tastes like pineapple and rum. I haven't tried it before.

'What is it?' I ask Carol curiously.

'It's called Australian Virgin. It has rum, white wine, pineapple juice and beer syrup. It is shaken with ice and served through a strainer.'

Carol seems to be an expert at this cocktail thing.

# Saturday, 4th November, 2017

It's after four o'clock in the morning. Time has passed without us noticing.

We dance all night and drink; we drink a lot. More than we can count. Guys come over and invite us for drinks. Carol can't say no. She has lost control and dances among men around her. I watch her sitting on a sofa. My feet hurt. Carol is rampant, I have to get her out of here or she will end up in an alcoholic coma.

I get up and go straight to where Carol is pushing past among the people.

'Carol, let's go. Please,' I say, as I grab her arm and pull her towards me.

'I don't want to go. I'm having a great time.'

That is obvious. She doesn't stop wiggling among the boys.

'You're not well. You can hardly stand up. Let's take a break.'

'No. I want to stay a little longer. Dance with me.'

She holds my hands and tries to make me dance with her. She no longer vocalizes well and I don't understand half of what she says.

'Please, Carol. Let's go now' I insist.

'No' She pushes me away and goes to dance with a man who's been looking at her and gesturing at her all night.

I sit on the sofa again. A man approaches me to invite me to dance. I answer him with a refusal. My purpose now is to convince Carol to let me take her home and sleep. I stare at her with my mouth open. She doesn't look like the same girl I knew. You can tell that her assistant's stood up has affected her. She doesn't stop drinking. One drink after another. The guys don't stop rubbing themselves in her and Carol does nothing about it. I'm ashamed of her.

I get up and go to her, this time determined to get her out of here, and I don't take no for an answer.

After much insistence and begging, she finally accepts.

'It's okay. As you wish' she agrees.

Good! Al last she has come to her senses. She says goodbye to the men by throwing kisses at them. They look as if they can't take a girl to their bed tonight. Some other time! Not tonight, gentlemen. If we can call them gentlemen. I doubt it.

We come out in the crowd almost in a hurry. There are a lot of people and most of them are out of control.

'Carol, give me the car keys. You're not well and you can't drive.'

'I can. I'm all right,' she babbles.

'You?' I say almost yelling. 'If you don't give me the keys, I'll take a taxi.' I threaten her without success. And I remember that I have the card of the taxi driver who brought me from the airport in my wallet.

Carol doesn't listen to me and gets into the car. In the driver's seat.

'Very good. Do whatever you want. I won't get in with you.'

I take the card and the mobile out of my bag and call the taxi driver, who answers after the first ring. I ask him if he can come and he accepts immediately. He says he'll be right away.

Carol drives away and I stay waiting for the taxi that doesn't take a long time to arrive.

'Good night, Miss.'

The taxi driver gets out of the car and opens the back door for me.

'Good night. Thanks for coming.'

I'm worried about Carol.

'The same address from the other day?' he asks.

'Yes, please.'

The taxi driver starts the car. He looks at me several times through the central mirror. He notices my concern.

'Why was a beautiful girl like you so alone at this hour?'

'I wasn't alone. Actually, I was with a friend, but she left in her car and I didn't want to go with her.'

'Why? If it's not too much to ask.'

'She drank a lot and, despite asking her for the keys so that she wouldn't drive, she didn't listen to me and left.'

'Oh!'

'I hope she arrived safely.'

It took us a little over ten minutes to get there. There was no traffic on the road. The taxi driver gets out and opens the door for me.

'Thank you very much. How much is it?' I ask.

'Nothing, Miss. This trip is on me.'

'I can't accept that' I say it while I take the money out of my purse.

'No, I won't accept it.'

'Well, then, please, call me by my name and don't treat me so politely.'

'All right, Daniela. As you wish.' He throws me an intoxicating smile. 'Same to you. By the way, my name in Charlie.'

'I know. It's on the card you gave me.' I blink faster than usual showing my charms.

Charlie says goodbye to me with a wink and a big smile. He's cute!

I look on both sides of the street, but I can't see Carol's car. Has she arrived? Maybe it's parked on another street. Has something happened to her? I'm worried. I put the key in the door and I go in the house. I go to Carol's room, knock on the door, but nobody answers.

I walk in.

I need to make sure she's OK. She's not there. Where could she be? I call her. She doesn't answer either. I choose to leave her a

*WhatsApp* message hoping that she reads it and the two ticks turn blue. Nothing. Where is she? It was very unwise of her to take the car in her condition. I should've stopped her from taking the car.

I'm moving around in bed, from one side to the other. I can't sleep. Carol is not here and her absence increases my concern. I look at my mobile hoping that she has seen my messages. I am saddened to see that those I have sent haven't turned blue.

I end up surrendering to so much thinking and worrying, and I fall asleep.

I wake up because the sun is burning my face through the window. I forgot to close the curtains. I don't know what time it is.

I look at the clock. It's two in the afternoon.

I also look at the *WhatsApp* I sent Carol. It's still the same. She hasn't seen it. I have to know if she got here safely. I get up and go straight to her room. I try and knock on the door. I go in. It's still empty. The bed is the same as yesterday. She didn't spend the night here. Where did she sleep? Will she be all right?

Her room is the largest. She has her own bathroom and the furniture is similar to those in my room.

It has a light pink wall and the rest is white. It is very tidy. Like the rest of the house.

'*Buongiorno, signorina*!'

What a scare! I let out a scream. I turn my head at full speed. A young boy, about twenty years old, is standing on the threshold of the door. He's tall and dark. He has huge green eyes, and black wavy hair. He is wearing black and white short pyjama.

'You scared me,' I say still with my hand on my heart.

'Sorry for scaring you. I didn't mean to do so. My name is Luca.' He extends his arm to me, and I respond to his action yet with my heart in my throat.

'Carol told me that you would arrive on Monday.'

'Yes... Well...'

He doesn't seem to want to talk about it. I change the subject radically.

'Well, yesterday, Carol and I went out. She passed on the drinks. I asked her for the car keys and she refused. I didn't want to come with her and I called a taxi. When I arrived, I thought she would be here, but nothing. I called her, sent her a *WhatsApp* message and she didn't answer, she didn't even see it. I thought she would be here by now...' I let out a sigh.

'Don't worry. It's not the first time she's done it. She might be at David's house,' he says casually. He knows her better than I do.

'David?'

'Yes. He's her assistant.'

'Ah!' Carol didn't mention the name.

'By the way, you can speak to me in Spanish. I speak and understand it perfectly.'

'Ah. Well, good for me. So much talking in English has got my brain all over the place.'

'Well, I'll be in my room. Don't hesitate to come if you need anything.'

I nod my head and, although Luca is very calm, I can't stop worrying about where Carol might be.

I go to my room, take a clean change of clothes, a striped shirt and some short leggings and go to the bathroom. The shower feels more than good. The water is fresh.

It is warm.

I leave my hair wet, I don't feel like using the hairdryer. I leave the bathroom, already dressed and go to the kitchen. I'm hungry. I prepare myself something to eat.

I hear the door. Carol arrives with a guilty look on her face. I run to her.

'Where were you? I was so worried about you.'

I sound just like my mother. She used to say the same thing to me when I was late.

She comes in barefoot. She brings her shoes in one hand and her jacket in her arm. She carries her bag hanging down the other arm, and the house keys in her hand. She looks like she hasn't slept all night.

'I'm sorry. I was very unconscious. I'll talk to you later. I have a terrible headache.'

She leaves me with the doubt and goes to her room.

I go to the living room with my plate of food, turn on the TV and sit down to eat. At least my worries is gone. Luca sits next to me with his plate.

'I had a fight with my boyfriend' he tells me.

His confession takes me by surprise. I drop my fork on the floor. Boyfriend? Do my ears betray me? I swallow. Carol could've told me that our housemate was gay so I wouldn't have this stupid look on my face. Luca is going to think I'm stupid or something.

'Huh?' The expression on my face suddenly changes. I arch an eyebrow.

'We were spending a week's holiday getting to know Australia and I saw a message from his ex-boyfriend on his mobile phone.'

'But that's nothing serious. It doesn't mean anything.' I try to sound normal.

'The messages weren't a simple "Hello" or "How are you?" They were hot messages. I gave him a chance to explain, but he simply nodded his head and the only phrase that came out of his mouth in a whisper was "I'm sorry".'

Luca is unable to hold back and breaks down in tears. A fragile child stands before me and all he needs is a hug.

All I do is hug him and repeat that everything will be fine. I'm grateful that he's trusted me to tell me his problems without even knowing me.

'*Grazie,*' he says with tears in his eyes.

'You're welcome. You don't know how well I understand you.'

'When did you get here?' he asks, changing the subject.

'Two days ago.'

'I guess you're still on a different schedule. It happened to me.'

'It was like that yesterday. Today I'm better already.'

We end up talking about how his trip went and I explain to him how mine went. They were practically the same.

Carol appears in the middle of the afternoon. She looks like a zombie. She is wearing pink pyjamas and white slippers. She goes to the kitchen. She prepares a sandwich. Luca and I look at her, waiting for her to say something. A "hello" would be nice. Nothing. She doesn't say or make a sound. She just makes the sandwich, puts it on a plate and disappears down the corridor. Luca and I look at each other and burst out laughing.

'Do you feel like going out tonight?' Luca says to me out of the blue. Wasn't it that he was that bad after what his boyfriend did to him?

'Yes,' I accept immediately. 'I just hope you don't do the same as Carol,' I warn him. 'I wouldn't want to go through the same thing twice.'

He nods his head and smiles maliciously.

'You'll see how much fun we'll have. Do you like Latin music?'

That sounds like blessed glory to me. My brain is already remembering the dance steps I learned six years ago. The night is promising.

'Yes, I love it.'

'Then I'm going to take you to a place that will blow your mind.'

He proposes me to order something for dinner.

'We can order some pizzas,' he says.

'Yes. I like pizza.'

Luca looks for his mobile in his room and enters a restaurant search application. He looks at one near his home that has pizzas and does the shopping.

'I'll pay,' I say, taking my card.

'You're late, honey. I have my card details saved and I've already paid.'

He looks at me with an "I have beaten you" face.

I have no choice but to resign myself to the speed of my favourite Italian.

The delivery man isn't long in coming. The pizza smells wonderful.

Luca sits at the kitchen bar and cuts the pizza into pieces while I set the table with two small plates, napkins and glasses. I take a bottle of *Coke* I bought days ago from the fridge and serve it.

We eat.

Carol is still locked in her room and doesn't show any signs of life. Luca and I are getting ready for the night ahead. He has dressed up very handsome. He's wearing worn out jeans and a tight black T-shirt that fits him very well.

'*Sei bellissima.*'

'Liar,' I tell him with half a smile.

'It's true, that dress looks great on you.'

I've chosen a short dress in navy blue, with an asymmetric neckline with only one strap on the left shoulder.

'You look very handsome too' I say with sincerity.

Luca doesn't have a car. I remember Charlie and I call him.

He answers right away.

He'll be here in ten minutes. Before I go I want to stop by Carol's room. I want to know if she's OK.

I knock on her door.

'May I?' I ask cautiously.

'Come in.'

'Are you all right? Do you need anything?'

'No. Thank you. I want to rest.'

Carol is lying on the bed typing on her laptop. The room is a mess. Nothing like the way I saw her this morning.

'Luca asked me out. You in?'

'No. I have a headache. Have a good time.'

I leave the room and close the door again. Luca is waiting for me impatiently at the entrance door.

'Come on! The taxi is already here.'

Charlie is standing on a black car. It's not the taxi. He's wearing a pair of worn out jeans, a pair of *Nike* shoes and a white linen shirt.

'What about this car?' I ask with surprise.

'I'm not working today.'

'But…'

'Yes, I know what you're going to tell me. I just couldn't say no to you.'

He looks into my eyes and his go dark. It makes me blush. I change the subject. I've been very good at it lately.

'This is Luca. He lives with me.'

'Nice to meet you.' Charlie gives Luca a handshake and he stares at him.

It seems that Luca hasn't been indifferent to the taxi driver. *Don't go that way! I think you're wrong.*

Charlie opens the copilot's door for me to sit down. The seat is very comfortable. Luca sits behind me and shows the direction to the handsome taxi driver, who starts right away.

'Have you lived here long?' Charlie asks Luca.

'I arrived in September. I'm doing a master's degree.'

'Oh.'

'Are you from here?' Luca is curious.

'Yes. I was born and raised here. Although I feel like travelling, but I've never been able to or had the time.'

'Whenever you want, you can come to Italy with me.'

Luca is clearly hitting on Charlie. I think he's making a mistake. I don't think Charlie is interested in that kind of relationship. The tension can be cut with a knife. I have to think about what to do or say to change the subject.

I look back. Luca is staring at his mobile phone.

'Is it far from here?' I interrupt Luca.

'No. We're getting there.'

'I hope we have a parking space nearby because there's usually not much room in the area where the club is,' explains Charlie.

It's almost midnight. Charlie goes through several streets in search of a parking space. First he goes down one, then another. He can't find any available spot. We go through the same streets again. Luca suggests a street where there is usually a parking lot and

Charlie listens to him. In the distance I see a car coming out of a car park.

'Charlie, look! There!' I say, pointing to the car coming out.

Charlie accelerates and parks quickly in the empty space.

'Finally' he says rubbing his forehead. 'I was starting to get desperate.'

'Yes, I noticed that,' I answer laughing.

We parked a bit far from the premises. The walk will do me good to lower the pizza we had for dinner.

I grab Luca's arm and we walk through the crowded streets of Sydney. Charlie comes with us.

## Sunday, 5th November, 2017

The Cuban Place is brimming with people. You can hardly dance. Luca has been missing for a while and, no matter how hard I look, I can't find him.

Charlie is by my side. You can tell that this music is not his favourite, but, in spite of that, he is here, keeping me company.

We drink some *mojitos* that go down my throat as if they were water.

'Shall we dance?' Charlie is in high spirits.

'Yes.' I was looking forward to it. 'Do you know how to dance?' I ask, raising an eyebrow.

'No. But you teach me.' His look is funny and seductive.

He takes me by the hand to the centre of the dance floor. *Reggaeton* is being played. Charlie pulls me into his arms. I can feel his agitated breath on my neck. My heart is racing. It seems that it's going to come out of my mouth. We look at each other and laugh without really knowing why.

Don't let the night end! I don't want it to end. We dance as if there were no one else on the dance floor. He caresses my cheek gently and my body shakes. His fingers run around the corner of my lips. We are closer and closer and I feel more and more heat. His lips are coming closer to mine without asking permission. I don't care because that's what I want now.

'What's up, little couple?'

It… may… not… be… Really? He hasn't shown up all night and he has to show up now. Luca surrounds us with his arms above our shoulders with a malicious smile from ear to ear. What a bastard! He just ruined the "movie" moment I was having with Charlie. Even my brain is laughing at me.

Luca has gone too far with the drinks and is euphoric. He grabs my arm and pulls me away from Charlie, who has a poker face.

'What are you doing?' I ask between anger and bewilderment.

'Come, dance with me, Dani.'

'Luca! Are you crazy?' I say with laughter. 'I can't leave Charlie alone,' I say, pointing at him. I see him going towards the bar.

Luca insists and ends up convincing me. He's apparently happy, but it's just a facade. Deep down he is sad about what has happened to him. Maybe it's his way of escaping from reality. Although for me it is not the best. I experienced it last night with Carol and I don't want it to happen again.

Luca moves very well, you can tell he knows what he's doing. I hardly remember what I learned in my Latin dance classes. He keeps spinning me around. I try to follow his rhythm, although sometimes I get lost and trip over my own feet.

A *salsa* song begins to play. People step aside and leave the dance floor free. I don't really know what's going on.

I look through the people on tiptoe and see a couple walking towards the dance floor holding hands. The girl is wearing a minidress with red and black transparencies and the guy is wearing a short sleeved shirt in the same colour as the girl's dress and black linen trousers.

I am fascinated by the Adonis who is in the centre of the stage. He is a handsome man, his skin is a chocolate colour, and his hair is short and very curly. He is tall; he looks like a *Calvin Klein* model. The girl is brunette, but not as much as the man and she is also tall, has a black, curly and very long hair, almost up to the waist.

They move around the dance floor with great ease. They are incredible. The movements they make are so symmetrical that they look as if they were just one person.

'His name is Raúl.'

'Huh? Who?' Luca interrupts my visual journey to the Adonis.

'Don't play dumb, I've seen how you look at him.'

I try to look as if I don't know what he's talking about. In fact, I found out at first sight.

From a distance he looks like Hugo. He is also tall and dark, but not as dark as this spectacular man.

'I'm looking at the two dancers. I haven't noticed anyone in particular.'

I'm trying to look convincing, although I don't think I've succeeded.

For a moment I forgot about Charlie and what was about to happen before we were interrupted by Luca.

I look for him among people. I look from one side to the other. I see him. He's at the bar talking to a lush redhead. She has a dizzying cleavage and doesn't mind showing her charms to Charlie.

I keep dancing with Luca in a corner of the dance floor, almost ashamed comparing us with the brunette and the Adonis. I am thirsty. It's too hot.

'I'll go to get something to drink' I say to Luca shouting.

'I'm going with you. I'm thirsty too.'

We pass among the people, who are dancing without any worries, juggling so as not to take a hit. I go to the bar where Charlie is with the exuberant redhead and ask for another *mojito* while I look at them from the side. I am not jealous. *"Are you sure?"* my subconscious asks me. I don't even listen to it.

I'm a little dizzy. I don't know how many *mojitos* I have on me. Five. Six. Maybe seven. I don't know. I need to sit down. Luca leads me to an area where there are sofas. They are very comfortable.

Charlie comes with a tray on which he brings about twelve shots. He puts it on the table.

'Let's drink,' says Charlie with a shot in his hand.

'I can't take it anymore.'

It´s true.

Luca takes a shot and gives me another one. I'll make an effort.

We toast and drink one after another until all the glasses are empty. I'm so dizzy. Everything is spinning. I feel nauseous.

The guys don't seem to be much better off than I am. Some suggest we go home, I don't know which one of us. I accept because I need to get into bed and sleep.

We walk towards the car, stumbling. I'm holding Luca's arm. It seems that the car is further away than where we left it parked. It takes forever.

Charlie opens the car by pressing all the buttons on the remote control until he hits the right button.

I clumsily get into the back of the car and Luca sits down next to me.


My head hurts and I still feel nauseous. I get images in my head from the night, as if they were flashes.

How comfortable I am in bed! Both the pillow and the mattress are very soft. I don't know how I got here. The last thing I remember is when I got into Charlie's car.

Shit! I think I'm not alone in my bed. I felt a movement next to me. I shyly open one eye. *It's Luca!* My subconscious whispers to me. *What is he doing in my bed?* I lift the sheets, looking at the worst.

*No. No. No.* I repeat to myself again and again. We're completely naked. *No way! But what have I done?* I turn around. I don't want to look.

No! Shit! This must be a hidden camera. Charlie's on the other side of the bed. I pick up the sheets again. He's naked too. I scowl. This has to be a dream. Worse, a nightmare. I nod my head. I snort. I pass my hand over my forehead. What do I do?

I find a T-shirt and put it on quickly. I get out of bed by crawling to the bottom. I take a pair of panties and sweatpants and go to the bathroom.

I walk around the bathroom, from the door to the window and back. I try to remember something, but I can't. I leave the bathroom and go to the kitchen window. Charlie's car is parked in front.

What have I done? I repeat to myself over and over again. I haven't been here a week and I've already done the craziest thing in my twenty-four years of life.

I sigh.

I'm sure everything has an explanation or that I'm trying to make my little brain believe that it still doesn't assimilate the state in which I've got up. I deny with my head. I rub my face with my hands and cover my eyes, hoping that it will be easier to overcome this moment. I look at the kitchen. I don't feel like eating anything. My stomach is upside down. I don't know what time it is. I look at the clock on the kitchen wall. It's a quarter past two. I just want this day to pass quickly so I can get on with my life.

I hear a door open. I look out into the corridor from the corner of the kitchen. Someone comes out of my room. It's Luca. He's tiptoeing out of my room, with his clothes hanging on one arm and his slippers in his hand, and he's going to his room.

He hasn't seen me, thank goodness. I wouldn't know what to say to him either. Nothing like this or similar has ever happened to me. The only positive thing that I draw from this madness is that I haven't remembered Hugo. Well... I do now. *"Get out!"* I shout to my little head. Not today. I have enough to think about in this mess.

Earth, swallow me!

Someone's coming down the hall. I stick my head out again. It's Carol. Thank goodness for that. For a second I thought it was Charlie.

I take a deep breath.

'That was quite a party last night, wasn't it?'

Carol passes behind me and gives me two little pats on the back.

'Party?'

I shrug my shoulders.

'Yes. I couldn't sleep with your laughter.'

I don't remember anything at all. My face makes a thousand different gestures.

'Who did you have so much fun with?' she smiles slightly mischievously.

'Bah! No one.'

'No one? Well, it didn't look like "nobody".'

At the end I'll have to confess so that she doesn't keep questioning me.

'A boy I met last night.' I lie. Of course I'm not going to tell her the truth because even I don't know it.

'Oh.'

I need to find out, but I don't dare. I doubt that Luca will remember, he was drunker than me or that's how I remember him before the treacherous shots.

Carol raises an eyebrow and I can see a half smile on her face. I don't think she's quite convinced.

'I'm going to make something to eat. Do you want some?' Her question is sincere.

'No, thanks. I'm not hungry.'

I'm going to the living room. I need to sit down and keep thinking. I have a headache and not because of the drink, but because I think so much. I hear Carol preparing the meal.

It smells good.

I'm sitting in the single sofa with my back to the kitchen. My legs are shrunken and my knees are at chest level. I wrap my arms around my legs and in one of my hands I have the remote control.

I turn on the TV and zap in search of something interesting to watch. I play with the remote control while I think. I don't get anything out of it.

I snort.

I don't know how I'm going to deal with this problem. I frown. How could my life get so complicated in such a short time? *"It's nothing, woman"*, says the Jiminy Cricket I have in my subconscious. *"If you say so..."* I reply with irony.

'G... Good afternoon.'

That voice... It's Charlie! I curl up more on the sofa so that he doesn't see me.

'Good afternoon. What can I do for you?' Carol asks him.

'My name is Charlie. Have you seen Daniela by any chance?'

I waggle my index finger over the back of Carol in the hope that she will notice and say no.

'Mmm... Well...'

Carol hesitates. *"Tell him no"*, I shout to myself.

'No. I haven't seen her.'

I sigh. Thank goodness. She has seen my signs.

'Oh. I have to go. If you see her, could you tell her to call me, please?'

'Yes. I'll tell her.'

'Thank you very much.'

I can hear the door closing. I exhale. I get up and go straight to my room. Carol comes behind me.

'Wasn't that the taxi driver?'

Carol is at the door with her arms crossed, smiling and scrutinizing me with her eyes.

'Yes' I say almost whispering.

Carol comes in, closes the door and sits on the bed next to me.

'The boy is not bad,' she says as she pulls my hair out of my face. She starts to laugh and I can't help but laugh too. She is right.

'What a shame!' I cover my face with my hands.

'It's no shame. By the way. The handsome taxi driver told me you should call him.'

'Yes. I heard him from here. I'll do it tomorrow.'

Luca enters the room without asking.

'What a night' he says without strains.

I don't want him to say anything.

'Yes. We had a good time. We danced a lot' I interrupt him so he doesn't keep talking.

'I know, I'm in,' says Carol suspiciously.

Just thinking about how we could have ended up the four of us drunk... I shake my head and get that thought out of my head. If three are a crowd, I don't want to imagine four.

'I'll go to the shower.'

I want them to leave the room and not talk anymore, so that Luca doesn't lose his tongue.

As soon as they come out, I make sure that Luca goes to his room alone and I go in without knocking. I close the door.

'Don't say anything,' I warn him.

'Yes, don't worry. I wasn't planning to. Besides, I don't remember very well what happened.' He seems sincere. 'I only remember getting into your friend's car and waking up in your bed with you beside me,' he adds.

'It's the same for me. I woke up and I was in the middle of both of you.'

I blush.

I turn around and go to the bathroom. A shower will do me good. The water falls warm on my body and relaxes me.

We are sitting at the kitchen bar, Luca, Carol and I. The television is on and there is a comedy show. It's nine o'clock at night and we're eating *pasta* prepared by Luca. It's exquisite. You can tell he's Italian.

'Nervous?' Carol asks me.

'Very much so,' I answer sincerely.

'Calm down, woman. Everything is going to be fine.' Luca winks at me.

I feel nervous and calm at the same time. My boss seems like a very serious guy and the clinic is fantastic.

Luca and Carol talk about things from before I arrived. I don't really understand what they're talking about. We talk about the weekend, the day I spent with Carol and the day I spent with Luca, of course, without going into detail.

I'm in bed looking at the ceiling. I pick up the phone on the bedside table and call my mother hoping she'll answer. I haven't had time to talk to her, only to my sister. We have written a few messages to each other. It takes her a while to answer, but she finally does it.

She is in the hospital.

'Hello, mummy. How are you? I didn't know you were working.'

I need to see my mother.

'Hello, daughter. I'm very well. Missing you.' She's shedding a tear. 'Hey, baby. Today I have a morning shift, although I'm on a short break.'

There is a lot of background noise.

'I needed to see you.'

'Are you all right?'

How well she knows me.

'Yes, mummy. It's hard to be so far away, but I'm fine. How are Dad and Jonathan doing?'

'Well... As always, daughter. Your father is very busy at work and your brother between video games and girls... You don't get him out of there.'

'Oh.'

'What time is it there?'

I look at the clock on my mobile.

'It's eleven o'clock at night.'

'It's one o'clock here.'

'I know, mum. My mobile shows me both times. The one here and the one in Madrid.'

'Well, Dani. I have to work. They are waiting for me to give the medication to the patients.'

'Okay, mummy. I'll try to call you tomorrow. I can't promise anything, though.'

'Okay, daughter. Good luck on your first day of work.'

'Thank you, mummy. I love you.'

'I love you too, Dani.'

I feel a bit empty. The conversation was very short, but it's working. I understand.

It's been a crazy weekend. First, with Carol, and then with Luca and Charlie. I hope to be able to solve it soon, although I confess that I am a little embarrassed to ask Charlie if he knows what happened.

I set the alarm on my mobile for seven o'clock. I check on *Facebook* and see the photos that my friends have posted. They are all without me. I am saddened.

I go to bed and fall asleep thinking about the craziness of the previous night.

## Monday, 6th November, 2017

The mobile phone alarm wakes me up with a start "how I hate it!" and keeps the dark thoughts of the night away from me. I'm not going to think about that. Today is a new day. Today is the day. I'm starting my new job. My life's job. I love animals. They give me the peace and quiet that the rest of humans take away from me.

I get out of bed and open the curtains to let the sun's rays flood the room. They've been asking to come in for a while now. I look at my mobile phone. The clock reads twenty degrees centigrade and it's three minutes past seven in the morning.

I'm going to the bathroom. I pick up my hair with tweezers so as not to wet it in the shower; I have it clean from yesterday. The shower is almost cold and it wakes me up.

I go back to the room wrapped in a towel. I look in the wardrobe for some leggings and a sleeveless T-shirt. I put on some ballerina style shoes and go to the kitchen. Carol is already up and beautiful, with a dark grey skirt and jacket, some black high heeled shoes and she's already combed and made up. She looks like a model.

She has a cup of coffee in one hand and the phone in the other; she is speaking in legal jargon. I don't understand anything.

'Good morning,' says Carol as soon as she hangs up the phone.

'Good morning, Carol. How busy you look this morning.'

'You see, the phone hasn't stopped ringing since first thing. Coffee?' She points to a cup.

'No, thank you. I don't feel like it. I'll buy something on the way. I want to get to work early.'

'If you want, I can give you a lift in my car. I've got time.'

'No. No need. I'd rather walk. It's a great day. Thank you.'

'You're welcome. Well, I'll be off then. I have a lot of work today.'

She grabs her purse from the kitchen counter, leaves the cup in the sink and goes out the door at the speed of light.

There is fruit in a green glass fruit bowl, I take a banana and put it in my bag. I go to the bathroom, brush my teeth, put on my makeup and comb my hair a little.


I walk down Old South Head Road. There are a lot of people around. The sun warms my body. There is not a single cloud. The sky is a clear blue and smells like the sea. It always smells of the sea here. I love it.

I have to buy some sunglasses because my eyes hurt. It bothers me a lot. Later, when I finish my work, I'll go to an optician's.

Images of the crazy night come to my mind. Luca has told me that he doesn't remember anything. Is it true or is he lying to avoid making me feel bad? I don't know. After work I'll get the courage from where I don't have it to call Charlie and talk to him. I hope he remembers, because I have to get out of this doubt.

I arrive at the clinic at ten to eight. Kayla is in the reception. She greets me warmly and I wait sitting in the waiting room. Darel doesn't take five minutes to arrive. We go to his office and he gives me a sheet with the schedule and the duty days. He also offers me a white jacket. I'm surprised, because it has my name printed in black on the right side: "Miss D. Duarte". It makes me feel important for a moment.

I look at the time sheet out of the corner of my eye. We are nine veterinarians. Four on the morning shift, four on the afternoon shift and one on the night shift. Seven assistants, three on the morning shift, three on the afternoon shift and one on the night shift; plus, two receptionists.

The morning shift runs from seven in the morning to two in the afternoon. In the afternoon, from two to nine o'clock night. In addition, there are duties on weekends.

I'm on duty next weekend.

'I hope you're happy with the schedule.'

'Yes. Sounds good to me.'

I have no complaints.

I have a morning shift this week. Next weekend I work from Friday at nine o'clock at night until Monday at seven o'clock in the morning.

'Today you will work all day with me so that you get familiar with the clinic and learn where all the things you might need are.'

I nod with my head. I agree with everything.

'We have the first appointment at half past eight. If you want, we can have a cup of coffee.'

'Yes. I haven't had any breakfast.'

I was already in need of a cup of coffee.

We go up to the first floor. There are several people in the kitchen area. Darel introduces them to me: Jack, the other vet, is young, not very handsome, but he seems nice. Angela, Rose and Sarah are three young, blond, middle aged assistants.

Darel makes a very strong black coffee for me. He brings me the cup with the coffee and sugar. I like it sweet, so I add three spoons. I drink it hot; I don't like it to get cold. They offer me biscuits that come in a box. There is a lot of variety. They talk among themselves about the animals in the clinic.

There are two dogs admitted and recently operated on.

'They are doing well,' says Darel. 'We are treating a snake bite on a German shepherd's leg.'

Darel goes quickly to the pharmaceutical store, brings an antidote and injects it.

'It will need to be observed' warns Darel to the German shepherd's owner.

'Yes, Mr. Williams.'

Darel and Angela carry the German shepherd on a stretcher in the lift to the first floor and put him in a cage adapted for him. Darel returns immediately. We continue to work all morning almost without rest. Now I understand why there are so many vets in the clinic.

My mobile rings. I look at it. It's a *WhatsApp*... from Charlie.

> *Good morning, Daniela. How are you? Can we meet today?*

I don't feel like answering now. I'll do that later. When my shift is over, I have to face this problem now and move on. Well, at last and after all, it's an experience that, of course, will not be repeated. I can't get drunk like that anymore.

The morning passes very quickly. There's only an hour left to finish the shift.

'Daniela, could you stay until three o'clock today? So you can meet the vets and the assistants of the afternoon shift.'

Darel is interested in me meeting all the staff.

'Yes, that's fine with me. I'm aware that I started later.'

'Tomorrow you will meet the night's shift colleagues. They leave when we arrive.'

'Okay.'

I like to meet new people and even more so my colleagues. I'm curious to see what they look like.

I write to Carol to let her know when I'm done and send her a picture of my schedule. She replies almost immediately with an OK. She must be very busy.

I'm exhausted. Today has been a hard day's work and the occasional emergency.

Two men and six women arrive several minutes apart. They are the afternoon's colleagues. Liam and Max are two veterinarians in their forties. Emma and Holly are the vets. Emma will be in her forties while Holly is younger. Grace, Ella and Eva are the middle aged auxiliaries as well as the morning auxiliaries and Beth is the receptionist. She's very young; I don't think she's in her twenties yet.

Everyone greets me very warmly. I hope I'm not mistaken about the names. Although it's hard not to make a mistake, almost all of them are tall, blue eyed blonds.

I help Emma in her practice. She doesn't seem to like me being with her very much; she looks at me with suspicion. I don't pay attention to her. I look at my watch every few minutes. Minutes don't go by. I don't like this woman. She doesn't inspire me with confidence and I don't know why; she doesn't like me either. The others are kind and patient with me.

'I'm leaving. My shift is over. Darel told me to go to at three' I inform Emma.

'So?' she says indifferently.

'W... Well, Darel told me to go out at this time,' I explain between cut and shy.

'OK.'

Emma turns around and continues cutting the nails of a Siamese. No "See you tomorrow" or "Nice to meet you". Nothing. If they draw my blood now, I'm sure not a drop would come out. She has left me cold. Will she be like that? Maybe I caught her on a bad day. If so, it's not my fault. I take the folded work schedule sheet out of my dressing jacket pocket.

Well. We don't have the same shift or any duties together. For now. Thank goodness for that. I can't imagine working seven hours with her, let alone fifty-eight. Phew!

I'll say goodbye to the rest of the staff. I leave my dressing jacket in a small room with lockers next to the reception and take my bag and my jacket; I say goodbye to Beth.

The afternoon is very hot. The mobile phone shows 32 degrees. The heat is so dry that it makes my throat dry. I go into a small shop of groceries. I buy a bottle of ice water and a bag of chips to quiet my stomach, which is replicating its right to eat.

The streets are crowded and I find it hard to walk without bumping into a passerby. The traffic is impossible and the drivers are honking their horns in desperation thinking that this will ease the congestion a bit. The truth is that this doesn't work, all they do is pollute acoustically as if there wasn't enough noise.

I remember that I have my headphones in my bag and I connect them to my mobile. I need to isolate myself from the ambient noise, it reminds me of Madrid.

*Fito and Fitipaldis* come directly into my ears, and their catchy music makes me walk to the rhythm of the song.

Nobody is home. I leave my things in the room and put on my short pyjamas. I go to the kitchen, I feel like cooking. I go to prepare something for when Carol and Luca arrive. I look for everything I need to make a potato omelette. I'm not bragging, but they're really good.

I peel the potatoes and cut them into small, thin pieces. I also chop the onion into very small pieces. I throw them in the frying pan with the hot fire. As soon as the onion browns, I add the potatoes. I turn it with the wooden spoon and under the fire so that it does not burn. While the potatoes are being made, I take the opportunity to beat the eggs in a bowl.

I have the omelette on a white plate, I prepare a salad. I place three plates on the kitchen bar with their respective glasses and forks. I put the omelette and the salad in the middle.

I hear the door open. It's Carol. She looks exhausted. Her mouth is open when she sees everything I've prepared and she smiles broadly.

'Did you make it?' she says, pointing to the food.

'Yes,' I answer proudly, with a smile from ear to ear.

'I'll change my clothes and we eat.'

'Okay. Will Luca be long in coming?'

'No, he should be here soon,' says Carol, walking away along the corridor.

Luca arrives a few minutes later.

Carol and Luca are delighted with the food. Everything is flattering. They make me blush.

'É *tutto squisito*,' says Luca.

'Thank you.'

'How was your first day?'

'Good. I can't complain. My boss is very kind.'

'How about you?' I ask Luca.

'*Bene*. The master's degree is going very well for me. I'm already looking forward to finishing and work.'

Carol is absorbed by her phone.

'Carol. How are you doing at work?' I interrupt her.

'Huh?'

She didn't hear what I asked. I repeat the same question.

'Ah!' she exclaims. 'Exhausting. I haven't stopped all day. I have had two trials and three conciliations.'

'Oh.'

As I pick up the dishes from the table, Luca is washing them. Carol has gone to take a shower.

The afternoon passes almost without me noticing it. I'm lying on the sofa, Luca is next to me. We look like two lazy people. It's hard for us to move to get the remote control on the table, just a few feet away from us.

'Make room for me.' Carol claims a space on the sofa.

'There's plenty of room,' answers Luca.

Carol, as always, has come with her laptop.

'Don't work so hard,' says Luca. 'A few so much and others so little'

Carol sticks out her tongue.

Luca makes a sandwich and brings Carol and me another one.

'Thank you,' Carol and I say at the same time.

'You're welcome, girls.'

I receive several messages from my friends. They are starting the day. It's barely nine o'clock in the morning in Madrid. They make me laugh.

They tell me about their adventures during the weekend and I tell them about my colleagues and about Carol and Luca.

I miss those nights when we didn't stop dancing from club to club, had breakfast at seven in the morning and arrived home already in the daytime.

I look at my mobile phone lying on my bed. I go into the messages. I see the message Charlie sent me. I forgot to answer it. I'll leave it for tomorrow, I don't want to think about it again; besides, it's already late to be sending messages.

I exchange several messages with my parents and my siblings. It's still early in Madrid.

> *How was your first day at work?*
> *Have you killed any critters yet?*

My little brother is always so nice.

> *Not today. Maybe, tomorrow.*

I play along.

> *I call you.*

My mother calls me on *Skype*. They are all there and talking at the same time. I find it hard to understand them.

'One by one, please' I ask them to be quiet.

'Daughter, how are you?' My mother's face is all sweetness.

'Good, mum. Very happy. I miss you very much.'

'Dani, when will you invite me to visit Sydney?'

My brother is looking forward to travelling.

'Whenever you like, Jonny.'

'How about your mates? Any interesting men?' My sister is always thinking about men.

'Well...' I'm silent for a few seconds.

'Is something wrong with you?' asks my mother.

'Nothing.' I try not to worry them with my nonsense. 'There are nine of us vets. This week I have a morning shift and on the weekend I have a duty from nine o'clock at night on Friday until seven o'clock in the morning on Monday' I explain.

Everyone is amazed.

'We're very happy for you, Daniela' my father says very proudly and that makes me excited.

'I'll send you a picture of my schedule later.'

'Okay,' they all respond at once.

I say goodbye to everyone. As always my mother shows an extra tear.

I have to sleep early because I get up at six tomorrow. I turn on the mobile phone alarm. I brush my teeth and go to bed. I fall asleep almost immediately. It's been a tiring day!

Luca is also in his room talking to his family. The times in Italy and Spain are the same and it's normal that we coincide when we talk to our families.

## Friday, 10th November, 2017

The week has passed in the blink of an eye. Charlie has been writing to me all week. I also have several missed calls. I haven't dared to answer the messages or return the calls.

Neither Luca nor I have talked again about what happened last Saturday. I've only been thinking about work, about the new people I met at the clinic. Except for Emma, the others are amazing with me.

The work has been exhausting. I'm not used to working so many hours and I still have to go back at night and stay until on Monday morning.

I have almost six hours to eat; rest and return to the clinic.

I'm home alone because both Luca and Carol told me they would be late. Carol because of work; and Luca because of university.

I make myself a French omelette and a salad for lunch and sit in the living room while I watch TV and make a list of things I'm going to take with me to spend the weekend at work.

I'm preparing a backpack with some clothes to change into if I need to. A toiletry bag with a toothbrush and toothpaste, and some other things. I've never worked so many hours in a row.

While studying at university, I worked part time in a supermarket as a cashier.

Luca knocks on the door.

'*Posso entrare?*' he says cautiously.

'Yes. Come in.'

He sits down on the bed. He has just come from the university.

'What a pity you can't stay this weekend to go out to dance,' he says laughing.

'I don't like those jokes.'

I get serious.

'I'm sorry. Don't be offended.'

I laugh out loud.

'What are you laughing at?'

'The look on your face. I'm joking. I don't mind what you said.'

'Seriously?'

'Yes. What has happened, happened. We shouldn't give it more importance. I only have the doubt of knowing what really happened.'

'Didn't you talk to Charlie?'

'No. He sent me several messages and called me, but I haven't been able to answer. Maybe I'll do it during my shift.'

'And when will you be back?'

'Monday morning. I go in today at nine o'clock at night and leave on Monday at seven o'clock in the morning' I explain.

'Wow! Nothing much. Take it easy.' He pats me on the back as a comfort.

'I will try' I say with resignation.

I finish putting everything I need in the backpack and leave it at the entrance.

Carol arrived a while ago and is preparing dinner for everyone. She has set the table and we are sitting down to dinner.

First there is a shrimp cocktail. It's delicious. I taste it little by little to savour the explosion of flavours. The dish is made up of peeled prawns, lettuce leaves, a sauce I don't know about and lemon juice.

'What is this sauce?' I ask with curiosity.

'It's English sauce. Do you like it?'

'It's exquisite. You are a great cook.'

Carol smiles gratefully and Luca nods his head. He agrees with me.

Carol takes the dishes off the table and brings a tray with fish that she has prepared in the oven. I don't know what kind of fish it is.

'What fish is it?' I want to know.

'Barramundi. It's a local fish. Its name comes from the aboriginal language of Queensland and means large scale river fish.'

Wow! Now that's a full blown explanation. I am speechless.

I try it. Not bad at all.

'Do you like it?' Carol is impatient for my answer.

'Yes. It tastes different from what I'm used to.'

I am full. I can't eat anymore and I'm not the only one. Carol and Luca are just like me.

'I have to go now, otherwise I'll be late for work' I say looking at the clock.

'I'll take you,' says Carol.

'Don't worry. I'm going for a walk.'

'No, woman. I'll take you,' she insists and I accept.

'*Ti accompagno*' Luca invites himself.

'He always does the same thing.' Carol seems to know him well. 'He wants to know where you work.' Carol laughs because she knows that Luca has heard her.

'*NON SONO COSÌ!*' he shouts from his bedroom door. I go to the bathroom and brush my teeth. I straighten my hair a little.


We go in the car listening to the radio and talking about dinner. I still have it in my stomach. We arrive in a little over five minutes. There was no traffic, and Carol parks in front of the clinic.

'If you need anything, tell me and I'll bring it to you.'

Carol is very kind to me.

'I think I've brought everything I need,' I'm checking the backpack. 'If I need anything, I'll let you know.'

I say goodbye to Carol and Luca with a kiss. I get out of the car. Jack comes walking on the pavement. We go up the stairs of the clinic together. I look back and Luca and Carol are still in the car. How gossipy! They are smiling maliciously. I look at them wrinkling my forehead and moving my head from right to left several times.

As we have arrived early, Jack suggests that we go up to get something to drink. He brought some refreshments.

'Do you want one?' He extends a can of *Coke*.

'Yes. Thank you.'

The afternoon shifts colleagues say goodbye to us in the entrance and Jack locks the door.

'Now, at night, we lock the door for safety,' he explains.

'Better. You never know.'

'Now we only deal with emergencies and monitor the condition of the animals in our care.'

'Right.'

'Don't worry. Even if it's a lot of hours, the work is not very heavy.'

'How long have you been working here?'

'Well...' he thinks about it. 'It will be four years in two months.'

'I've never worked in a clinic, I was just an intern.'

'Well. Don't worry, I'll help you with everything you need.'

That reassures me.

We go up to the kitchen and make ourselves a cup of coffee. Jack turns on the TV. We check how the animals are doing. They are sleeping.

The medication gets them very relaxed or sleep most of the time.

We are sitting on the sofa, drinking the third cup of coffee and watching a typical series from here. I don't know it. Jack laughs while watching the series and I take a look at my mobile phone. I think about answering Charlie's messages, but I'm still not ready to face the truth.

I sigh.

'Are you all right?'

I look up and see Jack watching me.

'Yes. A little nervous.'

'Because of the duty?'

'Yes.' I lie. The truth is that I'm nervous about what Charlie might tell me.

'Keep calm' He puts his arms around me. 'You'll see how everything will be fine.'

I'm uncomfortable that he has touched me and I leave immediately with the excuse of preparing a cup of tea.

The doorbell rings. We go down.

At the entrance there's a man with a mongrel dog. He is nervous. Charlie immediately opens the door.

'G… good night. My dog… My dog. Well… he's… hurt.' The man can't stop stuttering.

'Calm down. Don't worry,' says Jack, trying to calm him down.

'Pass through here' I say pointing to the corridor where the consultations are.

We put the dog on the metal table.

'What is the dog's name?' I ask the gentleman.

'His name is Darko.'

I am sitting in front of the computer to cover the data of both the dog and the man. This is mandatory.

'Is it new or do you already have a vet's card?'

'No. It's my first time here. I have just moved here.'

I ask him for all the necessary data: name, address, telephone number, pet's name, age… When I'm done, I help Jack, who has already shaved the wound area on the left leg and cleaned it.

'It's not too deep, so no stitches are needed' Jack explains himself very clearly.

I open a cupboard where there are all kinds of disinfectants and opt for an iodine solution. Jack applies it very carefully with the help of some gauze.

When he finishes, I leave the solution in the cupboard and take a bottle of healing ointment.

'You must be careful to ensure that he does not lick the wound. In any case, we will cover it with gauze and bandage it. We will also put an Elizabethan collar on it.'

I pass the gauze and bandage to Jack.

'The necklace is in the medicine room,' says Jack.

I run. I find it right away and give it to him. I help him put it on.

'Thank you very much.' The man was very grateful about our work. Or rather, with Jack's. I have only done the work of an assistant.

We go upstairs and check on the animals that have been admitted. They are still sleeping. We go back to the sofa and Jack suggests putting on a film. He has brought several. He is already used to these duties.

'What do you want to watch?' Jack has brought an arsenal of films. I don't know which one to choose. 'Would you like to watch Pirates of the Caribbean? I have all of them.'

I nod with my head.

'I have popcorn too,' he says, shaking the box. 'By the way, you've helped me out very well' Jack congratulates me while he puts the film on the DVD and puts the popcorn in the microwave.

'Thank you. I just did my job.'

'The man was very nervous, but the wound actually was not deep,' he says.

'It's normal. Blood always impresses.'

'Yes. That's true.'

'And how long have you been living here?' he asks.

'Nearly nothing. I arrived last Thursday.'

'Ah! And why did you decide to come?'

I keep quiet.

'Well. If you don't want to talk about it, that's fine.'

'Thank you. The truth is that I don't feel like talking about that topic. Tell me something about you. Were you born here?' I want to know.

'I'm from Perth, the westernmost part of Australia. The region is called Western Australia. It is the area with the most hours of sunshine.'

'And why did you come to Sydney?'

'My mother and I moved here when I was six years old. After she separated from my father.'

'I'm sorry.'

'You have nothing to be sorry about. These things are very common.'

'And don't you miss Perth?'

'No. I have no one there except my father. We get on well. I visit him whenever I can.'

'Is it far away?'

'A little. I always go by plane because it takes more than forty hours by car.'

'Is it that long?' I'm impressed.

'Yes' he says. 'By plane it's five hours one way, and a bit more than four hours back' he adds.

'Wow! That's a lot of hours.'

'Not so many.'

'Well, if we compare it to my trip…Yes, it's not that many.'

'How many hours is it from Spain to Sydney?' I explain the whole journey. He is speechless and doesn't blink. 'That's a great trip.'

I nod with my head. He's right.

'I've never made such a big trip before.'

'Nothing less than a trip around the world. Do you have any family or friends here?'

'No. I met my roommate through a room search page and we started talking on *Skype*. There are three of us in the house. Carol is the owner and Luca is a tenant like me.'

'Oh.'

'I live with my mother. I don't want to leave her alone. She has always worked hard to get me through and she is very good.'

'I miss my parents and my brothers and sisters very much.'

A tear comes shyly out of my left eye without asking for permission.

'Don't cry. You'll see how soon you can be with them.'

'I hope so. I've just started here and I don't know when I'll have a holiday.'

'As soon as you've been here for three months you can ask for a holiday whenever you want, as long as it's not already taken. Darel is a very good boss.'

I find that comforting. Maybe in three months I'll be able to visit my family.

The film ends without us noticing. It's already late. Jack brings a folding bed, mounts it next to the sofa and brings some blankets and pillows.

'Where do you prefer to sleep?' asks Jack, pointing to the bed and the sofa.

'Where it's more comfortable,' I answer with a smile. 'I don't care, I don't have any preferences.'

'Then you sleep on the bed and I'll do it on the sofa. If any emergency comes up, we'll hear it.'

'Perfect.'

I toss and turn and take a while to fall asleep. Jack has been asleep for a while. He comes back to my mind. Hugo comes back. I miss him despite being such a coward and a liar to me.

I fall into a deep sleep.

# Monday, 13th November, 2017

The weekend has been very quiet; just a few minor emergencies. The animals that were admitted for observation are leaving today. Jack and I are reporting the animals for discharge to take the work off the morning shift.

I have missed calls from Charlie. I will have to write to him at some point. I also have a message from Carol.

> *Charlie has been here. I told him you were working. He told me you should call him and that he needs to talk to you.*

I answer with a simple OK and keep the phone in my dressing jacket. The first rays of morning come in without asking for permission through the window announcing that a new day is already here.

I feel like going home, getting into bed and getting some real rest. The folding bed is not bad, but it is not a latex mattress.

Jack opens the door, and the first couple of people arrive and greet us. Emma comes in and doesn't even look at me. She's already bitter in the morning. How awful! I feel sorry for those who work with her. This woman has taken it out on me.

It's time to get out. I leave the coat and take my things. I say goodbye to everyone and I'm out. Jack comes out behind me.

'Daniela, how do you get home?'

'I'm walking.'

'If you want, I'll give you a lift.'

I agree because I'm very tired. The streets are already full of people and cars.

'You'll get used to working shifts. There are duties where there are no emergencies and there are other duties that seem to be crazy, but they all get along well, you'll see.'

'I hope so.' I yawn. 'Do exotic animals come to the clinic?' I'm curious.

'If you refer koalas or kangaroos, my answer is no, although sometimes they call us to go to the areas where they are, in order to heal their wounds or something similar. But yes some snake or tarantula.'

'Well, maybe I'll have a little problem there…'

'Why?'

'I'm spider phobic.' I look terrified.

'Well, you've come to the wrong country. Here the spiders are huge, they look like crayfish.'

'I hope I don't find any.' I cross my fingers.

'Living in a house, I doubt it.' Jack laughs.

'Here we are,' I say, in front of my house. 'Thank you again.'

'You're welcome. Sleep tight!'

'Same to you.'

I'm going in. Carol is finishing getting ready to go to her work.

'Good morning, worker. How did it go?' Carol is very smiling.

'Good. Better than I expected.'

'I'm glad. Well, I'm off to work. See you later.'

Luca is still sleeping. I'm going straight to the room. I put on my short pyjamas and get into bed. It's soft and fluffy. It smells good.

I fall asleep right away.

The doorbell rings and wakes me up out of the blue. What a scare! My pulse has accelerated. I didn't count on this now. Who could it be? Maybe it's the postman; I don't know what time he's coming because I've never met him or her.

I get up and dress in a white cardigan and slippers. I walk down the small corridor, cross the middle of the living room and the kitchen and reach the door. I open it without asking.

Oh, shit! I should have asked. It's Charlie. He's leaning against the door frame with a stern look on his face. I raise an eyebrow. I know, I should have called him or at least answered his messages, but a day and another day went by and at the end I didn't even remember. Rather, I lacked the courage.

My subconscious looks at me with a "silly" face. It's a bit right. I ignore it. He's come for an explanation and I'm not ready to give one to him. I take a deep breath and invite him in.

'Please, come in and sit down,' I say pointing at the sofas.

He nods his head.

'I'm going to get dressed. I'll be right back.'

I shoot out into the room. I take the first tracksuit I see in the wardrobe and get dressed. I don't know what I'm going to say, I don't know if I want to know what happened or continue with my ignorance. Sometimes, living in ignorance is the best thing.

I remember when I was a child; I was so happy thinking that everything was perfect... Well, I'm not going to think about when I was little now. I take a deep breath. I'm short of breath.

I go to the bathroom and look in the mirror. What face I have and what hairs... I wash my face with soap, comb my hair as best as I can and brush my teeth.

I hate people who talk to me first thing in the morning and have the typical halitosis of the night.

I take courage from where I don't have it and go back to the living room. Charlie is sitting on the chaise longue. I sit in one of the individual chairs.

'Mmm...' I don't know what to say. 'W... Well...' I stutter.

Well, we're off to a good start.

'Nothing happened.' Charlie interrupts me.

I frown.

'Huh?' I don't understand anything.

'Nothing happened,' he repeats so that I understand. 'We were very drunk. When we got here, Luca invited me in and we went to your room. Luca brought more drinks and, well…, it was very hot, we got undressed and fell asleep,' he explains.

'Seriously?'

'Yes.' He sounds sincere. 'I don't understand why you haven't returned my calls or messages.'

'Well… I was embarrassed.' I blush.

'Why?'

'Because I thought something had happened between us.'

'Something could have happened.'

'How so?'

I don't know what he is talking about.

'At The Cuban Place. Your friend interrupted us, remember?'

Of course I remember. We were about to kiss when Luca arrived.

I press my lips and bend my head. I'm very embarrassed. Charlie comes up to me, holds my chin with one of his hands and pulls up to lift my head. The expression on his face is all sweetness, nothing like the face he had on the door a while ago.

'Don't worry. It's all right,' he says.

'When I woke up and saw myself in bed with both of you on either side, I feared the worst.'

I cover my face with my hands.

'Don't cover your face.'

He grabs my hands and pulls them away from my face. His hands are soft and big.

'I invite you to eat. Well… If you want…'

I didn't expect it. He just left me blank.

I accept.

'I have to change my clothes.'

'Don't worry. I'll wait for you here.'

I go back to the room and look for a dress in the wardrobe. I decide on a white one in strips and short. It is hot. It's always hot.

I put on some ballerinas of the same colour as the dress and go to the bathroom to comb my hair and makeup. I want to look beautiful. I'm excited for the first time in a long time.

We go along the M1; there is quite a lot of traffic. It's very similar to Madrid. It's almost two o'clock. Charlie has connected the air conditioning because it is very hot in the car. He has been in the sun while we were at home. On the LED screen on the dashboard it marks 26 degrees outside.

'Where are we going?' I'm curious.

I don't know this part of the city. In fact, I know almost nothing. I haven't had much time.

'It's a surprise,' he says, raising his eyebrows and half smiling.

I stay just as I was. With the same curiosity. I am intrigued. My stomach tells me that it is hungry. I haven't eaten anything since last night, when Jack ordered some pizzas for dinner.

We arrive at a port; there are many boats and yachts. There is a restaurant with a large window and a huge terrace with metal tables and wooden chairs.

A big sign says: *"Chiosco by Ormeggio"*, in black.

'Do you like it?' asks Charlie.

'And how could I not like it! It's an incredible place.'

We go in and sit down at a table in the terrace area. A large cream coloured pergola protects us from the sun. It has some plants hanging in each corner. From time to time, a mist maker placed in the central part of the pergola sprays water.

The waitress comes with two menu cards. I open it and look at it from top to bottom. The food they offer is mainly Italian, although there are also typical dishes from here. They have a lot of variety.

The prices are very affordable.

'I'm hesitant. I don't know what to order' I say.

'We can order a lobster grill first,' suggests Charlie.

'Whatever you order will be fine. I don't know any of these dishes or this restaurant.'

'Don't worry. Everything is very good.'

I nod with my head.

'As a second course we can order grilled salmon with cherry tomatoes and a lamb's lettuce salad to go with it.'

'Yes. I love salmon!'

'What do you want to drink?'

This is clear to me. No alcohol.

'Water for me. Thank you.'

The waitress comes and takes note of everything Charlie says to her without taking her eyes off him. I look at her with suspicion and she leaves with a bad face.

After a few minutes, the waitress comes back with the drinks. She serves us and leaves almost without looking at us.

'How have you been doing at work? Your friend told me that you were on duty all weekend.'

'It's been a long time, but I'm not really complaining. My partner has taught me very well. He has been very kind and patient with me.'

Charlie's face changes immediately. He reflects sadness or maybe it's jealousy. I don't know.

'I'm very happy for you' he ends by saying.

'Thank you.'

'What shifts do you have this week?'

He wants to know.

'This week I only work on Wednesday, Thursday and Friday from two in the afternoon to nine at night. And you?'

'I'm my own boss. I have a taxi company and I'm doing really well. I have several people working for me.'

'Oh.'

The waitress comes with the first course and interrupts our conversation.

'Here is your lobster grill. I hope you like it.'

It smells good!

The lobsters come in a large white rectangular dish on top of a few leaves of lettuce. Charlie serves me one.

'I hope you like it.'

Charlie is waiting impatiently for me to try it.

I delicately taste some lobster. It's still very hot. It tastes delicious, it has a mild flavour. It's salty and spicy too.

'It has an exquisite flavour.'

'I'm glad you like it. I was looking forward to seeing you and clearing up the misunderstanding we had.'

I blush remembering that moment.

'I'd rather turn the page. It's all forgotten now. Forgive me for not calling you.'

'Don't worry. It's all forgotten as far as I'm concerned too.'

We stare at each other for a few seconds. His look is seductive. I feel warm inside.

The waitress arrives and removes the empty plates and immediately returns with the second course.

The salmon comes with cherry tomatoes as the menu said. The dishes it comes in are square and navy blue.

It smells good. It's my favourite fish.

I savour the explosion of flavours slowly and deliciously. I enjoy every bite and the different flavours that this delicious dish offers me.

The salad is perfectly seasoned. Charlie, who has done it, has made the right choice of salt, oil and vinegar.

'It's the best salmon I've ever tasted in my life' I mean with sincerity.

'You don't know how happy I am to see you like this.'

'What?'

I don't know exactly what he means.

'Like this. Eating together. Happy. Cheerful. I thought I would never see you again.'

He makes me blush with every word he says to me. How does he do it?

'I've already explained why. I'm sorry.'

'No, no, no, I'm sorry. I didn't mean to make you feel bad. It was just a comment.'

'I think we were interrupted by the waitress earlier' I'm trying to change the conversation.

'Huh?'

'You were telling me about your company.'

'Oh. Yes, but you'd better tell me about yourself, about your work, about the shifts you have.'

I take the sheet of paper Darel gave me out of my bag.

'I work a week in the morning and a week in the afternoon. Every four weeks I'm on duty on the weekend and, when I'm on duty, I rest Monday and Tuesday or Wednesday and Thursday. It's a bit complicated to explain.'

'Not at all. I understood it at first. I'll write it down in my calendar so I know when I can see you.'

And again that feeling runs through my body.

'Would you like some dessert?'

The waitress caught us by surprise. She arrived so quietly that we didn't notice her.

'A black coffee and a *tiramisú* for me.'

Charlie orders the same as me.

The waitress, very attentive, picks up the dishes from the table and brings us the bill. Charlie takes his card out of his wallet and gives it to her.

The waitress returns immediately with the card and the receipt and we leave the restaurant.

We park in front of my house. Charlie gets out of the car, goes around it and opens the door for me to get out. A real gentleman. The kitchen curtains move slightly. I wouldn't be surprised if Luca and Carol were behind. They are gossiping.

Charlie opens the back door of the car, takes my jacket and my bag and gives them to me. That's quite a detail on his part.

'A delicious meal' I confess.

'I hope it's not the last time.' He winks at me. 'I don't want you to disappear again.'

I press my lips and move my head from side to side.

'I won't, I promise' I say by raising my right hand as if I was on trial. 'It was a misunderstanding. I'm sorry.'

'I have nothing to forgive, but I wish that from now on you could tell me anything without hiding.'

'I will.'

Charlie walks me to the door.

I look for the keys in the bag. I get distracted looking for them and Charlie takes advantage of my absent mindedness to pounce on me and give me a treacherous kiss on the lips.

My bag and jacket fall down. He took me by surprise. He surrounds me with his strong arms and I let myself go. I reciprocate and we kiss for several seconds. It is a strange moment. I surround him with my arms above his shoulders.

We separate.

My heart is racing. My breathing has accelerated and is irregular. I'm short of breath. I see that Charlie is just like me. But it's not he who occupies my mind. He is still present inside me. What I just felt happened to me because I was thinking about Hugo, not Charlie. I have to go.

We stare each other not knowing what to say. I am hot. More than usual. His eyes burn with desire as do mine. I try to normalize my breathing. I cannot.

I take my bag and my jacket from the floor. I quickly enter the house. I say goodbye to Charlie and close the door.

I have mixed feelings. Suddenly, he came to my mind as if he was calling me by telepathy. I want to go on with my life and leave it behind, but it is impossible for me.

At the kitchen bar, Carol and Luca are sitting with an apparent normality. It's a lie. Their faces give them away. They have been spying on me through the window.

'Gossipers!' I tell them without mincing words. 'I saw you through the window.'

They stand with their mouths open as if they were outraged by the accusation I am making.

'Now don't be offended. I have seen you' I insist.

'So?' asks Luca.

'What do you mean, "So"?'

'How did it go?' asks Carol with total normality.

I can't suppress the desire to tell what happened.

'Good. Really good. We talked. We laughed. He took me to lunch at an Italian restaurant in Mosman. In the port.'

'*Chiosco by Ormeggio*?' asks Carol.

'Yes. That same.'

'Wow!' That boy really likes you.

'I don't think so.' I'm playing it cool, even though my inner self is repeating *"Yes, yes"*, jumping up and down.

'He came for you on the weekend. That means something' says Luca in a mocking tone.

Carol doesn't know how I woke up that morning and I don't want her to know, although I know now that nothing happened.

I have to tell Luca when we are alone. I can't bite my tongue with this news. Although I have to wait until he's alone.

I take a warm shower while *Pablo Alborán* floods the entire bathroom with his sweet voice and his new songs. Ouch! How right you are in everything you say.

*"You come back*
*In every dream I have, I fall back into your net.*

*I know it takes a while to heal from you at once.
I had so many happy moments that I forget how sad it was to give you my soul,
what you spoiled..."*

"*Why did you spoil everything*", my mind repeats that question over and over again without getting an answer. I feel rage, anger and love. I'm still in love with him and I think about Charlie's kiss. Can it make me forget about Hugo? That's what would make me happiest right now, but…

I get dressed and go straight to Luca's room. I want to tell him what Charlie told me and take this weight off my mind and move on.

I knock on the door.

Luca opens the door. He's wearing short blue and black pyjamas. He lets me in and shows me the bed to sit on. I didn't know his room yet. It's very tidy. I'm not used to seeing a man's room so tidy. Honestly, I'm surprised.

He has a pile of books and notes on his desk. I guess he was studying.

'Am I disturbing you?' I ask cautiously.

'Not at all. You are always welcome in my humble lair.'

He bows as if I was a princess while he smiles.

'You have a very nice room. You should see my brother's,' I say, looking around.

'Is it that messy?' he asks, puzzled.

'Not at all. On the contrary. I was surprised to see the room so tidy.'

'*Grazie.*' He is flattered by my comments. 'By the way, what do you need?'

'Ah, yes. It'll just take a moment.'

'You tell me.'

'Nothing happened.'

'Huh? I don't understand. Nothing, what?'

I haven't been able to explain myself and it's clear that Luca doesn't know what I'm talking about.

'The other day, when Charlie, you and I went out and ended up in my bed...' That memory makes me blush. 'Nothing happened.' I can't hide my happiness and relief.

Luca hugs me.

'I'm very happy for you. I know how worried you've been about this.'

'Yes. Very much so.'

'Did the taxi driver tell you?'

'Yes. He arrived today while I was sleeping. I opened the door without even asking. At first I was afraid of what he might say, but when he cleared it all up...' I take a deep breath. 'Everything is cleared up.'

'He likes you and you know it.'

'Me? It can't be. That's impossible.'

'*Perché?*'

'Because I'm in love with a bastard who doesn't deserve it.'

'*Ma... lui non è' qui*. Right?'

'What do you mean by that?'

'Well... That being so far away, it's easy to forget. No one dies of love.'

There you are right. That is true.

'I know. But it's been more than two months and I still think about him.'

'I have an idea.'

*An idea?* My eyes open wide because I know that behind that little face of a good boy hides a mischievous and very naughty one.

'Why don't you come with me to the dance classes?'

'To dance?'

'*Se*, *salsa* and *bachata*.' His eyes are filled with hope.

'I haven't danced for six years. I don't even remember anymore.'

'Come on... *Prego*...' He begs me almost on his knees.

I hesitate for several seconds while Luca's face fades away, thinking that I'm going to give him a negative answer.

'Yes!' I exclaim.

I have to start thinking about myself and enjoying life.

'Yes?' asks Luca in a doubtful tone.

I nod with my head and Luca jumps around the room as if he were a small child.

'The classes are at Bondi Dance Company on Tuesdays and Thursdays, from 9.30pm to 10.30pm.'

He said it so quickly that it takes my brain a few seconds to assimilate it.

'Well, I'll leave you to continue studying. I'll write down the days of the dance classes in my calendar so I don't forget them' I say leaving the room while Luca stays with a smile on his face.

I'm in my room, lying on the bed, as I'm used to doing these days. I'm looking at the white, dull ceiling and the halogens

Carol has gone to bed early because she was very tired and Luca said he would stay up all night studying. The poor guy has a lot of studying to do. I still remember the pile of books he had on his desk.

Tomorrow I'm going to try my little dance skills. I hope I'll remember something. I wouldn't want to make a fool of myself. I would die of shame. I take that absurd idea out of my head and throw it in the trash can that my little brain has reserved for these things.

Positive mind. Right.

I also have the day off tomorrow and I'll try to rest what I haven't rested today because of Charlie's unexpected visit. I remember his look at the doorway. It gives me goose bumps.

*What are you doing?* That question is repeated in my subconscious, time after time, tormenting me. *I have to forget you and go on with my life as you probably have done.*

I am curious.

I could ask my sister or my mother, it wouldn't be difficult. They work together. They see each other almost every day in the hospital.

I dismiss that idea immediately.

## Tuesday, 14th November, 2017

Today I woke up very optimistic, thinking that it will be a great day and with a new challenge to overcome.

The clock reads 11:06.

Carol is at work and Luca is at university. I have the whole house to myself. Finally a little peace and quiet after my resounding arrival in this country and with all the things I've experienced these days.

Today I feel like having a leisurely breakfast and something other than just a coffee. I'm squeezing oranges with Carol's electric juicer and I'm also making coffee. I peel an apple and a banana and I also make toast with butter and jam.

I sit at the kitchen bar. I have breakfast watching a Spanish series on my laptop. I miss those nights when, after dinner, I would sit in the living room with my little brother and watch our favourite series. Even though I'm eight years older than him, we have a lot of things in common and we enjoyed doing the ones we liked together.

I see something like a little brother in Luca.

I also take advantage of the morning to do some cleaning. First with the kitchen, then with the bathroom, and finally I clean the dust in my room and in the living room and I vacuum.

I prepare the food for the three of us while I send some messages to my mother. She's working at night so I guess she'll read them soon.

I leave the set table and go to my room. I check the emails I have pending. Almost everything is spam. I look at flights for February hoping with some luck to be able to go to Spain.

I look at several different combinations. There is a flight for eleven hundred dollars. I would leave on the thirteenth of February and arrive on the fourteenth, my birthday. The return trip could be on the twenty-seventh, arriving here two days later. Dreaming is free. But I would like to be able to celebrate my birthday with my family and friends.

I enter my *Facebook* account and see all the photos my friends put up of their night time parties. I'm missing in those photos. Suddenly, I feel nostalgia and tears come to my eyes without being able to avoid it.

For a moment I feel like entering Hugo's profile and seeing if he has written anything or uploaded any photos. Maybe he's been tagged in one. No. I can't do that, that would only hurt me more and those feelings that I'm trying so hard to eliminate would come out.

A message enters on my mobile phone. It is my mother. She tells me everything is fine. As usual. She barely has an hour left to finish her shift. I wish she was here now and gave me one of those loving hugs she gives.

Carol and Luca arrive. I leave the room drying my tears and go to the kitchen.

'Shall we eat?' I tell them trying to hide my sadness.

'Mmm... How nice it smells!' Carol and Luca say in unison.

While we eat, Luca tells us everything he has done at the university and Carol talks about her trials and her pending cases.

'I've had two trials and several appointments at the office today,' Carol says.

'That means that you are very good at your job' I emphasize.

'Thank you. I try.'

Luca finishes eating and goes to his room to continue his work. He apologizes for not staying to clear the table. I don't mind. I understand that he has a lot to study. I remember that time when I spent the day in my room or in the library studying.

'I'll help you clear the table,' says Carol.

'That's not necessary. I'll do it. You go and rest.'

Carol has reluctantly gone to her room. She insisted on helping me, but she was very tired and I can do it by myself.

I just finished washing up and cleaning up the kitchen. I collapse on the sofa to enjoy a moment of relaxation. I'm looking for an interesting programme to watch.

Luca has gone out to buy some things he needs and Carol is still in her room.

There's a knock at the door.

I get up. I go to the entrance and, as always, I open the door without asking.

'Good afternoon. Is Luca here?'

There's a tall, broad shouldered, dark boy in front of me, with dishevelled hair, brown eyes and dressed in a pair of torn jeans, a white T-shirt and sandals.

'No. He went out a moment ago. If you want I can leave him a message.'

The face of the mysterious boy reflects frustration.

'No. Thank you.'

He turns around and leaves the way he came. I arch my eyebrow surprised and at the same time a little confused by this unexpected visit. He gets into a navy blue car and gets out very quickly, so fast that his wheels squeal.

I had never seen the mystery boy before, but something makes me think that he's the same boy Luca was with. The one he came for earlier than I expected when I met him. The boy doesn't have bad taste. The mystery boy is very handsome.

Carol comes out of her room very well dressed. She looks spectacular. Although it is not very difficult in her. She always looks good in whatever she wears.

She's wearing a long white dress up to her knees that fits very well with her skin colour. She wears matching shoes with a scandalous heel and her hair with some tufts of hair that are gathered and the rest falling in waves on her shoulders. She carries a handbag to match her dress and shoes.

'I'm going out to dinner. Don't wait up for me,' she says in a mocking tone winking at me with a wide smile.

'Good luck with your dinner. Whatever it is,' I reply mischievously.

Carol walks out the door wiggling like a Victoria Secret model.

I write a message to Luca, who hasn't arrived yet.

> *Hi. How about dinner somewhere?*

Luca answers a couple of minutes later.

> *Yes.* Va bene. *If you want, we can meet near the dance school.*

> *Okay. But I don't know where it is.*

> *The classes are at the Seagull Room, in Bondi Pavilion. Do you know where that is? It's next to the beach.*

> *Yes. I know where it is. I was eating there a few days ago.*

> *Go down O'Brien Street and then Roscoe Street. When you get to Campbell Parade, wait for me there.*

> *All right. What time?*

> *Is 8:30 okay with you?*

> *Perfect.*

I look at the time and I still have half an hour left. I check the route on my mobile's GPS. It will only take me ten minutes to get there, so I have plenty of time to take a shower and get ready.

I'm waiting punctually at the place Luca told me. I look on both sides of the street, but I don't see him. Someone covers my eyes.

'Who am I?' he says.

'It's you, Luca. Your accent is unmistakable.'

I turn around and there he is, as handsome as ever. With his tight T´shirt; this time he has changed the jeans for a pair of sport trousers. And I'm dressed more or less the same as him.

'*Merda*! Next time I'll try to put an Australian accent' he says disappointed.

I can't help but laugh.

Luca looks at me in confusion.

'*Posso farlo.*'

'I don't doubt your abilities.' I try to suppress a smile, but it's almost inevitable.

'We can have dinner at the McDonald's next door,' he says changing the subject. Maybe he didn't like my joke.

I nod my head.

We wait in line at McDonald's. There are a lot of people. I look at the diversity of hamburgers. I don't know which one to order. I opt for a Chicken *Big Mac* and a *Coke*. Luca orders a *McFeast* and another *Coke*.

We sit at one of the few free tables by the window. You can see the sea in the distance. It is very calm. We wait until our order is ready and talk about the dance classes.

'You're going to love them. Today we have *salsa* and on Thursday we'll dance *bachata*.'

'I hope to remember something I learned in my youth.'

Luca laughs.

'Oh, as if you were very old.'

'I'll be twenty-five in February.'

'What day?'

'The worst day of the month of February.'

'The 30th?' he says, kidding, clearly.

'You know which one I mean' I make it clear to him by rolling my eyes and tilting the head.

'And since I assume you're saying this for the 14th, I'll ask you why you say it's the worst day ever. Although I guess it's because of what you told me.'

'For that very reason. Love sucks. And, on top of that, I had to be born on Valentine's Day.' I don't like that day at all. 'By the way, someone came looking for you today. I almost forgot to tell you.'

'*Chi?*' He's intrigued, almost as much as I am.

'He wouldn't tell me his name. The only thing I can tell you is that he was tall, broad shouldered, had a dishevelled hairline and brown eyes.'

Luca's face changes radically. As if I was telling him that a relative had died.

'Who is it? It's clear that by the face you've made is someone who affects you a lot.'

A blonde girl shouts out our order number and Luca rushes out to get it. Maybe he doesn't want to tell me anything. I have to respect that. Maybe he didn't like the question I asked him. Maybe I shouldn't have told him that this mystery guy came asking for him.

'He is Victor, my ex-boyfriend. The one I told you about the other day. The one whose messages were a bit too hot, and who couldn't explain anything.'

Luca sits down and gives me what I asked for while he tells me his love afflictions. We are so similar…

'You don't know how well I understand you. Someday I will tell you my drama. But now I just want to think about going dancing and enjoying myself.'

'I totally agree.'

We devour our hamburgers as if we haven't eaten in days. From time to time we feel like eating junk food. I don't know what sauce they add to it, but it's almost addictive. I would eat another one, but that would no longer be good for my arteries.

It only takes a few minutes to get to Bondi Pavilion, where the classes are held.

'*Pronto*?' asks Luca.

'Huh? I don't understand you.'

'I'm sorry. Are you ready?'

I let out a sigh and nodded my head with rather little security.

'Now it's our turn to cut down on the extra calories we just ate' he adds.

That's right.

The memories of my first year in college and the first friends I had there come to mind. I don't remember who had the idea to go to Latin dance classes, but that year was the best of my life. Because it wasn't all about studying. We went on our parties and more than once we went to classes without sleeping. I can still remember the anger the teacher gave us because we couldn't stop laughing.

The teacher who taught us Latin rhythms wasn't bad at all. I still remember that, when we discovered that he didn't have a girlfriend, we made a bet to see who would hit on him first. Alicia won. They are still together. They're getting married next year.

The room is full of people, they look like professional dancers. I don't know what I'm doing here. I'm getting more and more nervous. My hands are sweating.

Luca is talking to two girls. He looks very integrated in this place. I think about running away. Luca grabs my arm. I think he's realised my intentions. Has he read my mind? Impossible, that doesn't exist.

Everything occurs to my subconscious... Luckily no one can hear what I think. They'd think I am crazy.

The classroom is big, white and one of the walls is orange. It has a large mirror that occupies an entire wall and on the opposite side of the mirror there are three windows from which you can see the beach.

More people are coming. It is almost time. I count over and, more or less, we are about thirty people.

No... it... cannot be... The dance teacher has just come in. The Adonis from The Cuban Place, that is the one. He arrived holding the hand of the girl who was with him the other night. My mouth is open and a cold sweat runs down my back.

'Good night. I'm Raúl. Although many of you already know me, I see new faces. Today I am accompanied by Elizabeth. She will help the girls with the dance steps.'

He looks me directly in the eyes or maybe it is me who is beginning to imagine what there is not. I think I'm starting to lose my mind. Besides, it's clear that the girl he's arrived with is his girlfriend, they were holding hands.

'For those of you who don't know me yet, I'm the *salsa* teacher. I hope you like the class. The membership for three months costs 39 dollars a week. For six months it's 35 dollars and for one year it's 29 dollars. Outside, in reception, you have more information about what is included with each fee.'

I don't even know what the Adonis said. I just think about that scandalous body and those intense black eyes he has. He has me hypnotized. Not only me, but half the class. I look sideways and the other girls are just like me, drooling over the beautiful teacher.

'Well. Let's start the class. First we'll go over the steps we've learned so that the new ones can catch up, and then we'll learn two new steps.'

I grab Luca's arm a little harder than usual and bring him closer to me.

'Why didn't you tell me that the man from The Cuban Place was the teacher?' I whisper in his ear.

'Because I'm sure you wouldn't agree to come,' he answers with a wink.

I look at him closing my eyes slightly, wanting to hold him by the neck. I can't. I laugh to myself, thinking about the funny faces Luca makes when he behaves so naughty.

Raúl explains the steps one by one, slowly. I still remember some of them. I practise them with Luca. He's a real professional. I let myself go.

'Come on, guys. One, two, three. Five, six, seven.'

Raúl encourages us and repeats the steps over and over again.

'With joy, which are very easy. Now, you ladies stay where you are, following the pace; and men, please change partners.'

Luca goes with the girl on my left and the guy on my right grabs hold of me and we continue dancing. He introduces himself. His name is John. The girl with whom he has come is his partner. They've been together for two years. He is from Canberra and she is from here.

The Adonis also swapped partners. I feel more and more shivers down my spine. He's only two girls away from me.

I see Luca in the distance, on the other side of the room. He smiles and talks to every girl he dances with. I wish I could be like him. After all, he's always happy. I can't say the same for me. Smiling seems to me to be a somewhat complicated task.

'Now let's practise a new step' says the Adonis.

He first explains the step to the guys. The girl who is now with him is delighted. She has a smile that doesn't fit on her face.

Then, Elizabeth explains the step to the ladies.

'Come on, now it's your turn. The ladies have to stretch their arms. Very sensual, as my partner explained.'

Almost without realising it, I have Raúl in front of me, looking at me with those black eyes. He is even more handsome up close. I feel warm inside. I'm going to melt like an ice cream in the sun. He holds me by the waist tightly while we do the basic step. Now I realise that what I feel for Charlie is nothing compared to what this Adonis makes me feel.

'Do you like the class?'

Huh? He's talking to me. My heart is racing.

'Yes. Very much' I'm almost out of breath.

'I hope to see you on Thursday.'

What? My face couldn't be more expressive. My eyes are opening more than usual. I swallow saliva. My mouth is dry.

'The *bachata* class.'

I'm starting to have killer instincts towards Luca. I look at him over Raúl's shoulder, but he twists my face. *"He's made a mess of you"*, my inner self tells me. How right it is.

'Eh... m... I think...' I stutter. I look silly.

'I'm saying this because I've seen you come with Luca and I suppose you'll come because he comes on Tuesdays and Thursdays.'

The Adonis doesn't miss a thing. He arches an eyebrow. My breathing increases, and not only because of the dancing, but also because of the handsome man who stares at me. I close my eyes for a few moments thinking that he will stop looking at me, but it doesn't work.

'Are you all right?'

How did he notice?

'Yes.' I hide. 'I'm just a little tired. That's all.'

I feel some envy in some of the looks in the room. If looks killed I would be dead. This Adonis attracts more girls than candy at a school gate.

Raúl turns me around and makes different steps from the ones we have been practising. I keep up with him as much as I can. He laughs. He has a perfect smile. He has no imperfections. At least, not at first sight.

I change partners and the Adonis goes away leaving in me his smell and his penetrating black eyes.

We take two more steps and intertwine all the steps we have learnt today. Luckily I let myself go, because I'm not able to think clearly.

'What's wrong with you?' whispers Luca, who has come to me without realising it.

'Nothing. It's just fatigue.'

He looks at me with half open eyes, without really believing it. I look away. Luca's technique. It always works. I smile.

'We're done for today. I hope you liked what we learned and, to the new faces, I hope to see you again.'

Raúl looks directly at me. He doesn't hold back.

I blush.

'I am going to the reception to ask about the different rates that the teacher has mentioned' I say to Luca. 'Wait for me outside if you want.'

Luca goes out chatting with some people in the class and I talk to the receptionist.

'Yes, the twenty-nine dollar a week voucher is fine. Do you accept cards?'

I give the card to the receptionist and, while I wait for her to give me back the card; someone grabs me by the waist and raises my *"bilirubina"* like *Juan Luis Guerra* in the song.

'What are you going to do now? Would you like to come and have a drink with me?'

Raúl's words echo in my head. *Have a drink with the Adonis?* I'm sure he'll say the same thing to all the other girls. He must be a ladies' man. I can't believe he's asking me that with his girlfriend still in the classroom.

'I can't. I'm working early tomorrow.'

*"Liar!"* my subconscious yells at me, *"you have an afternoon shift at the clinic"*. I know. I'm afraid to be alone with this guy.

'Well, some other time. It's just that we usually meet up with some students and some teachers after school.'

Disappointment and sadness take hold of me in an instant. I had just been hoping that this Adonis was asking me out, but no. He was just trying to look good for me as well as for the rest of the people.

He winks at me and leaves. I stand there, with the typical face of a stray dog, watching him wander away from that magazine model body.

I sigh.

The receptionist brings me back to reality.

'Your card, Miss.'

'Thank you.'

We walk slowly back home. I'm disappointed. I can't go through life having illusions, especially with a man of that calibre. It was clear that such an Adonis wouldn't look at me that way. "What's wrong with me? Nothing", I answer myself.

'Something is wrong with you.' Luca has been watching me for a while without me noticing.

'Nothing important,' I'm shameless.

'You can't lie to me. That face isn't about anything important, it's about disappointment.'

That's right. He's hit the nail on the head.

'A foolish one. Raúl told me to meet him and I, silly me, thought that it was a date. Clearly, it was not.'

'*Calmati!*' He comforts me by running his arm over my shoulders and approaching me.

Luca is a love. I love him as if I knew him forever.

We arrive home. It's empty. Carol hasn't come home from her dinner yet.

'And Carol?' asks Luca.

'Ah!' I exclaim. 'I forgot to tell you that she went to dinner. She came out very pretty and very well dressed with a smile from ear to ear.'

'I'm sure she's meeting her assistant,' he smiled maliciously.

'You know more than you're saying,' I tell him suspiciously.

'*Un po',*' he says, gesturing with his index finger and thumb.

'Tell me, please,' I beg him, interlacing his fingers.

He grimaces with his mouth and makes himself beg.

'*Va bene!*' he exclaims resignedly. 'Carol has been entangled with her assistant for a long time. More or less, since he was assigned to her. About a month and a half ago. I think. But they are in a tug-of-war. One day good; two days bad. No one understands them.'

'Do you know him?' I'm intrigued.

'I saw him once. He's a young man. I think a little younger than her. And handsome, very handsome. Blond hair and green eyes.'

'Wow! By the way. How old is Carol?'

'She turned twenty-seven last month.'

'And how about her assistant?' curiosity invades me.

'I'll be twenty-three in March...' He thinks, 'I wouldn't know, but I think he's younger than me. I think he's a law student.'

'Oh.'

Luca takes a shower while I brush my teeth. We've reached that point on confidence where we can be in the bathroom at the same time. That's the good thing about him being gay.

We talk about today's class and the next class. Despite the disappointment, I had a great time.

I fall asleep thinking about him. This time it's not Hugo. For the first time in a long time it's someone else who's hogging my thoughts. This time it's Raúl who occupies my entire subconscious and I feel frustration and sadness for having had illusions.

## Wednesday, 15th November, 2017

I'm walking on my way to work. The sun is radiant. There is not a single cloud in the sky. The morning has gone by faster than I expected. I sent some emails, a few messages to my friends and family, tidied up my room and ate.

I am early. It's fifteen minutes to two in the afternoon. I say hello to Kayla. She always works in the mornings because Beth, the afternoon receptionist, is studying in the morning at the university and can only work in the afternoons.

I go up to the kitchen and make myself a cup of coffee. Darel and Henry are here, Jack is resting today and tomorrow. The assistants Angela, Rose and Sarah arrive shortly afterwards as does Beth.

'Good afternoon, everyone. Angela, you will be with Henry today, Rose with Daniela and Sarah, you will be with me.'

Darel gives us instructions.

'If there is no problem, tomorrow we will work in the same way as today,' he adds.

Rose and I talk between appointments. It's the first time we work together and we hadn't gone beyond a "Hello" or a "Good morning". She's very nice. The afternoon passes quickly.

'Well, I've been working here for a year now. I am very happy. Darel is a very good boss' Rose boasts.

'I, too, am very happy at the moment. In Spain there are not the same opportunities as here. The only problem to enter Australia is having to apply for the visa and all the documents that they ask for.'

'Is it so difficult to enter here?' she asks curiously.

'Quite a lot. Above all, you have to fill in many forms.'

'I was born on Philadelphia, in the United States, but I came to live here with my family when I was only three years old.'

'I have always lived in Madrid, with my parents and my siblings. My sister went to live with her boyfriend two years ago. She is two years older than me. My brother is still sixteen years old.'

'I have two older sisters. They are married and have two children each. Do you live alone here or do you have any relatives?' she asks me.

'I live with a girl I met on a room search website and with another guy who lives in the house. I don't have any relatives here. They all live in Spain.'

'I'm sure you miss them a lot, don't you?'

That's where I got the sensitive touch.

'Very much. Every day. But now I'm getting better at it. The good thing is that we can talk on *Skype* or *WhatsApp*. The only drawback is the time change. There are ten hours less in Spain.' Rose looks at her watch. 'Here it's ten past seven in the evening and there it's ten past nine in the morning.'

'Exactly.'

Rose helps me hold a Belgian shepherd so that I can administer an injection. The owner holds his head.

'If he doesn't let us, we'll have to put him to sleep' I warn the owner of the dog.

'There is no problem. Whatever is necessary.'

I manage to put the injection in after a lot of effort.

Rose is cutting a cat's nails while I fill in the dog's details for the injection and a few other things that have been left pending.

My mobile phone vibrates. It's a message from Luca.

> *Ciao bella, come stai? I bet you don't know who asked me for your phone number?*

Coming from Luca, anything can happen. I'm intrigued by his question. I finish writing the information on the computer and I answer him.

> *Who?*

> *Your stud from last night.*

> *How? You're laughing at me, right? That's impossible.*

> *È vero. He wrote to me a while ago and asked me about you and if I could give him your number.*

> *Did you give it to him?*

> *Of course not! I told him that I had to ask you first.*

If I say no, I'll be missing the chance to get his number. But I don't want to get my hopes up like last night either. Maybe they weren't false expectations. Maybe he wanted to meet me so that we could talk and get to know each other better. A silly giggle escapes me and Rose looks at me in puzzlement. I have to pretend. I look like a teenager. My hormones are shot and my heart is racing. I don't know what to say to Luca.

> *Ciaooooo. Are you there?*

Luca asks me.

> *You're online and you don't answer me. What do I tell Raúl?*

> *Mmm... I don't know. What would you do if you were me?*

At the moment I'm already regretting having asked him that. I already know the answer.

> *Come on. I'm diving into the pool. Tell him yes.*

Nerves come to the surface and I am no longer able to hold my mobile phone with strength. I have to keep working normally. Work comes first. I continue to carry out my work with complete normality. I left my phone on my desk so I wouldn't be tempted to pick it up every five seconds.

Rose has noticed something because she looks at me trying to guess what I'm thinking. I still don't have enough confidence with her to tell her about my love affair.

It's almost time to go out. We are sitting in the living room. Talking about the day and the different anecdotes that have happened to us today. I remember that I left my phone on the desk in the examination room and I go down to look for it with the illusion that the Adonis has written to me.

I enter the room so quickly that I slip, and if it wasn't for grabbing a piece of furniture next to the door, I would have fallen. Luckily, nobody saw me. What a shame!

I take my mobile phone and look if there is one message notification.

Yes.

The *WhatsApp* icon appears at the top of the screen. I open it with my heart in my fist thinking that Raúl has written to me. My mind wanders with the different quotes we may have. Maybe he invites me to lunch, dinner or something better. Maybe to dance.

My illusion disappears the moment I see that the message is from Charlie.

> *Hello, beautiful. Would you like to have dinner with me?*

I feel an overwhelming sadness inside me because I would have preferred the message to have come from the Adonis. I like Charlie very much and we have kissed. Besides, he's very handsome, I can't deny it, but Raúl has something that makes me shudder at the mere sight of him and makes me forget everything around me.

> *Yes. I'm off in ten minutes.*

I don't want to be rude to Charlie. He's been very good to me.

> *Yes, I know. I'm out there waiting for you.*

I didn't expect this answer. I thought maybe he would tell me that he would come and get me at home.

He remembered my work schedule.

I say goodbye to my colleagues and go to Charlie's car. He is waiting for me with a smile. He's a stud. There's no doubt about it. He opens the car door for me to get in.

'Good evening, Dani. I was already looking forward to seeing you again.'

'Good evening. How was your day?' I don't know if I can say the same. Right now it's not exactly him I want to see.

'Very good. It was a good day. And you?'

'I have no complaints. The colleagues are very nice.' I try to hide my disappointment.

'You seem a little sad. Has something happened to you?' He's noticed. I am very expressive.

'No. Not at all. I miss my family. That's all,' I pretend.

'Would you like to have dinner in a Mexican restaurant?' He tries to cheer me up. His eyes are full of hope.

I nod my head. My guts are roaring. I haven't eaten anything since noon.

It took us about ten minutes to get there. There wasn't much traffic. Charlie parks in front of the restaurant. The Mexican one is next to the Italian restaurant I came to with Carol.

We go upstairs and go inside.

'Good evening. Table for two?' A waiter welcomes us at the entrance.

'Yes,' answers Charlie.

A waiter leads us to a table.

It is obvious that it is an elegant place. It is spacious. It has a big lamp in the entrance.

There are lamps with big black tulips on top of the tables. They are held up by grey beams.

The walls are painted in different colours. One wall is painted in intense pink with wide black lines in both diagonal and horizontal directions. Another wall is painted in a greyish colour above the brick, also with black lines in curved shapes, and another wall has large rectangular tiles in grey with the same black curves as the brick wall.

There is a long table in the centre of the restaurant supported by concrete blocks divided into sections of two chairs between the blocks, thus separating each section of the table for four diners.

The floor is also painted with a large circle with some rhombuses and others shapes that I do not know.

The bar is made of wood and is fixed on an illuminated panel.

At the back there are some small round tables with three armchairs also rounded to match with the table.

The waiter brings us the menu. I leaf through it from top to bottom. The prices are not cheap, but they are not too expensive either. The waiter comes back to take notes. We ask for a tasting of different types of tacos and water to drink.

The waiter comes back a few minutes later with a big jug of water, bread and guacamole as an appetizer.

'What are you going to do next weekend?' Charlie's question catches me off duty.

'Well, I don't know yet. I haven't thought about it.'

'If you want, we can go somewhere.'

*Alone? A whole weekend?* No way. I don't want Charlie to get his hopes up. He looks at me with bewilderment with his elbows on the table and his arms crossed. He waits for me to give him a yes, but I have to learn to say no more times. Charlie is going to get more excited about it.

The waiter comes back with dinner and it couldn't be more helpful because I'm not able to give him an answer now.

The tacos are served on slate plates. Everything is very well presented. There are several dishes with two tacos in each and different flavours.

My cheeks are on fire and not from a compliment that a man can tell me, but from the spiciness. I drink several glasses of water in a row to ease the burning in my throat. They are exquisite in taste. I try to give air to my throat with my hands. Charlie laughs at me. He eats the tacos as if the spice didn't affect him.

'You still haven't answered the question I asked you before.' Charlie is anxious.

I hesitate for a few moments.

'Look... It's just...' I'm not sure what excuse to use. 'I have to do general cleaning at home with Carol and Luca.' I sound credible.

'Well...' Charlie is a little disappointed.

'If you want, we can go another weekend' I don't like being so sharp and I give him a minimum of hope.

His eyes light up with the opportunity I have just offered him. Although I only did it not to see him sad.

'We can go back to dinner tomorrow if you want.'

'I can't tomorrow. I'm going to dance classes.'

'Dance? Since when?' His eyes are getting dark. He didn't like my new hobby at all.

'I started yesterday. Luca insisted. I already went to Latin dance classes in Spain six years ago.'

His eyes soften at the mention of Luca's name. He doesn't know that Raúl exists and that I'm so attracted to him. If he has been bothered by me going to dance, I can't imagine if he knew that the instructor is a teacher who looks like a model.

'Ah,' he exclaims, 'and what kind of classes are they?' He wants to know.

'*Salsa* classes on Tuesdays and *bachata* classes on Thursdays, from 9.30pm to 10.30pm at Bondi Pavilion.' And now I feel it's one of those moments when I've talked too much.

I don't know, but I feel that it's not going to be so quiet. He's going to want to know more.

'Maybe I will go to see my family in February, for my birthday.' I change the subject radically so that he doesn't keep asking me more questions about dance classes.

'I would love to get to know Spain.'

Is that a hint? Maybe that's how he thinks I'll invite him to come with me. We've just kissed, but I think Charlie thinks we're dating or something. I have to try to get that idea out of his head.

'Well...' I have no idea what to say. 'I'm looking forward to seeing other countries too. I've always wanted to get to know Latin America.' Phew! I think it was a good start.

'You said your birthday. What day is it?' Not a single one thing escapes him.

'The fourteenth.'

'What a coincidence! It's Valentine's Day.'

'Yes,' I say with resignation. 'Everyone tells me the same thing. When is yours?'

'On the fifth of August I'll be thirty. How old are you?'

'A few less' I say with a mischievous smile. 'Twenty-five' I add.

Charlie raises his hand and moves his fingers indicating that there is only five years difference. We laugh.

The waiter comes and takes away our dishes.

'Would you like some dessert?' asks the young man cordially.

I look at the dessert menu.

'A margarita cheese cake for me, please.' The waiter takes note of my order.

'I want a cucumber and jalapeño slushie,' says Charlie.

The waiter returns with our desserts. I give Charlie a piece of my cake to taste and he gives me a taste of his slushie. They are really good.

The night is spent talking and the restaurant is empty. The waiter kindly tells us that they are going to close.

It's almost half past eleven at night.

Dinner was fun, although at times there was some tension.

'They throw us out,' says Charlie, raising his shoulders and smiling broadly. 'I must confess that this is the first time I've lost track of time in this way and I have to be told to leave a restaurant.'

'I confess that me too.' I raise my eyebrows and laugh.

'I'm taking you home. It's very late and I'm up early tomorrow.'

'If you want, I'll come back in a taxi.' I said it without thinking

Charlie looks at me with bewilderment.

'And what am I?' he asks.

'Yes, I know. I only said it in case you wanted to go home now.'

'Come on. Let's not waste anymore time.'

We say goodbye with embarrassment to the staff who are already lifting the chairs and sweeping the restaurant.

Charlie, as always, opens the car door for me to come in. The streets are empty. We arrive immediately.

Charlie parks the car and unbuckles his seat belt. He pounces on me without giving me time to react and kisses me while holding my face with his hands so that I can't escape.

One of his hands goes down to my thigh and starts to go up to the elastic part of my panties. He makes an effort to pull them down.

I struggle and try to pull him away from me, but he's stronger than I am. His kiss is very passionate, but at the same time it's very aggressive, as if he was trying to claim that I'm his property.

I try to get rid of him, but it is impossible. He is literally on top of me. I have my seatbelt on and that makes it difficult for me to get out of the car.

I try to take it off.

'No!' I scream.

Charlie stops his action immediately.

'I'm sorry,' he says panting, 'I didn't mean to force you into anything. I am sorry. It won't happen again.'

'I hope so' I answer almost breathlessly.

Charlie apologizes to me again and again in shame. I didn't imagine that he could do this to me. I am really angry. I can't hide it. I look at him with hate.

He tries to calm me down by holding my hand, but I immediately take it off. I don't even want to feel his skin.

I take off my belt, take my bag and run out of the car. Charlie gets out of the car and follows me to the house door and, as I didn't have time to take the keys out of the bag, Charlie catches up with me.

'Please don't touch me' I tell him before he tries to do so.

'Just listen to me, please,' he says in a pleading tone.

I'm nodding.

'I was very jealous of what you said to me in the restaurant.' He runs his hand through his hair, nervously. He sighs. 'I know there is nothing between us, but I like you a lot' he confesses.

'You said it. There's nothing between us' I'm stressing every word. 'I don't want you to be confused with me. We have kissed once. Well... twice with tonight's.' I gesture with my hands more than usual. I'm nervous.

'I'm sorry. I thought we connected. That you felt the same way I did, but I was wrong. I was fascinated by your eyes from the moment I saw them through the mirror of my taxi. Forgive me.' Mere words of apology come out of his mouth.

I look in the bag for the keys. They don't appear. It looks like a bottomless bag. I stir my hand again and again looking. I don't want to talk to Charlie anymore. I just want to go home now and forget about this moment.

At last I find them hidden in one of the inner pockets. I look up. Charlie is kneeling in front of me. This is a nightmare. I pinch my left arm.

No.

It's not a nightmare. It is real.

'Get up' I command him.

'Forgive me,' he pleads.

I look at him, he seems sincere.

'I forgive you, but get up.'

Finally he stands up when he hears my forgiveness. He is looking down at the floor. He is not able to raise his eyes.

'Go away, please. I need to rest. We'll talk tomorrow.'

I say goodbye with a slight hand gesture. I open the door, enter the house and close it without looking back.

I put my back to the door and drop my bag. I run both hands through my hair. I take a deep breath while moving my head from left to right repeatedly.

I'm still in shock from what just happened a few minutes ago. The gentleman is no longer a gentleman and I don't like these unfounded jealousies at all.

I take my bag and when I look into the room I see Luca and Carol watching me without blinking and wanting to know. I don't want to talk about my end of the night. It was a real disaster.

'What are you doing up so late? It's almost midnight.'

'We were worried about you,' answers Luca.

'You could have warned us that you would be late.' Carol scolds me.

'You're right. I'm going to sleep.' I disappear down the corridor before Luca or Carol start asking questions.

I go into the room and lock the door.

I take my mobile phone out of my bag. I have ten messages. Two are from my sister asking me how my day went. She would never guess what I just went through. I answer her by saying that everything went well.

The other eight messages are from Charlie. He apologises to me in each of them. He has written them in Spanish. He must have thought that I didn't understand him when he said it to me in the car and on the doorstep.

I don't reply.

I shuffle off to bed. I can't get what the dark gentleman did to me out of my mind. Nothing like this has ever happened to me before. I end up exhausted and fall asleep with that nightmare in my head.

## Thursday, 16th November, 2017

I leave home for work early. I don't feel like walking. I'm going to the bus stop. I've thought about eating something somewhere. I don't feel like cooking or doing anything in general. I don't hate Charlie anymore, I'm disappointed. Yes. I am disappointed. A feeling that accompanies me more often than I would like.

The bus is full and I have no choice but to keep standing.

I look in my mobile phone at some restaurant near the clinic that has door-to-door service and in the kitchen at work, unhurriedly and quietly.

I order food from a Chinese restaurant. I wait in the reception of the clinic. Kayla is busy looking at the computer screen while typing at high speed.

'Good afternoon, Daniela. You're so early today!'

Kayla has stopped doing her tasks. She has got up from her chair and is standing next to me. I'm at the door waiting for the delivery man.

'I didn't feel like cooking. I'm waiting for the delivery man to bring me my food.'

'Where did you order the food?' she asks.

'At Bambusia. Do you know it?'

'Yes. It is very close by. I have also ordered food there once.'

Darel parks in front of the clinic. He is also early. Behind him comes the delivery man. I pay him and he gives me the bag of food.

'How nice it smells!' says Darel.

'It's Chinese food. I'm going to have a taste of it,' I say, holding up the bag.

I go upstairs and sit on the sofa in the living room. I've ordered a mixed appetizer with spring rolls, tiger prawn toast and pork dim sum. I've also ordered sweet and sour chicken; it comes with rice and salad.

I have a bottle of water in the fridge to drink.

Darel is coming. He turns on the TV and prepares a cup of coffee.

'Do you want some?' he asks, holding the coffee pot and shaking it.

'No. Thank you. Maybe later.'

'I have something to tell you.' Darel sits down next to me and I swallow. I have no idea what he wants to talk about. Maybe he's unhappy with my job, although I think I'm doing quite well. 'You'll see. Today Rose will be with you and Emma.'

'Emma?' I ask in bewilderment.

I mentally review the shift sheet and the schedule and I seem to remember that Emma and I didn't coincide on any shift.

'She had to change her shift. She had things to do this morning. You don't mind, do you?'

What do I care? Darel is the boss. If he says we have to share the assistant, then we have to share the assistant. I hope Emma is in a better mood and we have a pacific evening.

I nod with my head in resignation as I get up and throw away the wrappers and food scraps.

The food was excellent.

Darel and I are talking about work sitting on the sofa when Rose, Angela, Sarah, Henry and Beth arrive. They sit with us. Darel tells us about the evolution of two mastiffs who arrived this morning and are in treatment for a pit bull attack.

'They are evolving favourably. Now we have to make sure that the bites on their necks do not become infected. They are sedated, so there is no problem in treating them. We will have them here all weekend and if they evolve favourably, we will release them on Monday. Can you take care of that, Henry?' Darel explains himself very well. He is very professional.

'Yes' Henry answers with satisfaction.

Emma arrives and greets everyone, but she doesn't even look at me. This girl has taken it out on me. I don't know why. She is very strange. I look at her out of the corner of my eye. She walks around. She looks nervous. She makes herself a cup of coffee with her trembling hands.

'Emma, today you and Daniela will have to share Rose.' Darel tells Emma of his decision and she doesn't hesitate.

'I hope you won't make me work too hard,' says Rose, laughing.

'I will only call you for the essentials,' I answer with a wink.

Emma turns and looks up and down at me with the strangest look. She didn't like what I said to Rose at all. She'll think I said it with her in mind. I never mentioned her. Besides, what I said to Rose was a joke.

Darel puts his arm around my shoulders.

'I hope you have a good afternoon. If you have any problems, call me.' Darel caresses my cheek and leaves for his office.

Emma looks at me. This time with hatred, with her mouth open, while she holds the cup with one hand and with the other she stirs the coffee again and again. She's scary. Her gaze has darkened.

This looks bad.

'Rose, are you coming?' I say as I grab her by the arm and pull her.

'Yes. Let's go,' she answers. I think she noticed the way Emma looked at me.

I go through reception and Beth passes me the list of appointments I have today. Rose and I go into the examination room; we finish the details and check that there is everything on the furniture.

'Rose, please. You can send in the first patient now. Thank you.'

Rose obeys and goes out the door to call the first patient. I take the opportunity to turn on the computer and enter my session.

'Don't think you're staying with Darel.'

I look up. Emma is leaning on the door with her arms crossed, scrutinizing me with her eyes.

'Pardon?' I don't understand what she means.

'You heard me. He is mine.'

Rose bursts into the office with my first patient and his owner. I don't like the look on that woman's face. I'm afraid she's trying to make my life miserable.

I have nothing to fear. I am not doing anything to that witch.

I inject the vaccines to the poodle.

'Next week he has to come for the last vaccination. You will be given an appointment at the reception.'

'Thank you very much, Miss.'

Rose accompanies the gentleman to the reception and comes back almost running. She comes in and closes the door.

'Be careful with the witch,' she warns me.

'Huh?' I look at her raising both eyebrows.

I'm sitting at the desk finishing writing the poodle's vaccinations on his chart. Rose sits down in front of me. She lies down on the back of the chair and crosses her arms. I put my elbows on the table and listen to her carefully.

'Let's see... Let me explain. Emma is bad. Very bad. You must be careful. She's been in love with Darel since I've been here and she's capable of making life impossible for anyone who sets eyes on him.'

'Is she that powerful?'

'It's not power. It's just that she's looking for a way to make the one who likes Darel resign or the other way round.'

'Thank you for the advice. I will be careful.'

'If you need anything, just let me know. I'll help you with pleasure. My advice is not to let Darel touch you or look at you.'

'I don't like Darel.'

'I know. But he seems to like you. He's a born seducer. When a new, young and beautiful girl arrives at the clinic, he launches himself into a plate, and Emma can't stand that.'

'I don't think so. I think he just wants to be nice to me.'

'That's how he starts with everyone. Take care of yourself.'

Rose's words stick in my brain. I must be very careful with that woman. I know she's going to try to find a way to get me out of here, but she's not going to make it.

This is my dream job. I love what I do and no mentally ill witch is going to change that.

I hear them yelling Rose's name. It's Emma. How unpleasant it is. She must think she's her maid or something. It's no one's fault that she has such an empty life. How hard is it for her to get out of her office and ask her nicely for help? What a woman.

I need help with a Great Dane, but Rose is busy with Emma and I'm not going to shout at her like she did before. The owner helps me while I go to the wardrobe and take out everything I need to treat the dog. Rose comes to help me. She has passed by the hallway and has seen me in the situation I am in and she walks in.

Emma comes looking for Rose and shouts at her to get out of my office and into hers. This makes me very angry. I leave the dog's treatment half way through, go to her and take her out of my practice by grabbing her arm. I drag her to her office and close the door.

'Let this be the last time you barge into my practice like this' I warn her.

'Who do you think you are to take me out of the office like that?' Her face is all anger.

'It's not a question of who I am or what I'm not. It's about you having no education. I don't know why you are like that with me. I haven't done anything to you and Rose has done even less. Don't ever come into my practice again. Let's be peaceful.'

I turn around and walk out the door when Emma grabs my arm tightly.

'You don't know what you've just done,' she whispers in my ear.

I shudder.

'I'm not afraid of you,' I say in a defiant tone.

'You should be. You don't know what I'm capable of.'

'Is that a threat?'

'No. It's a warning.'

I get out of it and slam the door. I walk into my consulting room where both Rose and the dog's owner are standing there with their mouths open. I have only words of apology for them. I hope it is just a one off, although because of Emma's warning I don't think it will stay that way.

The afternoon passes very slowly, it seems that time has stopped. I take my mobile phone out of my dressing jacket.

5:02 p.m.

I still have four more hours of putting up with the witch. I hope this is the first and last time we will coincide in working. I feel panic at the thought of losing my job because of Emma.

> Ciao, *Luca. I'll be late for the classes about 10 minutes. The bus doesn't leave until 21:12 and I can't leave earlier.*

I leave Luca the message so he doesn't wait for me at home. When I leave here I go straight to *bachata* classes

His answer soon arrives.

*When are you going to have dinner?*

> *Relax. Don't worry. I'll have dinner after class.*

*I'll wait for you and we'll have dinner together.*

> *No need. You can have dinner earlier.*

> *I want to have dinner with you so we can talk.*

> *Is something wrong with you?*

I'm intrigued by this talk. Is she back with the mystery guy? Or a new love? Whatever it is, I'll know after my classes.

I smile.

These messages have made me forget for a moment the encounter with the evil witch. Good thing she doesn't know what I call her. I don't want to imagine how she would be if she did. I pass my hand over my forehead.

> *I'll tell you about it!*

I put my mobile phone back in my dressing jacket pocket and continue working. I try not to think about the bad things. I think about the classes, about having fun and enjoying myself. And about Raúl.

I blush and the heat takes over.

Darel enters my office and asks Rose nicely to leave. I'm afraid he hasn't come for good at all. I stir in the chair. His look is intimidating. He sits down in front of me and puts his elbows on the table.

He interlaces his fingers at chin level.

'I'm sorry to interrupt you like this, but I heard the warm conversation between you and Emma. I warn you that I don't like this kind of altercation, especially when there are people in the clinic.'

'I'm sorry.' I can hardly talk. I feel a pressure on my chest.

I rub my face with my hands and treacherous tears come out of my eyes. I am in shock. This is the second time in less than 24 hours.

'Well, woman. Don't be like that.' He holds my hands and softens my gaze. He's not as angry as when he arrived.

'Emma came screaming because Rose was helping me and all I did was to defend her.'

Darel nods his head as I explain in detail everything that happened and what Emma told me. I don't care what he thinks. I don't care how I look like those kids who have to tell the teacher at school what their classmates are doing so that I don't lose my job.

I call Rose to corroborate my version of events. She tells him the same thing I told her.

'Perfect. Everything is clear. Thank you, Daniela. Forgive me for the way I spoke to you before.' He hugs me and gives me a kiss on the cheek. He strokes my hair. 'You can come out now if you want. There's only a quarter of an hour left until nine.'

'Thank you. I need it.'

'Rose. You too.'

We go out together while Emma watches us from the end of the corridor. I see her from reception entering Darel's office. I don't think today will end well for her.

'Where are you going?' asks Rose.

'I'm going to Bondi Pavilion.'

'If you like, I'll give you a lift. I live on Brighton Boulevard.'

'I don't know Sydney well yet.'

'I live in a flat near the cliff that can be seen from Bondi Beach.'

'Oh.'

'Whenever you want, you can come to my house and we can have lunch together.'

'That would be nice. I live on Wellington Street.'

Rose gives me her phone number as she starts the car and we are on our way.

> *Hi. I'm off work. I'll be on time. See you at the front door.*

E quello?

This man forgets that I don't understand Italian.

> *I'll tell you later. I'm going in a colleague's car.*

> *OK. How long will it take?*

I ask Rose.

> *Rose tells me 9:15 or so.*

> Va bene. *See you at the entrance. I'm leaving the house now.*

Rose double parks on Campbell Parade.

'Thank you very much for the lift. Thanks to you I won't be late for class. See you tomorrow.'

'You're welcome. See you tomorrow.' Rose says goodbye to me and goes on her way.

In the distance I see Luca. Unmistakable. He's handsome even from afar. Too bad he's gay. He runs over and gives me a big hug that cracks my back.

'What do you have to tell me? You have left me intrigued' I ask as I look for the answer in his eyes.

'I'll tell you later at dinner. Now let's just enjoy the *bachata* class.'

We are holding each other's arms. I laugh at the adventures he tells me about at the university. It reminds me of me when I was studying. It was an adventure every day.

Today there is light in his eyes and the most beautiful smile. I'm very happy to see him like that. I hope I will see myself like this one day. When it seems that my life cannot get any worse, something always happens. Sometimes I wonder why I can't find someone to share my life with. Someone who is sincere, kind and caring. Is that too much to ask?

Luca gives me a pat on the back and takes me out of my wandering mind.

'We're here.'

'Already?' I ask.

'Yes. Where is your head?'

'I was thinking about my things. Nothing important,' I say.

Raúl is already in class. He's in front of the mirror practising some *bachata* steps with Elizabeth. He looks so professional and so handsome... There are some students in a corner of the classroom whispering as they point at him in disguise. He is a real charmer. You just have to look at him.

There are couples I already know from Tuesday and also new ones.

Raúl stands in front of us and gives us instructions to stretch our muscles before dancing.

'Good evening, ladies and gentlemen. Today, first we'll go over the steps we've learned so far so that the new faces can catch up, and then we'll continue with new steps.'

Raúl looks at me and surprises me by watching him. I look away immediately. I die of shame. My cheeks are burning. My breathing has accelerated without being able to avoid it.

'Do you feel well?' asks Luca.

'Yes, I feel fine.'

'*Mamma mia*! You're burning up,' he says, touching my cheeks.

'It's just that it's hot.'

Luca runs to his backpack and brings me some water. I drink endlessly, almost finishing the half litre bottle.

We are in a couple dancing the basic steps of *bachata*. What good memories I have of this. Luca is overjoyed, more than usual. I would like to have his same energy, to see life as he sees it.

Raúl comes to us. I have him right behind me with his hands on my waist and his breath on my neck while he corrects my posture. I can't help but blush.

My whole body shakes, my body temperature rises automatically and I lose control of what I was doing.

'You've lost your balance' Luca scolds me.

'Sorry, it was unintentional.' I look at him with a good girl's face.

'Don't let it happen again.' He winks at me and puts back that mischievous smile.

I look down.

Luca releases his hand from my waist, grabs my chin and pulls it up to look at him.

'Don't be ashamed. That reaction is normal.'

'Huh?'

'Look at the girls around us. They look just like you.'

We look around and I check.

'Just put some bibs on them' I say smiling.

'We change partners... Girls stay where you are and guys take the girl on your right. Go on. One, two, three, four.'

I feel a choking sensation when I look around and see that Raúl is close. My body temperature inexplicably rises again and my throat becomes dry when I see our glances crossing.

I had only had a similar feeling when I first saw Hugo. In his blue hospital pyjamas, his eyes, his hair, his voice…

'Are you here?'

I look up and it's Raúl who just asked me that question. Lately I am more in the clouds than on Earth.

The Adonis is in front of me, waiting for me to return from wherever I am to continue dancing.

I put my hand on his shoulder and with the other hand I hold his, which is waiting impatiently. I feel electricity between us. He looks at me and I feel warmth in his gaze.

I gulp.

'I've asked Luca for your telephone number. I hope it didn't bother you.'

His words fill me with relief, and at the same time with frustration.

'No,' I answer.

'I wanted to call you, but I didn't have time.'

Those words comfort me and make a ray of hope come out of a little corner of my heart. My inner self dances *bachata* while I don't take my eyes off the Adonis in front of me, although I can't believe that having a girlfriend he dares to flirt with me like that.

I watch him closely and I can look at every corner of his body. He has strong arms and his body is sculptural. You can tell that he takes care of himself and goes to the gym.

'Switching partners.'

Raúl leaves with the girl on my left who is more than happy and takes a little piece of me with him.

We are leaving the class. Luca and I talk about where to have dinner. Some girls have stayed talking to the Adonis. I watch him out of the corner of my eye and, although the girls are very willing to try to flirt with Raúl, he follows me with his eyes. At that moment I feel important, my ego rises to a level I've never felt before. The girls look at me with envy and the only thing that comes out of me is a smile.

We go to Campbell Parade when Raúl comes running towards us. My heart is pounding. He is here and alone. Where did he leave Elizabeth?

'Did you have dinner?' he asks.

'Not yet,' answers Luca.

I've lost the ability to speak and I can't make a sound.

'I'll go with you,' he says.

My inner self jumps with joy. *"This one, yes, this one,"* it repeats. I make it shut up. I don't want to get my hopes up, although I think I've had them for a while now. He has a girlfriend. That makes my inner self stop jumping.

'We can buy some *kebabs* and eat them on the beach. Would you like to?'

Luca and I look at each other and we don't need to say anything to know that we both agree.

'Yes' I can say that.

'I'm buying.'

We are in the bite box waiting for dinner to be served.

'Where are you from?' Raúl asks us.

'I am from Italy and Daniela is from Spain.' Luca goes ahead of me and answers for both of us.

'And what are we doing talking in English?'

'Huh?'

'I'm from Cuba. I speak Spanish perfectly.'

I could tell by the colour of his skin, the features of his face, his curly hair and how well he moves when he dances.

'Have you lived here long?' I'm curious.

'I came here when I was ten years old with my parents and my brothers' he comments. 'And you?' he adds.

'I've only been here for two weeks,' I reply.

'*Io, un po 'di più*. Arrived at the end of August,' says Luca.

'Your food.' The friendly shop assistant tells us.

He gives Raúl the bag with the food and drinks he has ordered.

We walk to the beach. The food in the bag smells very good. Raúl passes his arm over my shoulder. I let him do so. I feel like in a fairy tale.

Luca throws a mischievous smile at me.

We sit on the sand, facing the sea. It's sixty-six Fahrenheit's. The wind is blowing weakly.

Raúl takes the food out of the bag and places it on top of some plastic plates that we have been given at the restaurant.

We eat.

'It's delicious,' I say.

'I'm glad you like it. How about you?' he asks Luca.

'Yes,' he answers with his mouth full.

I look at the sky in search of the moon. A very thin line shows up in the black and starry sky. It's a waning moon. The stars look very big. I would say bigger than in Madrid.

'It's a very beautiful sky, isn't it?' says the Adonis.

'Yes, it's beautiful,' I answer without being able to take my eyes off the sky.

'If you like the stars, you have to go to the Observatory. Now it is an interactive museum where people go at night to observe the stars and planets through a very modern telescope or also with an old one, which I think is the oldest one still in use.'

'I have to go,' says Luca, interrupting Raúl's explanation. 'I have to get up early tomorrow.'

I look at him and tell him not to go. I don't think I'm ready to stay with this monument of a man.

'Stay,' I beg him.

'Go if you want to,' says Raúl, 'I'll take care of her,' he says, leaning his body against me.

I shudder.

'You are in good hands. *Buona notte*!' Luca winks at me.

I squint and move my head from one side to the other while behind Luca is moving away from us.

'I'm not going to eat you.'

Raúl looks at me and his face is all lust.

He leaves me speechless.

'Did you like the lessons?'

'Yes. Very much' I answer sincerely.

'I hope you'll come again. I like to see you dance.'

My body temperature rises again as if I was exposed to the sun.

'Mmm... I suppose... Yes' I say half heartedly. 'As long as work allows me' I continue.

'What do you do for a living?'

'I'm a vet in a clinic. What about you? Do you work alone as a teacher or do you have another job?'

'In the morning I work in a school as a physical education teacher.'

'Ah.'

'Why did you come to live in Sydney?'

'Because it has more job opportunities than Spain. For the same job the salary in Spain is half of what it is here.'

Raúl looks at me with bewilderment.

'Are you going to stay here long?'

'I don't know yet. I have a one year contract at work.'

'That means I will be able to see you for at least a whole year.'

A silly smile lights up my face.

Raúl slowly approaches me. He caresses my cheek with one hand, and with the other he surrounds my waist.

'I love those blue eyes of yours. They are so big and expressive…'

I don't know what to say. I feel my heart beating in my throat. They are beating very fast and my breathing has accelerated.

'I have to go.'

I get up in one jump. This is going too fast. I don't want the same thing that happened to me with Charlie.

'Why are you leaving? It's not too late.' Raúl has stood up and put his arms around me.

We are alone. The few people who were walking have already left. It's a beautiful night. But I don't want to spoil this moment. I'd rather leave now, than let it become a big deal.

Raúl pulls me towards him.

'You're beautiful. You know that? I liked you from the moment I saw you.'

'You… I… Well…' I can't say a proper sentence.

I'm at this Adonis' mercy. I want to tell him how handsome he is. That I like him since I saw him at The Cuban Place.

I restrain myself. He has a girlfriend, I repeat to myself. Although right now he controls my breathing, my heartbeat and even my temperature. He only needs to touch one inch of my skin for my temperature to shoot up.

I have to go and I have to do it now, otherwise this is going to end up in more than just a dinner at the beach.

I take a deep breath.

'I already knew you' I confess.

Raúl raises his eyebrows.

'Where? When?'

'At The Cuban Place a little more than a week ago.'

'I go there every weekend.'

'Ah.'

'I've seen you and your...' I keep quiet.

'She is my sister.'

'Elizabeth? Is she your sister?'

'Yes' Raúl says. Now I've made the biggest fool of my life. *His sister* repeats my inner self jumping for joy. *She is not his girlfriend.* I repeat to myself. A smile is drawn on my mouth without being able to avoid it.

'Did you think she was my girlfriend?' he asks, laughing.

I nod my head in shame. I look down at the floor. I am unable to look at his face.

He laughs out loud and I end up laughing too.

He holds me by the waist with strength and pulls me even more towards him, making me feel his heartbeat. They are almost as strong as mine.

He asks my permission to kiss me with his eyes. His eyes burn in desire and I can't help it.

He kisses me sweetly on the lips while I feel his heart beating in time with mine. He tastes like *kebab* and *Coke*. His lips are soft and tender. His tongue explores inside my mouth looking for mine until they meet. I stand on tiptoe and wrap my arms around him at shoulder height. It's a magical moment.

Images come to mind of last night and of Hugo. He comes back to my mind to haunt this delicious moment.

I push Raúl away from me almost at a moment's notice.

'What's wrong with you?' he asks, wondering.

'I'm sorry. I can't. I have to go.'

I run away without looking back and leave him there alone, on the beach.

I walk down Roscoe Street. I think about what I have just done. I've just lost my last chance to find the love of my life. I may never find him. The streets are empty. Many fast food places are closing. I feel like crying.

I try to hold back.

## Saturday, 18th November, 2017

I'm in bed. The sun comes in through the window. It warms up the room and I'm very comfortable here, between the sheets. I start thinking about Raúl and the kiss on the beach, about Charlie and the struggle in the car, and about Hugo and his betrayal. All this has happened in such a short time... I sigh.

I am confused. I don't know what to do. This is when I most need my mother's hug and those afternoons of girls sitting on the sofa drinking coffee, with her and my sister, in the village house, by the fireplace and surrounded by blankets.

I look at the clock. It is 12:22.

Yesterday Jack invited me to dinner, but I refused. I wouldn't want him to be confused with me. I just like him as a friend, nothing more.

Darel was very different with me, he hardly spoke to me. Everyone at the clinic realised that. Maybe Emma told him something that turned him against me.

That worries me because I don't want to lose my job, and even less because of that bitch. She is bad.

Rose has been with me all afternoon and that has made it happen quickly, as she talks to me and tells me stories that make me laugh. She is very nice and pleasant.

I think about getting up, but it's so nice in bed without doing anything... The truth is that I have nothing to do. I could stay here all day, between the sheets and with the smell of the sea coming in through the window and flooding the room with its fresh scent. It's like having the beach inside the room.

Yesterday I couldn't see Luca. When I arrived from work, he had already left for dinner with a "friend".

I laugh.

I guess which friend it was. At the end we didn't talk about what he wanted to tell me last Thursday because Raúl signed up for our dinner. I was intrigued by that.

At night I didn't hear him arrive and I slept late watching my favourite series on my laptop. He may have also slept over.

There are several missed messages and calls on my phone. They are from Raúl and Charlie.

> *Good morning, beautiful. How are you? Although the way you ran off the other night... You're in shape.*

Raúl is right. I have been a coward. I haven't been able to face the situation I was going through at the time.

> *Good afternoon. I'm fine. Enjoying the day off.*

He's online, but he hasn't seen my message. I take this opportunity to look at Charlie's message, although I can imagine what he might have written. It will all be words of apology.

> *Hi. I hope you're not mad at me. I got jealous for no reason and I crossed a line with you. Forgive me. This situation hurts me a lot.*

I believe that he is sorry, although I still find it hard to forgive him. I can't believe how we have come to this. He was such a gentleman, but he decided to go over to the dark side like in Star Wars. On the other hand, I am not a spiteful person.

I answer.

> *Well, I forgive you. But don't expect us to have the relationship that we had a few days ago. It will take me a long time to trust you again.*

He answers instantly, as if he had been waiting for my message stuck to the phone.

> *Thank you very much. I needed so much for you to forgive me... I haven't called you or sent you any messages before so as not to burden you.*

I thank you.

> *I wasn't ready to talk to you either. I don't understand your jealousy. We were only just friends....*

> *I like you and I got confused. I'm sorry. It won't happen again.*

Of course it won't happen again because it's going to be a long time before I get back to trust him. I will never be alone with the dark knight again.

> *I just hope you don't go to get confused again.*

> *I promise you.*

A message from the Adonis enters. I get nervous thinking about what he has written to me. I open it.

> *I hope you enjoy your day off. I still have those blue eyes stuck in my mind.*

I blush.

I leave my mobile phone on the little table next to my bed, get up and go to the bathroom to take a shower.

As the water runs through my body, I think of Raúl and I get chills.

He is very handsome. I don't think he's for me. I think about those girls in the dance classes: so tall, so blonde, so thin and so beautiful that I get depressed.

I look at myself in the mirror in the bathroom steaming with hot water. What do I have that I the others don't I have to learn to be more optimistic, like Carol. She gives off that security that I lack.

I leave my room clean and tidy. I look at my mobile in case Raúl has written to me. Nothing. I look at my *Facebook* profile. I go to The Cuban Place page; there are photos of the night I was there.

I check them one by one.

In some photos I appear from afar with Charlie. There are many of the Adonis and his sister. I let out a silly smile. And I thought she was his girlfriend. He doesn't have a girlfriend. That relieves me and at the same time it worries me. There are many candidates interested in that position. I can't compete with all those girls.

There is one photo that particularly catches my eye. It is Raúl. He is leaning on one of the columns observing something, but I don't know exactly what. I zoom in on the photo. Huh? In one corner of the photo there is Charlie, Luca and me drinking. For a moment, I think that he could be watching me. I don't think so. But I look again and again at the picture and that's what it looks like. I don't know if my eyes are betraying me or if I'm already delirious.

I get out of bed and go to the door. I have to ask Luca. I want him to give me an unbiased opinion on this photo.

What a scare! When I open the door I meet Luca.

'We have telepathy,' I say to him in surprise.

'*Perché?*'

'I was just coming to find you.'

'Well, I'm here now,' he says, pointing to himself.

'Come in and sit down. I need your opinion on something.'

'What is it?' He's intrigued.

'Look,' I say, showing him the photo. 'Tell me if Raúl is looking at me or not in this picture.'

Luca looks at it carefully. He zooms in and out several times.

'Yes, he's looking at you,' he says in a very calm tone.

'You said it as if you were not surprised.'

'I'm not surprised because that night you and he danced together.'

'Huh?' I can't believe my ears. 'That's impossible.'

'*Vero*! He came up to you and invited you to dance,' he explains.

'When? I remember that after drinking on that sofa we left.'

'You are wrong. Before we left, you danced with him and very tightly, by the way. You have been the envy of many girls and perhaps some other guys.'

My temperature just goes up a few degrees at once. I don't remember any of that. I run my hand through my hair and pull it away from my face. I close my eyes and try to remember. I squeeze them with strength.

Nothing.

'I don't remember anything' I confess.

'Don't torment yourself with that. It's over now. You'd better tell me. How did it go with Raúl?'

'Good.' I'm breathing deeply. 'I'm furious.'

'Why? If you just said good.'

'Because I confessed that I had met him at The Cuban Place and he didn't tell me that we had already danced together. I feel like...' I bite my tongue.

'Maybe he didn't want you to feel bad, because you have to accept that you were very drunk. Rather, the three of us were very drunk that night.'

'That's true. Maybe I said something out of place.' I cover my mouth with my hand. I die of shame.

Luca passes his arm over my shoulders.

'Well. Don't think about it anymore. Come on; tell me what you did with Raúl the other night.' He wants to know.

'Well... We finished dinner. We talked. By the way, did you know that he's a physical education teacher in a school?'

'No.'

Luca seems as surprised as I was.

'And then?' Luca insists.

'And he kissed me.'

'He kissed you? *Mamma mia!*' His eyes open very wide.

'Yes.'

I blush when I remember that moment.

'How does he kiss?'

'So why am I going to lie to you? He kisses like the devil, but I don't want to get my hopes up. I don't want the same thing to happen to me as with Hugo.'

'You still haven't told me who this Hugo is.'

I inhale and exhale a couple of times before I start telling the story that brought me here. I run my hand through my hair.

'A year and a half ago I met a boy. He is a doctor and works in the same hospital as my mother and sister. They are nurses. We started dating. He came to my career graduation ceremony. We were very happy, or so I thought.'

I start crying and can't help it and Luca gives me a big hug.

'If you can't go on, it's okay.'

'Yes. I want to tell you about it. I proposed to him to move in together several times, but he was evasive. When we spent the night together it was in a hotel, like when we went somewhere on holiday. They were always short. Two or three days. I suspected that he was hiding something from me, because he never wanted us to go to his house. So I looked into his social networks, but he had it all completely private. We were together for about fifteen months.'

I can't talk anymore. I'm crying so much that I can't articulate another word.

'Calm down. It's over now.'

Luca keeps hugging me, stroking my cheeks and wiping my tears with his pyjama shirt.

Impotence takes hold of me. That traitor doesn't deserve my tears. He promised me the sky and the stars. I believed him. I was a fool. He deceived me as if I was a child.

'He tricked me,' I said in a voice over.

'Don't talk anymore. Stay calm.' Luca puts me to bed and covers me with a small blanket that I have on a chair. 'I'll get you a glass of water.'

Luca leaves the room and closes the door. I look around. I miss him. As much as I try to hate him, I can't. I miss his kisses, his caresses and the way he made love to me. It was all like in a storybook, but without a happy ending.

The result has been to be more than 17 thousand kilometres away. And, even so, with this long distance that separates us, I am unable to forget about you.

What have you done to me? I have your eyes stuck in my mind. Every time I close my eyes, I see yours. I remember your skin touching mine. Your warmth, your breath, and your words. Those words that have been so encouraging, and so destructive at the same time.

Luca returns with the glass of water. I want to change the subject. I'll ask him about what he wanted to tell me the other day. Oh, Raúl! You've come into my life with such positive energy. I'd like not to share you in my thoughts, but I can't control my heart or my thoughts.

I stand up and sit next to Luca. I drink the whole glass of water in one gulp.

'By the way, Luca, what did you want to tell me the other day?'

'Ah! I didn't even remember anymore. Remember the boy who came asking for me?'

I nod my head while I finish drying my tears.

'He's the same boy I told you about. On Thursday he called me and asked me for a chance. Yesterday we went to dinner and you can imagine how we ended up.' He giggles like a schoolgirl.

He's in love. You can see it in his eyes.

Carol knocks on the door, comes in and sits down on the chair next to him to the desk.

'It's not good to tell each other things in secret, huh?' Carol complains.

'I was just telling her what you and I talked about yesterday,' replies Luca.

'Your boyfriend?' asks Carol.

Luca says yes with his head.

'Shall we eat?'

'Yes!' exclaim Luca and I in unison.

Carol has prepared food. Everything smells good. I am hungry. Yesterday I didn't have dinner and today I didn't have breakfast either.

Luca has an ear-to-ear smile. He has given his boyfriend a second chance. I just hope he doesn't fail him again and that he ends up just like when I met him.

Carol has admitted that she has a relationship with her assistant.

I keep quiet. I think that I could go back to Spain. Leave everything here and go back to Hugo.

Luca and I clear the table and do the dishes. Carol has cooked and it seems fair to us to divide the tasks in this way. We leave everything clean.

I'm lying on the bed, looking out the window at the wonderful day today. While Carol was talking about her assistant and Luca about her boyfriend, I have forgotten for a moment the tears I have shed talking about Hugo.

What might he be doing? Is he still with his crazy girlfriend or has he already left her definitely? He promised me that he would leave her so many times that I got tired of waiting for that moment to come.

I still remember the time we met in the same club. I was with some friends and he arrived with her. I wanted to die when I discovered that one of my friends was a close friend of his girlfriend.

Hugo tried to get rid of her by using my friend to be with me for a while. That day was the most humiliating day of my life.

I don't think I deserve to be anyone's second best, let alone have to hide in order to see us.

Luca enters without knocking.

'*Migliore*?' he asks with concern.

'Yes.' I lie.

'You were very quiet during the meal.'

'I didn't feel like talking, you know? The saddest day of my life was when I followed him to find out where he lived and saw him holding the hand of that madwoman. That day my world collapsed, that day all my dreams fell apart. I wanted the earth to swallow me up.'

'Oh.' Luca lies down next to me. 'The same thing happened to me. I had a boyfriend in Italy, he was with me and with someone else at the same time.'

'With another girl?' I raise an eyebrow.

'Yes, with another girl. I got so angry that I told the girl. Obviously, she didn't know anything.'

'I wanted to have done the same, but I didn't have the courage. Hugo told me so many times that he was going to leave her that I believed it. He told me that she was not well. That she was a disturbed woman and that no matter how much he told her to leave his house, she wouldn't leave.' I sigh. 'At the end I got tired and this is the result' I add.

'Why do you think I live here?'

His question is very obvious. Same reason I am doing it.

'Oh.'

Luca's story and mine are not so different from one another. We are both here out of love and trying to rebuild our lives. Luca seems to have succeeded.

I hope I become like him and forget Hugo forever. He doesn't even deserve that I remember his name.

'Should we go out tonight?'

'I don't feel like it. Thanks, Luca. I'm meeting my family tonight.'

'Oh.'

Luca left a little upset with my answer.

I'm thinking of sending Raúl a message and confronting him. He's known me since the night of The Cuban Place and he didn't say anything to me. Maybe I said something silly and that's why he didn't want to tell me. I let out a little smile. I blush thinking that we have already danced together. I would have liked to remember that moment.

I take the mobile phone from the little table and keep checking the photos from that night in the hope of seeing one where we can be seen together.

There are too many photos.

There it is! The long awaited photo. We are very close together. I'm surrounding him with my arms over his shoulders, while Raúl is holding me by the waist. Why did I have to drink so much? I would have liked to remember that wonderful moment.

How handsome he is! He's one of the most beautiful men I've ever met. I watch him carefully.

I decide to write to him.

> *You already knew me and didn't tell me anything.*

I send him the message and also the photo of that night. I await his reply. He is not on line. I'm afraid I'll have to wait.

I take advantage and tag myself in all the photos I appear in so that my friends can see that we don't only know how to have fun in Spain.

I get a message.

> *Yes. It's true. We danced a bachata song, but you were a little... You weren't exactly up for dancing.*
> *You weren't at all, honestly. Your friends took you right away.*

What a shame!

> *Did I say something out of place?*

He's online, though he's slow to answer. I'm sure I said some... nonsense. If I know, I don't ask him anything.

> *I'll only answer if you agree to go out with me.*

My temperature has just risen as if I was inside an espresso pot. I snort. Do I accept? Do I want to know if I said something absurd or not? I don't know what to do. I get out of bed and run to Luca's room. I need his advice.

'Luca!' I exclaim his name as I enter his room without knocking on the door.

'Ah!' he shouts. I just gave him the scare of his life. He took his hand to his chest. 'Tell me,' he says, trying to catch his breath.

'I sent Raúl a message to clear up the picture from the other day. He said he would tell me what I said that night if I agreed to meet him. What do I do?' I ask him, shaking him by the shoulders. I am very nervous.

'*Aspetta, Rallenta, non ti capisco…*'

I spoke so fast because of my nerves that Luca didn't understand me.

'Sorry' I apologize while I write in the translator of my mobile phone everything I just said and translate it into Italian so that he understands.

'*Buono*! Accept. This way you get out of doubts.' Luca encourages me.

'What if I said something I shouldn't have?'

'If you don't go, you'll never know. Throw yourself into the pool. You have nothing to lose'

'You're right. Thank you'

I kiss him on the cheek and leave the room jumping for joy as I send a message to the Adonis.

> *Okay. I accept. Where do we meet?*

> *The other night's beach in half an hour. Is that okay?*

> *Yes. I live nearby.*

> *Bring your bikini and we'll go for a swim, it's a very nice day.*

An image of the Adonis in a swimming suit comes to mind. Without a T-shirt. Together on the beach. My imagination goes wild. My body temperature rises quickly.

I leave my mobile phone on the bed and look for a bikini. I have doubts. I don't know which one to wear. I decide on a sky blue one. I take a white linen dress and some sandals. I put sun cream and a towel in my beach bag.

I leave the room and inform Luca of my plans. He gives me a hug and wishes me all the best. I'm excited to see the handsome Cuban in swimming shorts. I bite my lips.

I go to the beach with determined and firm steps. A smile lights up my face. I listen to music with my headphones.

I'm on the promenade. I'm looking for Raúl. There are too many people and no matter how hard I look for him I don't see him. The sun is shining very brightly and it is very hot. From time to time, a light breeze refreshes me.

I call Raúl on the phone. He answers me right away. He tells me that he is in front of Bondi Pavilion. I go there.

Raúl is surrounded by some women who wiggle around of him as if they were flies.

I approach him with certain shyness.

'Hi...' I say stuttering as I touch Raúl's back.

'Hello' he exclaims. 'How are you?' Raúl turns around and gives me a big hug and a kiss on the cheek ignoring the flies around him.

He wraps his arm around me and we move away from those harpies who look at me with a scowl. They stand there muttering.

'You look very pretty,' he says.

'Thank you,' I blush, 'you too.'

I take the towel out of my bag and put it on the sand. I take off my dress and put it away with the sandals. I take out the sunscreen and start pouring it on my arms and belly.

Raúl takes the cream off my hands.

'Lie down on your stomach. I'm going to pour cream on your back.'

I do what he says without a word. I am delighted.

He pours the cream directly on my back. It's cold and he begins to spread it out with his hands, massaging my whole back.

I feel again that electricity between his skin and mine.

He finishes with his sweet massage and I get up and sit on the towel.

'Did you like it?' he asks.

I nod with my head.

'Come on. Let's go for a swim.'

He takes me by the hand and lifts me from the towel in one go. We go into the water. It's warm. It's the first time I've bathed in the sea since I arrived. The waves are a little bigger than in the Mediterranean.

Raúl holds me up so that I don't get out of balance with the rolling of the waves.

'And what did I say?' I ask straight out.

'Nothing.'

'Nothing?'

'No. Nothing.'

'You told me that if I came you would tell me.' I feel disappointed.

'I lied to you. I wanted you to come and I needed an excuse for that. You made it quite easy for me.'

I am speechless.

This Adonis has seen my stupid face. I am angry. That's a lie. I'm great in this man's arms.

He pulls me closer to him. I feel his skin touching mine. I embrace him at the height of his neck. I have to stand on my tiptoes. He caresses my cheek gently and I wait impatiently for a sweet kiss from his lips. Up close he is even more handsome. I caress his hair, his arms, his face…

He kisses me. It is a passionate and sweet kiss. The waves sway us and we fall.

We laugh and a new wave hits our face. Raúl gets up and helps me to get up too and we go to our towels.

'You are a liar' I tell him with laughter.

'A little. But it was for a good cause.'

'Do you miss Cuba?'

'Pretty much. I haven't been there for three years. Life there is totally different from the one here.'

'What part of Cuba are you from?'

'From La Habana. And you?'

'I'm from Madrid. There is no beach there. Everything is noise and traffic jams. Although there is a lot to visit. What I miss most is my family and friends.'

'I have all my friends here because I was very young when I came. I have my grandparents, cousins and uncles in Cuba. We talk on *Skype* from time to time.'

'I also talk to my family on *Skype*. The only inconvenience is the timing change. Today I have arranged to talk to them at ten at night because in Madrid it will be twelve noon.'

'Now it's six o'clock here,' he says, looking at his mobile. 'In La Habana it's still one in the morning. To be able to talk to them I have to do it in the early morning so that it's daytime there.'

'You have it worse than I do,' I say, lifting both shoulders.

He nods his head.

We lie down on the towels and sunbathe. Raúl is sideways towards me. His eyes are closed. I don't know if he's sleeping, but I take the opportunity to observe him carefully. He has a scandalous body.

I fall asleep.

Raúl wakes me up with a kiss.

'Sleepy. If you stay in this position any longer, you're going to burn yourself.'

He's stood upright and almost on top of me.

'Thank you.' I turn around and face down.

'If you want, we can have a soda later,' he suggests.

'Yes.'

I still want to get some colour. I'm a little pale.


We are on one of the terraces of the Bondi Pavilion. It's overflowing. It has the parasols unfolded and the water sprays at maximum speed.

We have ordered *Coke*.

'We can go out tonight, what do you think?' The Adonis is asking me out.

'No' I say almost regretting it. I told him the same thing I told Luca. 'Tonight I want to rest. Besides, I'm going to talk to my family.'

'Well...' he frowns.

'We can meet up again another night if you like.' I'm trying to change that look on his face.

'Yes. Next Friday. Let's go to The Cuban Place.'

'Well... Okay.' I hesitate because I'm still embarrassed to remember how that night ended and after knowing that I danced with the handsome man next to me. 'Okay,' I accept.

'Are you coming to the classes next week?'

'Yes. I'm working in the mornings.'

'Do you work during weekends?'

'I work one weekend a month. Or rather every four weeks. I worked on the weekend from the 10th to the 12th.'

'But how many hours do you work?'

'When I have a morning shift, I go in at seven and leave at two. The afternoon shift is from two to nine, and when I'm on duty, I go in on Friday at nine at night and leave on Monday at seven in the morning. And I get off that Monday and Tuesday or Wednesday and Thursday. We take turns.'

'So, when you're on duty and don't get off until Wednesday, you work from the previous Friday until the following Monday morning and then come back in the afternoon.'

'Yes' I say without having him almost believing it. 'It seems like a lot of work, but it's not that bad. In the duties we only deal with emergencies and keep an eye on the animals that are admitted, if there are any,' I say.

'Mine is simpler. I teach physical education to primary and secondary school children. The earliest I come in is at eight in the morning and I usually leave at three in the afternoon.'

'Ah.'

If I had this teacher in secondary school, I'm sure I wouldn't have missed a single day of school. I can imagine how the girls would be watching Raúl stretch.

'I have to go,' I say.

'Already?' Raúl asks sadly.

'I want to take a shower, have dinner and then talk to my family.'

'I'll go with you. If you don't mind.'

'Not at all.'

We walk down the street. Raúl puts his arm around my shoulders. I'm on a cloud. The girls look at me. They will think what that Adonis is doing with that simple woman. I just smile.

He tells me about the classes with the primary school children. I love to listen to him talk. I tell him that I prefer animals. They are more loving and grateful. He agrees with me on that.

And he comes back to my mind. And those walks on the beach in Valencia in one of the getaways we took. I get that thought right out of my head. Now I am with the Adonis.

'I live here' I say pointing to the house.

'Very beautiful.'

'Thank you. The house is not mine,' I laugh. 'It belongs to Carol, a girl who also lives in the house apart from Luca.'

'Ah.'

'Good. I'll go in now, I have things to do.'

'Won't you say goodbye to me?'

Huh? He leaves me petrify. I stand on my tiptoes and give him a kiss on the cheek. Raúl turns around and our lips meet again. We kiss passionately. His tongue and mine come into contact again and I remember the first kiss we had on the beach. His hands run along my waist and he hugs me tightly. I caress his cheek gently. We separate and stare at each other.

I burn with desire. Raúl has an intense look and makes me shiver.

'I have to go in,' I tell him as I open the door.

'I hope to see you again soon.'

I nod my head while a smile is drawn on my face.

I'm taking a shower with almost cold water. I have to lower my body temperature. I think about the kiss a while ago at the door. My body is shaking again. I keep smiling at myself with that silly smile I had just now. It seems that this time it will be possible for me to forget Hugo.

I still have in mind what happened with Charlie. I've forgiven him, but I haven't forgotten about it.

I'll make myself a salad. Luca and Carol are going out tonight. I prefer to stay and rest. I go back to the room and turn on my laptop, put it on the desk and call my mother.

I'm sitting down, eating the salad while my family tells me how the week has gone. My mother is making plans for my birthday, in case I finally go in February. My father is a bit overwhelmed by work. Being a bank manager is not easy. My brother is preparing the exams for the first evaluation. My sister is not there, she has gone with her boyfriend for the weekend.

I tell them that I have started taking dance classes. My mother is very happy. She encourages me to continue. With my handsome teacher, as if I didn't want to go. Although I don't tell her that. I'd rather keep it to myself. I don't want them to get their hopes up about something that might become nothing.

They say goodbye to me. My mother is going to start making the food, my father is going to go out to collect the bread and my brother will surely start playing PlayStation, as usual.

I'm in bed. I get a message. It's from Raúl.

> *Good night, beautiful eyes. Hope to see you before class.*

> *Good night. I'll call you. Have a good rest.*

> *Too bad you didn't want to go out tonight. I would have liked to*

*dance with you again, but this time in a conscious state.*

I blush.

*Maybe next weekend.*

And I fall asleep thinking about the handsome dance teacher. I predict that tonight I will have some extremely passionate dreams. I hope they are not tarnished by the traitor's shadow.

## Monday, 20th November, 2017

I'm running to work. I fell asleep. Yesterday I was talking late to Raúl. He called me on the phone and the hours went by as if they were seconds. And when I was starting to fall asleep at last, Luca was up all night talking to his family, and not in a low tone, but quite the opposite. It's normal that he won't go to university today, he'll be exhausted.

I arrive two minutes before seven. They are all in their coats. I go quickly to my locker. I leave my jacket and my bag there, and I put on my dressing jacket.

Darel assigns me consultation number two. Kayla gives me the list of patients and Rose is again my assistant and also Jack's. Today he is assigned practice number three. Darel is in room one and Henry is in room four. Angela is Darel's assistant and Sarah is Henry's assistant.

There is a lot of work. It's twelve o'clock and I haven't even had a cup of coffee yet. The others are just like me. It seems that today the owners of the animals have agreed to bring them for consultation.

Rose keeps going from one practice to another. I try not to bother her too much. Jack also does some of the work without her help.

'If you want, you can go for a cup of coffee. You don't have appointments for the following a half an hour' Rose tells me from the door.

'Thank you. I already needed one. And you, are you coming with me?' I ask her.

'I finish up a few things and then I go.'

'Very well.'

I get up from my chair and go up to the kitchen. Jack is preparing a coffee.

'Do you want one?' He asks me, pointing at the coffee can.

'Yes, please.'

'How are you doing?'

'Good. A little tired.'

'You're almost late today.'

Huh? Is he checking up on me?

'I went to bed late yesterday.'

'Maybe they didn't let you sleep.'

I don't believe what my ears are hearing. It sounds like a lure. His tone of voice has nothing to do with the tone of when we first met. Maybe it has something to do with the fact that I never wanted to meet him for dinner. I remember that he invited me on one occasion and I refused.

'They let me sleep perfectly, thank you.' I'm being sarcastic.

He leaves the coffee cup he made for me back on the table, just in a little tap. I get up, take the sugar, milk and a spoon. Jack leaves with the coffee cup in his hand without saying goodbye. He didn't like my answer.

I don't know what's wrong with him. On Friday he talked to me about the most normal things. The weekend must not have suited him at all. I don't know what's wrong with him. Nothing he tells me can affect me.

Rose arrives and makes herself a cup of tea.

'Do you know what's wrong with Jack? He's very strange,' I ask her.

'I have no idea. He arrived in the morning a bit upset. If you want, I'll ask him.'

'No!' I exclaim, almost with a shout. 'I don't want him to think that I sent you.'

'Don't worry. I know how to do it.' She winks at me and giggles maliciously.

I'm in my office, sitting in my chair with my coffee cup on my desk. I take advantage of the time I have left to check if I have any news on my mobile phone.

I have a new message. I open it.

> *Hello, beautiful. How did you get started on Monday?*

I love that Raúl gives me compliments. It raises my self esteem.

> *Hi. I'm very sleepy. You didn't let me sleep at night.*

It feels like we've spent the night together. I regret to have written that at the time of sending it.

> *I wish it wasn't because I had been talking, but because we were together.*

I blush instantly. I can't think of what to say to him. He has disarmed me with his message.

> *I have to work. I'll talk to you later.*

> *I'm working too, Miss. We'll talk later for sure.*

I exhale.

Rose arrives to tell me that I already have another patient waiting. I tell her to send him in now. I can't wait for two o'clock in the afternoon.

I vaccinate the poodle. The owner is a typical old lady. She talks so much that I don't know which vaccine to give the poor animal and I almost injected the wrong one.

Luckily Rose gave me a signal. We look at each other. I raise an eyebrow and say no with my head.

I finish my workday by curing a cat.

'It's time to go out,' says Rose happily.

'Yes, thank goodness. I'm exhausted.'

'Should I take you home?'

'Well, I'm not going to say no. I don't really feel like walking. I'm going to have to think about buying a car.'

'If you plan to stay here for a long time, you can get your Australian driving licence.'

'Is it very difficult?'

I might be interested. That way I wouldn't depend on anyone and I could move around Sydney freely. The difficult thing will be to drive on the left.

'No. You only need to have a driving licence from your home country.'

'Yes, I do.'

'You also need to have a valid passport, debit or credit card, fill in a form, certificate from the bank where you are registered and it will cost you approximately 80 dollars.'

'Ah. And where can I do that?'

'On the Internet. I'll look it up and tell you.'

'Thank you. Are cars very expensive?'

'There are all kinds of prices.'

Rose and I leave and go to her car. Jack gets out behind her, mumbles goodbye and gets into his car.

Rose drives very calmly. The traffic is impossible.

'I asked Jack why he was so strange this morning.'

'So?' I am intrigued.

'He thinks you have a thing for Darel. Someone told him what happened last Thursday and he's clearly jealous. Plus, the fact that you didn't want to have dinner with him on Friday.'

'And why would he be jealous? He and I have only shared one duty, apart from you, of course' I'm pointing out. 'I didn't want to have dinner with him precisely to avoid this.'

Rose laughs and passes on her joy to me. She always takes everything with that positivity that makes everything bad seem less bad.

I go inside. It's still empty. Carol is still at work and Luca probably went to the university.

I'm going straight to my room. I leave my bag and jacket on top from the desk chair and change my clothes.

I sit on the sofa, turn on the TV and check my mobile phone messages. I go into Charlie's. We haven't spoken or seen each other since he apologised to me. I hope he's okay. I'm not capable of holding a grudge for long. It hurts me that he thought I was his property or even that there was some kind of relationship between us, but that has only happened in his head.

I would like to write to him and ask him how his day is going, but he still gets his hopes up again and it would be a step backwards.

I go on Hugo's *Facebook* profile. My curiosity is aroused. I've been repressing myself for a long time.

He has a lot of new photos. He's just as handsome in all of them. He's with her. With the crazy obsessed woman who won't leave him alone. It could have been me in those photos with him and not that girl. I don't know if I hate him or her more.

Hugo didn't know how to put her in her place and throw her out of his house. Maybe he didn't want to and everything he told me was just an invention to make me wait for him. It makes me very angry. I want to go and give him a good slap. That's what he deserves.

I have never told my family the cause of the break up and both my mother and sister treat him as if he was the best of people. Maybe I should tell them. I dismiss that idea immediately. I don't want them to have problems at work because of me.

My mother would be the first to talk to him.

I'm hungry, but I don't know what to do. I look in the fridge for something to inspire me. Nothing. Another salad. I don't feel like cooking. It is hot.

I make enough salad in case Luca or Carol feel like it. I cook some eggs. I add corn, tuna, cooked ham, fresh cheese, tomato and a lettuce. I prepare everything in a bowl and dress it.

I take a plate, pour some on it and go back to the sofa. I eat without enthusiasm.

> *Beautiful, how did you do today in work?*

Raúl's message makes my day and, as always, he raises my self esteem.

> *Hello. Good. Eating a salad and lying on the sofa.*

I'm not going to tell him what happened to me with my partner. I'm not going to make a mountain out of a molehill. It's not important.

> *That's fine. I just got off work. See you today?*

I'd like to see him, but I don't want to rush off with the Adonis, just to see if I'm going to fall on my face.

> *I really want to, but I need to rest.*

> *What a pity. I wanted to invite you to the cinema.*

The offer is not bad at all. I haven't been to the movies here yet. I like Raúl very much, but I can't get Hugo and his betrayal out of my mind. I'm afraid the same thing will happen to me again. I couldn't bear it.

*We're going to have to leave the cinema to the weekend.*

*Don't tell me that. I really wanted to see you without being in class. I can't be alone with you there.*

I giggle. Thank God I'm alone.

*Well, it'll have to be that way.*

I send him the message with an emoticon of a wide smile with a wink.

*I'm offering you a plan you can't refuse.*

*Tell me.*

*Dinner, cinema and dance. Friday night. A complete package. You can't say no to me».*

*Sounds good.*

*If you say no, I'm going to have to kidnap you.*

I suppose he's joking about that.

*You're not going to be a serial killer or something like that?*

*You're so funny. I'm still a long way from that level.*

His message is accompanied by an emoticon that laughs out loud. I'm more relaxed.

*Okay. I like the plan.*

*Perfect. I'll talk to you tomorrow.*
*Kisses.*

I'm gawking at Raúl's messages as I fork a piece of lettuce.

Luca sits next to me with another plate of salad. He comes in tired and doesn't feel like cooking. That makes two of us. Mondays are always the worst.

'How was your morning?' he asks.

'Well, except for one colleague who was very strange.'

'And what was wrong with him?'

'My colleague Rose told me that it was because she was jealous. She thought that Darel, my boss, and I were together. But that's not the case' I clarify.

'And if so, why should she be jealous?'

'I ask myself the same question. Other than that, the rest is fine. With a lot of work. And you?'

'Good. I had an exam.'

'I guess you did well. I saw that you studied a lot.'

'Yes. I was nervous, but I think I did pretty well.'

'Raúl wrote to me and invited me to dinner, the cinema and dancing.'

'*Quando?*' Luca's mouth is open.

'On Friday.'

'Do you know that you're going to be the envy of everyone?'

A chill runs through my body. I wouldn't like to have more problems with anyone. I have enough with Emma, with Charlie and now with Jack.

'I'd better tell him no.'

'Don't even think about doing that!' he exclaims.

'Why?' I say with my mobile phone in my hand.

Luca pulls my mobile out of my hands. I stare at it in disbelief.

'What do you want? To lose the opportunity of a lifetime?'

'I don't want to get into trouble.'

'Problems?'

'Yes. My colleague, Emma, hates me and I don't really know why. Jack's really weird with me because he thinks I'm involved with the boss, and Charlie...' I'm quiet.

'What about Charlie?'

I just messed up. I mean the whole body.

'Mmm... So we had a friction.'

'What kind of friction?'

Until I tell him, he's not going to stop asking.

'He got the wrong idea about me.' I won't go into detail.

'Well, he'll get over it. Focus on what's there now. A handsome dance and physical education teacher is inviting you, among many candidates, to spend a spectacular night by his side. What is the problem? I don't see where it is.'

Luca is always very expressive when he talks. He makes me laugh.

'Maybe you're right.'

'Maybe? I'm always right,' he says with an air of grandeur.

We laugh out loud.

'How vain you are' I affirm.

'*Un po*' he answers with a smile.

Luca has gone to his room. He has to keep studying because he has exams all week.

Carol has arrived, showered, changed clothes and left because she had some agreements to make. She looked a bit overwhelmed. She hasn't eaten.

I'm bored; I'm not sure what to do. Maybe I should have accepted Raúl's date. It's still dark in Spain and I can't talk to my family or friends. What should I do? Go to the beach. Alone? No! I don't like to go alone. I could call Rose. Maybe she's not doing anything and can meet me.

I'll call her.

Rose told me she's free. She was bored at home as I was. We are going to the beach and then she invited me to her house for dinner. She said I could take a shower there so I wouldn't have to go back to mine again. I take a change of clothes and put them in my bag, also a towel and sunscreen.

We meet in front of Bondi Pavilion. Rose is lying on the towel, sunbathing. She is wearing big sunglasses. She doesn't see me coming, so I take advantage and give her a fright.

'You scared me!' shouts Rose.

I laugh out loud at the look on her face.

'Have you been waiting for me for a long time?' I ask.

'Not long,' she answers, still a little angry.

'Come on, don't be angry. It was just a little joke. I'll buy you an ice cream.'

Rose accepts. I go to the bar in the Pavilion and order two large jars with two chocolate balls and one vanilla ball.

We are sitting and looking at the sea while we eat the ice creams. I love chocolate. I think about the night I had dinner here with Raúl and Luca or the afternoon when Raúl invited me to come. It was only a few days ago and it seems like a long time ago.

I can't help but remember the first time Hugo and I went to the beach. I don't want to remember that anymore, but I can't control what I think.

'What are you thinking about?' Rose takes me out of that bad memory.

'Well... Memories I have from a long time ago.' I can't help it if the sadness gets stuck in my face.

'Come on, don't be sad anymore. You're here in Sydney,' she runs her arm behind my back. 'With a super friend.' She points to herself as she laughs. She makes me laugh too.

'You're right' I say.

'And look at the number of boys there are,' she says as she looks over her glasses at all the boys on the beach.

We laugh out loud and the people next to us they look at us, but we don't care.

Jack arrives by surprise, or at least for me, because Rose prays not to be surprised at all. My laughter turns into a big serious face.

'What are you doing here?' I ask.

'Dani, don't be like that. I told him to come.'

I don't know if it bothers me more that Jack is here or that Rose invited him.

'I think you two need to talk' says Rose as she stands up from her towel.

I don't have time to tell her anything because she got up very quickly. Jack sits down next to me.

'Rose is not to blame. I just wanted to apologize.' He seems sincere. 'I was very rude to you this morning,' he continues.

'It doesn't matter. It's all forgotten now.'

'It's not true. Your face doesn't say the same thing.'

Are you a psychologist now? I thought he was a veterinarian.

'That's not true. I was remembering things from my past.'

'So, friends?' He extends his arm to me.

I nod my head as we shake hands in a sign of cordiality.

Rose comes with three sodas. She couldn't have come at a better time; my throat was already drying up. I drink. It is very cold. It refreshes my whole body.

'By the way, Jack, who told you that Dani and Darel were together?' Rose asks.

'Emma told me on Friday at the shift change. She was very furious,' he explains.

Feelings of hatred are awakened within me. If I had Emma in front of me now, I would grab her by the hair and drag her all over the beach. She is very hateful. She has made it up so that her colleagues hate me and so force me to leave. She's not going to make it.

'Don't tell her anything, please,' Jack pleads.

'She won't know anything about me,' says Rose.

'I won't say anything either,' I say.

What is clear is that I will do something to let her know that she will not be able to do it with me.

I'm going to lie down and sunbathe. I think about what I could do to scare Emma, although I can't think of anything.

I sigh.

I hate her. Yes. I hate her very much, as much as or more than Hugo. *"Liar!"* my subconscious replies. *"You don't hate Hugo, you wish you did"*. My subconscious is always right. I stick out my tongue.

Rose has invited Jack to dinner. She has a one room flat. It's quite spacious. The kitchen is American style, very similar to Carol's. The bathroom has a large bathtub.

She has prepared spaghetti *carbonara* for dinner.

I receive a message from Luca.

> *Are you coming for dinner?*

I forgot to tell you that I didn't have dinner at home. We always warn each other about everything.

> *I'm having dinner with a friend from work.*

> *I was worried about you.*

> *I know. I'm sorry. I should have warned, but I forgot.*

> Va bene. *I forgive you because it is you.*

> *I love you.*

*I love you too.*

I leave the phone in my bag and sit down to dinner. I try Rose's spaghetti. Not bad at all. They're *au dente,* just the way I like them.

Jack congratulates the cook.

We talk about work, about Emma and Darel. Jack explains that Emma has been working with Darel for at least eight years. They had a relationship over four years ago.

'Darel left Emma for a new girl who came to work and since then she has been jealous of all the pretty girls who come to work. She does everything she can to make them quit.'

'And why doesn't Darel throw her out?' I'm curious.

'I don't know.'

'I knew that she was jealous of all the new girls that came in, but what I didn't know was that there had been a relationship between her and Darel,' says Rose, incredulously.

We finished dinner and Rose removed the dishes. She comes back and brings it is a large tray with a wide variety of fruit.

'Well, boys. I'm leaving now' I tell them.

'I'll take you' Jack offers himself. I think about it for a few moments because I don't want him to have any illusions, but I'm also very tired and I don't feel like walking home at this hour.

I accept.

I say goodbye to Rose, who's left to do the dishes in the kitchen. I take my bag which is on the sofa in the living room. Jack opens the entrance door for me to go in first and we go down in the lift to the doorway.

Jack's car is just a few feet away. As you know my home address, you don't need to enter it in the GPS. He'll be on his way in no time.

'Once again I apologise. I was very rude to you this morning, Jack' explains.

'It's all right. It's already forgotten.' I'm sincere. 'Someone told me you were jealous.'

'And why would I be jealous?' he asks with a scowl.

'It's going to sound a bit self centred, but they think it's because you like me' Jack laughs while I look at him puzzled.

'Why are you laughing? Do you think that might be impossible?'

'No, that's not why. Someday I'll tell you about it.'

Jack leaves me just as I was.

'You can leave me here,' I say as I walk down the street next to mine.

'As you wish. I don't mind leaving you at home.'

'It's very close. Don't worry about it.'

'Okay,' he says, resignedly.

He parks on O'Brien Street where it's on the corner with my street. I say goodbye to Jack and get out of the car.

Jack starts when he can't see me anymore. I'm just a few feet away from my house.

Luca is in his room, studying. I greet him and go to rest. It's been a long day and a bit strange, but at the end everything has gone well. Jack has apologised to me and I trust that there will be no more problems. I keep thinking about the problem with Emma and how to solve it.

I'll think of something.

## Tuesday, 21st November, 2017

Today the day at work has been calmer. Jack and I have worked hand in hand. Rose has felt bad and has not come to work.

Darel has been indifferent to all of us. According to Kayla, he has had personal problems. He didn't want to go into details.

The morning went by relatively quickly.

We had an emergency operation for a dog and Darel tested me by making me lead the operation. I have to confess that for a few moments I was quite nervous because it was the first time I had to do it, but it was a success and Darel congratulated me on it.

Jack brought me home. Lately it has become a nuisance to come by car and not on foot and, as always, there was no one at home.

I didn't feel like eating, I feel less and less every day. I'm too lazy to prepare it after work and, in this heat, I only feel like eating salads, so I've prepared one and I've given Carol and Luca plenty to eat.

I talked to my mother because she had a night shift and was quite free. He told me that my grandfather is sick. I've been quite worried about that. It's not the first time it's happened to him, but before I was there to look after him and now from here I feel helpless.

I've spent most of the afternoon checking the social networks and biting my nails in anger at how well my friends are coping with me not being there with them. They look so happy that they don't seem to need me anymore. That makes me sad.

Another of my new routines is to eat out when Luca and I go dancing.

We are in a pizza restaurant and, while Luca tells me how his day went, I wander around in my mind looking for the happiest memories of when I lived in Spain. I can't find them.

Everyone has moved on with their lives and I'm stuck with the bad memories, with him. In Hugo. And although now those memories are shared with those I have of Raúl, there are still more of the ungrateful, spoiled and lying ones.

I nod my head so that Luca thinks I'm listening to him, but I have no idea what he's talking about.

I'm not hungry. A lot has happened to me lately.

'How was your day? Hello? Daniela, are you there?' Luca passes my hand in front of my face and I come to my senses.

'Sorry! What were you saying?'

'You're in the clouds. I was asking you how your day had gone, but judging by your distraction, I'd say regular.' Luca looks at me with concern.

'The day has gone more than well.'

'So what's wrong with you?'

'I was thinking about Spain, my friends, my family. About a little bit of everything.'

'Ah.'

'The boss congratulated me on a successful operation I had to lead urgently.'

'I'm very happy for you.' Luca gets up from his chair and gives me a hug and a kiss on the cheek.

'Thank you,' I say as Luca crushes me in his arms.

We walk towards Bondi Pavilion. Today, perhaps with less desire than other days.

'Cheer up, Dani. Please,' Luca begs.

'I'm trying.'

There are those from Raúl's fan club in the classroom who look at me when I enter as if I had monkeys on my face. I make a disgusting gesture so that they stop looking.

'Don't listen to them. They are jealous,' whispers Luca to me.

Raúl enters and, ignoring all the slugs that approach him, he comes straight to me, takes me by the hand and gives me a kiss on the cheek.

'Hello, beautiful. How was your day?'

'G... Good' I mean almost breathless.

The Adonis surprises me more and more every day with these gestures. He's a real soap opera stud. No wonder. He has the genes to be one. I am arousing a lot of envy among female students and perhaps some male students.

Raúl stands in front of us, turning his back on the big mirror. He shows us the steps to follow to warm up our muscles. Today his sister, Elizabeth, has not come.

We do everything he tells us in unison.

We stand in pairs. Luca and I, as always, together.

'Are you better?' Luca asks me, knowing the answer, because since the Adonis came in, I've had a smile on my face that I still can't remove.

I nod with my head.

'I'm very happy to see you like this. I don't want to see you sad anymore' he says in my ear.

Raúl follows me with his eyes and I follow him. It's as if we can't avoid it, as if it was an attraction. He smiles at me, and I smile back at him in the same way.

We learn several new steps and link them to what we already know. We are left with some very beautiful steps.

Raúl asks our permission to record our movements so as to help us individually where we make mistakes.

He approaches us with the camera and I can't help but blush.

'I love the colour of your cheeks' he says when he walks past me.

Again my whole body shakes. Luca looks at me and smiles.

'It seems you're serious,' says Luca.

'I don't want to get my hopes up,' I answer.

'*Buono*. You live day by day and don't think about the future.'

'Yes.'

'You let yourself go and forget the past.'

'I try, but it's not that easy.'

'*Ti capisco!* But you have to make an effort.'

He grips me tightly and spins me around.

'Change of partner,' Raúl says almost yelling.

And, as always, while the girls continue to make the base step on the site, the boy on my right comes and Luca walks away with the girl on my left.

One less boy to be with my Adonis.

Today we are learning many new steps and I like that. Raúl is a very good teacher and he explains to us how to position the arms to both boys and girls.

The girls are delighted when Raúl approaches them to explain well how to position some part of her body.

Now I am the one who looks at them suspiciously.

We change partners again. I look over my partner's shoulder to see where my Raúl is. I count mentally. Five more and it's my turn. My inner self claps for joy as it skips.

The guy I have as a partner keeps trying to hit on me. He keeps throwing compliments at me. I don't like him at all. Too white and blondish.

I have to lift his hand off my back several times because he has tried to put it a little lower than my waist. If he keeps this up, I'm going to have to ask for a change of partner.

'Please, hand on the waist' I warn him with a bad face.

He nods his head, but says nothing.

I can't wait for Raúl to arrive. I just want to dance with him. I look at him sideways and catch him looking at me. He smiles at me. He can light up the whole room with his smile.

I want him to come now. Time has stopped and I have to dance with this guy who doesn't stop talking nonsense to me. I don't listen to him. It feels like we've been here for hours.

Slowly the five couples that were between me and the Adonis are passing by. It's a Chinese torture. I want to have him for myself now.

Raúl stops the music, takes me by the hand and leads me in front of everyone. He talks about a new step. First he explains it. I am very nervous and I keep looking at the floor and my cheeks are red.

He surrounds me with his muscular arm around my waist and takes my hand, with which he is free. We walk slowly, while the rest of the students record us with their mobile phones. I'm ashamed of myself.

I don't like to draw attention to myself and this is just the opposite.

'Relax, darling' he whispers in my ear.

Did he call me darling? I must be dreaming. I'm on a cloud. I have the Adonis to myself. He has chosen me to practice one of his steps. The girl he usually does this with is looking at me jealously.

I ignore her.

We put ourselves in the place we were. Raúl asks again change of partner and we are finally together.

'Finally' he says.

I blush.

I was thinking exactly the same thing.

'You dance better every day' I'm flattered.

'That's thanks to you, who are a fantastic teacher.'

'Because you are a good student.'

'When I arrived, you were sad. Can you tell me why?'

'I was remembering things from the past.'

'Are you better?'

How could I not be better in this man's arms?

'Yes.'

Raúl spins me around so much that I get dizzy. Only he has the ability to make me forget about the bad things. We look into each other's eyes and sparks fly between us. He has a hypnotic smile that makes me unable to stop smiling when I look at him.

We finish the class.

'Wait for me.' Raúl holds me by the arm so that I don't come out.

I say yes with my head.

'I leave. I'll leave you with your boy. *Ciao signorina!*' Luca walks away with a big cheeky smile.

I am at the entrance of the Pavilion waiting for Raúl. I make a visual inspection of my mobile phone. I have no new messages or calls. On one of the benches a few dance partners are sitting. They are looking at me sideways and whispering.

It's bothering me a lot.

I come closer.

'Why are you talking about me?' I ask without any hesitation.

They're speechless. One of them stands up. With both hands she throws her hair back and looks at me angrily.

'You're a bitch,' she says while the others sitting down nod their heads.

'What?' I'm standing in front of the blonde with my arms crossed, my eyes wider than usual and one of my eyebrows raised.

'You've been chasing Raúl since you got here.'

I can't believe what my ears just heard. These girls are looking for war.

I breathe in.

I breathe out.

I do it several times with my eyes closed, before answering the dyed blonde. I think carefully about what I'm going to say to her.

'Hello, beautiful.'

Raúl is behind me. He has arrived just in time. He hugs my waist and gives me a kiss on the cheek. He presses me hard against him. The hateful girls look at me with jealousy, their eyes half open.

It's the best thing that could have happened because I was about to grab the hater in front of me by the hair and drag her all over the promenade.

'Hello' I say.

I turn around and hug him tightly and give him a sweet kiss on the lips. I have to stand on my tiptoes to do it.

The hateful women look at my Adonis drooling and I release a sarcastic smile as a sign of triumph.

We walk away through the small park around the Pavilion. For once in my life I feel like a winner. It is a very enriching feeling, I feel even bigger.

'And Luca?' Raúl asks.

'He left a while ago.'

'Ah!' His smile is clearly seductive.

'How was your day?' I want to know.

'Very well. The primary school pupils are still quite manageable. Secondary school pupils are more rebellious. But I get along with everyone. And you? I didn't think you had a good day. As I said before, I saw you very differently at the beginning of the class.'

'I told you I was thinking about the past.'

'Any old love?'

Exactly that. You hit the nail on the head. I don't want to remember the same thing again.

I just nod with my head.

'Nothing a good ice cream can't cure,' suggests and I accept. 'If we hurry, we can still reach an ice cream parlour very near here,' he says, looking at the clock.

He takes me by the hand and pulls me up to speed.

'You didn't come with Elizabeth today,' I change the subject.

'She doesn't feel well. She's a little cold,' he explains.

'Ah, poor thing, hope she gets better.'

'I'll tell her that from you.'

'Did you tell her about me?' I look at him with suspicion.

'Yes, of course. I talk about everything with my sister, we have no secrets. By the way, she thinks you're a nice girl and very pretty.' Raúl squeezes my hand while he throws me a fleeting smile.

We almost ran to Gelato Messina Bondi. I still find it hard to breathe. We arrived on time.

'What would you like?'

'Mmm...' I think, although the answer is always the same. 'Chocolate' I answer.

'You heard the lady,' said Raúl to the boy who was behind the counter. 'And for me, a creamy one. Thank you.'

The boy serves us the cones as fast as he can, it must be because it's almost eleven o'clock at night and that's the time the sign says it's closing time.

We eat the ice creams on the way to my house. Raúl insisted on accompanying me. He says he lives near where I live, but I don't know exactly where. That makes me not to trust him. The same thing happened to me with Hugo. And at the end he had a good reason for not telling me where he lived. As much as he had a girlfriend.

I deny with my head and take that moment of my life away from my mind. I don't want to think that Raúl can be just as much of a liar.

'What are you thinking about?' Raúl looks at me trying to decipher what I am thinking.

I didn't realize that.

'You told me that you live nearby, but I still don't know where' I say shrugging my shoulders.

'Is that why you're like this?'

'Yes,' I say, almost whispering.

He stands in front of me, raises my face with his free hand and fixes his eyes on mine.

I am shaking.

'Are you cold?' he asks.

I'm denying with my head.

'And why are you shaking?'

'It's because of the way you look at me. It makes me nervous.'

He laughs. I don't know if it's me or maybe it's what I said. He confuses me.

He takes out his mobile phone from his trouser pocket, enters the menu and opens the Maps application.

He inserts his address and mine.

'Look,' he says, showing me the screen.

He lives just a 10 minutes walk from my house. On the corner of Beach Road and Glenayr Avenue. Exactly in a flat of a building called Bondi Steel, number 57.

I blush with shame I feel. I have come to think that he didn't tell me because he was hiding something from me just like the other one did.

'We live nearby' I say by pointing out my house on the map.

'Yes.'

'Thank you for telling me.'

'Why shouldn't I tell you?'

'It's just that... Some time ago, I was with a boy, in Spain. And no matter how much I asked him where he lived, he always managed to change the subject. Until I found out why.'

'Let me guess. He had a girlfriend and you thought I was doing the same to you.'

'Yes' I say embarrassed.

He gives me a hug. I feel his heart beating. I look up, tiptoe and kiss him. It is a tender and passionate kiss. I surround him with my arms at the height of his neck while his arms surround my waist.

I feel the temperature rise between us. He kisses me more and more passionately. His tongue runs through my mouth and I follow him rhythmically.

'I have to go now. I have to be up early tomorrow.'

'Come to my house,' Raúl begs. I keep quiet. 'Please,' he pleads.

'I'm not ready yet,' I said sincerely.

'I'm sorry; I didn't mean to make you feel uncomfortable.'

He caresses my cheek, takes me by the hand and accompanies me to my house.

'Sleep well, beautiful.' He gives me a sweet and chaste kiss on the lips.

'You too. Send me a message to let me know you're home safely.'

'Yes, mum.' He winks at me, kisses me on the cheek and leaves.

I go in the house. Luca and Carol must be asleep by now.

Today, despite the strange day, I had a happy ending. I'm tempted and that's what I know reflects on my face and the smile I have in front of the mirror in my wardrobe, from ear to ear.

I look at my watch.

It is almost midnight. With the few hours I'm going to sleep, tomorrow I'm going to have dark circles under my eyes almost as big as my face.

I fall asleep thinking about Raúl's sweet kisses.

## Thursday, 23rd November, 2017

I overslept, again. I'm in a hurry to finish getting ready.

'Still at home?' says Carol looking at the time.

'I overslept. I'm going to be late for work.'

'I'll give you a lift. Don't worry. I don't have much work today.'

I take my bag and wait for Carol at the entrance door.

Carol parks a few feet from the entrance to the clinic. It's still eight minutes to seven.

'I'll finish early today. Would you like to have lunch together and catching up?' proposes Carol.

'Yes, I'm really looking forward to it. We have hardly spent any time together lately.'

I get out of the car and go to work.

How disgusting! The first thing I see when I get in is the witch Emma. Again? No way. She changed Henry's shift. Looks like that he does it on purpose to torment my life.

'Good morning, Kayla. Do I have many consultations today?'

'No, Daniela. Today will be a fairly relaxed day.'

'Much better.' I smile.

Kayla gives me the sheet with all the consultations of the day.

'Good morning, girls.'

I turn around and see Darel coming through the door with a big smile. Nothing to do with last Tuesday's Darel.

'Good morning', Kayla and I answer at the same time. Emma says nothing. In fact, she hasn't even looked at him.

'How are you?' Darel asks me, running his hand behind my back.

I don't like that gesture at all.

'Very good. Thank you,' I answer politely.

'I'm glad.'

He walks away and goes straight to his office. Emma looks at me and I ignore her.

I go to my locker, leave my bag there and take my dressing jacket.

I'm in the same office as I have been in all these days. Emma is in the fourth, in Henry's. Rose is my assistant and Jack's again.

I'm sitting at my desk turning on the computer. Rose is sitting in front of me.

'Did you see that Emma is here today?' she asks.

'Yes,' I say with a disgusted look on my face. 'It was the first thing I saw when I arrived.'

'How disgusting!' she says with laughter.

I look at her and, instantly, she has already infected me with her laughter.

'Ready for a new day?'

'Yes,' I answer with resignation.

Rose enters with the first patient of the day.

'Good morning,' I say.

'Good morning. My dog hasn't wanted to eat for a few days and I don't know what's wrong with him.'

'Good morning. Let's take a look at him and do some tests.'

'Very good.'

Rose helps me put the dog on the table. I explore it carefully.

'Rose, please bring me everything I need to take blood from him. Does the dog let himself be taken or do you want us to sedate him?' I ask the boy standing next to me.

'Normally they sedate him because he moves around a lot.'

'Very good. Rose, bring me the sedation material too, please.'

Rose does what I ask her to do with a lot of professionalism.

We sedate the animal, which stands still a few minutes later.

I start by shaving the leg where I am going to take the blood. I put the rubber around the leg and proceed to take the blood.

Shortly after finishing, the dog wakes up, stunned.

'We will analyse the blood and I will give you the results in half an hour. You can wait in the waiting room if you like.'

'Thank you.' The boy leaves the surgery with the dog still stumbling. Rose rushes to help him.

Rose returns and takes the dog's blood to an automatic analyser that we have in one area of the operating theatre.

While the test is not ready, I continue my consultation.

Emma passes by my surgery several times and looks at me with contempt. Rose is behind her making fun of her. I have to suppress the urge to laugh out loud.

I have the results of the analysis.

'Your dog has a little bit of anaemia and some dehydration, but the test shows no other abnormalities. I will be taking an X-ray of his stomach in case he has ingested something strange.'

The owner nods his head.

I observe the X-ray carefully. There is nothing in the stomach.

'Has your dog experienced any changes in the last few days that might have affected it?'

'We have just moved from our house and I had a baby a week ago.'

'Sometimes dogs are stressed by some strange situations and, in your case, between the change of house and the arrival of a new family member, the dog has become stressed and perhaps jealous.'

'Ah.'

'What you should do is not neglect your dog and pay the same attention to it as to the baby. Let your dog smell and lick the baby. Absolutely nothing will happen. The dog, as far as I can see, has all the vaccinations.'

'Yes.'

'If he persists in not eating, then we will have to admit him and give him some serum.'

'Okay. Thank you very much.'

'You're welcome.'

We have an opening. Jack, Rose and I went up to the kitchen and we drink coffee while we talk about work.

'I have only a few more consultations. Vaccinations and cure reviews basically,' says Jack.

'So do I. I've only got vaccines left and I think I'll cut the nails of two cats,' I say.

'I'm very happy to help you; I wouldn't like to have to help Emma again. Last time I had a hard time, I don't think you were there to help me,' says Rose, looking at me with a warm smile.

I smile.

'Darel sent for me to call you. He told me that he is waiting for you at your office.' Kayla gives me the message and returns to the reception.

'Good, guys. See you downstairs' I say goodbye to Jack and Rose.

I go downstairs with a coffee cup in my hand.

I approach Kayla.

'Do you know what Darel wants?' I ask her.

She shakes her head.

'Thank you,' I say as I walk away from the reception.

I knock on the office door.

'Come in,' says Darel.

He is sitting at his desk.

'Sit down,' he says, pointing to the chair that is available.

I can't quite make out his face. I don't know if he's happy or angry.

'You're wondering why I sent for you.'

I nod.

'You have shown me on Tuesday that you can work under pressure with a lot of professionalism.'

'Thank you.'

'Thank you. I see that I have made a good choice with you.'

He stands up and takes some documents from a file. This is my contract. I'm a little disoriented. He tells me that he is happy, but maybe, because of what happened the other day with Emma; he decides to restrict my contract.

I bite my nails.

'You currently earn about eight hundred and eighty dollars per week plus an extra bonus for the weekend duty.'

'Yes.'

'I know I told you you'd get the minimum because you were just starting out, but I'm going to give you a raise. As long as there is no repetition of what happened with Emma.'

'Yes. That subject is already forgotten' I hasten to say.

He shows me a new contract. The date is the same as last time.

'You can see that it is the same as the previous one only the weekly salary has gone up by 67 dollars more per week.'

I am more than happy, but I don't want it to be too noticeable, so he won't think I'm working for money.

'Since the salary is weekly, if you like I have put it in the week of December 4th, Monday. Is that OK?' he asks.

'Yes. All right. Thank you very much for trusting me.'

I have my hands on the desk, holding the contract I am reading. Darel extends his arms and puts his hands over mine.

The expression on his face has changed and I don't like it. I don't want to have any friction with this gentleman.

I move my hands away as fast as I can and smile with sarcasm.

'Any day you and I can go out for lunch or dinner.'

If I tell him no, he might throw me out of work and I wouldn't like that. If I say yes, it looks like I'm selling out. What a situation!

I take a deep breath.

'Perhaps one of these days.' I leave the door ajar.

'Very good.' He gets up from his chair and gives me his hand to get up.

We leave the office and Darel has his hand on my back. Emma comes down the stairs, looking at us with that look I don't like at all. I say goodbye to Darel and go towards my office, taking long strides.

I call Rose to bring the patient in the waiting room.

I look at the guinea pig vaccination's card. I have to give him a vaccination reminder.

Rose is busy, so I get it from the cupboard myself.

I open the tiny bottle. All of a sudden, I get a bad smell, like sodium hypochlorite. I bring the bottle closer to my nose. This is not good. It shouldn't smell like this.

I take out another one. It smells the same.

'Is there a problem?' asks the animal's owner.

'No, no problem.' I don't want to alarm her. 'I go out for a moment. Please wait here.'

I am leaving my office and going to Jack's office.

'May I?' I ask.

'Yes, come in. What is it?'

'Smell this,' I say, holding the bottle up to his nose.

'This is bleach!' he exclaims.

'That's what I thought. I'll take a vaccine from your cupboard.'

'Yes. Whatever you need.'

I open the vaccine I took from Jack's office cupboard. It clearly doesn't have the same liquid inside, even though they're the same colour.

Someone wanted to boycott my work.

'I go and give the vaccine to the guinea pig I left in my surgery and come back.'

'OK.'

I give it the vaccine. Fortunately, the good one. I open all the vaccine bottles and in all of them there is the same thing: bleach. I put my hand in my mouth and think about who wanted to hurt me in this way.

'It could only have been one person,' says Rose, who is leaning against the corner of the desk.

'I find it hard to believe that she tried to go that far.'

'You have to put a stop to it. She's not going to stop until you leave.'

'If she wants a war, she'll have a war.'

Jack enters without knocking.

'What happened?' he asks in frustration.

'Someone has exchanged all the vaccine bottles for bottles with bleach.'

'All of them?' he asks, surprised.

Rose and I say yes with our heads at the same time.

'That was Emma,' he says bluntly.

'That's what we think, too' rectifies Rose.

Now I'm really starting to be afraid of the witch. If she tried to get me to kill the animals, I don't know how far she'll go. I have to think about what I can do.

I can't tell Darel. I promised him I wouldn't have anymore trouble with Emma.

Finally, I'm done. I had to replace all the vaccines I had in the cupboard for vaccines in the pharmacy store. I could have taken the bottles to the witch's office and done the same, but I am incapable of having an animal die because of me. It is unethical.

Rose is gone. I didn't go with her today because I'm meeting Carol. I call her.

I have to do it twice for her to answer.

'Hi, Dani. Finished work already?'

'Yes. We had a lunch date.'

'Yes. I haven't forgotten.'

'Where do we eat?' I ask.

'Is Jamie's Italian OK for you? The same one we went to when you arrived.'

'Okay. I'm going to look at the buses. When I get there, I'll let you know.'

'I'm close by. I go in and book a table,' says Carol.

'Perfect.'

I look at the bus route. I go up to the Oxford Street stop on the corner of Denison Street. I get on bus number 440. It is very crowded.

I get off at Oxford Street, corner of Palmer Street and take the next bus.

The 373 bus arrives immediately.

I walk to the restaurant. It is almost three o'clock. I call Carol and inform her that I am arriving. She is already there. I can't stop thinking about what would have happened if I had injected the poor guinea pig with bleach.

I go into the restaurant and look for Carol. She is at the back. She waves her arm to me so that I can see her. There is someone sitting with her, but I don't know who it is. His back is turned.

I approach.

'Good afternoon. I am a little late because I came by bus and I had to change at Oxford Street' I explain.

Carol and her companion stand up. She gives me a kiss on the cheek and introduces me to her companion. It's David, her assistant. I finally meet him.

I sit next to Carol in front of David.

He is very young, as Luca had told me. And also very handsome. He is dressed in a black suit and white shirt, without a tie. He is tall and blond with green eyes. He makes a very good couple with Carol.

The waiter comes and takes note of everything we ask him. He tells us that the kitchen closes at four o'clock, but he still gives us time to eat.

'Carol told me that you are her assistant,' I ask David.

'Yes, I started a few months ago.'

'Are you a law student?'

'Yes, this year I'll finish my degree and then I'll do a master's degree,' he explains.

'Carol also told me about you. You're from Spain, aren't you?'

'Yes, I arrived recently and I work as a veterinarian in a clinic.'

We are almost finished. David goes ahead, pulls out his card and pays. I feel bad; I've tried to pay my share. He refuses outright. I don't think it's fair, because David is still a student, he'll have a lot of expenses and I don't think he has a big salary as Carol's assistant.

They say goodbye at the door of the restaurant with a kiss on the cheek.

Carol and I go to look for the car. It's parked in a parking lot near the restaurant.

'What about at work?' she asks.

'Well...' I hesitate to tell her. 'Good.' I lie.

'I'm glad you've adapted well.'

'Thank you. And you, how are you? It's been strange eating early with you.'

'Actually, yes. I only had a trial today and a meeting with the bosses. I've been walking around the centre since midday and have done some shopping.'

'Ah. That's good.'

We got home; it took us almost half an hour to get there. Luca is in the kitchen preparing a sandwich. He greets us and goes straight to his room with his plate. He has to keep studying.

I go to bed to take a nap. Something I haven't done for a long time. I think about what happened in the morning. I have to keep thinking about how to find a solution. I can't leave it like that. Today it was the vaccines, but tomorrow it could be the anaesthesia or any solution to make the cures.

The phone wakes me up. I have received a message. It's from Raúl.

> *Hi, beautiful. How was your day?*

I can get used to this. *"Yes"*, says my inner self. I love receiving his messages and more with compliments included.

> *Hello, prince. I was sleeping. I had a normal day today.*

> *Excuse me, my princess. I didn't mean to wake you up. If you were*

> *sleeping here, you wouldn't have to be sending messages.*

Huh? Now that's a direct one. It leaves me speechless.

> *I like my bed.*

> *I could be your pillow.*

> *I don't rule out your proposal. If I need a pillow, I'll call you.*

> *Are you coming to class today?*

> *Yes, I am.*

> *Tomorrow we'll meet, I hope you haven't forgotten.*

> *No. I have it in mind and written it down my diary.*

> *That's the way I like it. A tidy girl.*

You don't know that well. In my house they call me the maniac. Although I think they exaggerate. I'm just tidy.

> *See you later.*
> *Kiss.*

I say goodbye cordially. I leave the phone on the bed and take a shower. I woke up in a sweat, and Raúl's messages and the proposal to be my pillow didn't help.

I return to the room. I have a message on the phone. It's from Raúl, it's an emoticon of a kiss. I also have several new messages from my sister.

> *Hello, little sister. I have something important to tell you.*

> *It's something important.*

> *I hope you will answer me quickly.*

What will it be?

> *Hi. I was in the shower. What do you have to tell me? You left me half.*

A few seconds later, I get a voice message.

'*Carlos asked me to marry him and my answer was yes. He took me to a country house the past weekend and proposed me there. I'm sending you a picture of the ring.*'

She was breathless with that voice note.

> *I'm so happy for you, sis. It's about time. You deserve it. You've been around long enough to take that step. You just made my day with this news. I guess mum is looking forward to that day.*

> *Mum is impatient, but we don't have a date yet, although I imagine it will be in August or early September.*

> *Let me know in time. Well, now I'm going to finish getting ready for class. A kiss and a hug.*

> *You will be the first to know the date of the wedding. Lots of kisses and don't get tired of dancing so much.*

Luca is anxious for us to leave now.

'Are you ready?' he says from the corridor.

'I'll be right out. One moment, impatient' I laugh.

We are waiting for the *kebabs* we have ordered to be served. This is the same place where we ordered the food the time we had dinner with Raúl on the beach.

It doesn't take long for them to give us our food.

We are sitting on one of the benches at the entrance of Bondi Pavilion. The *kebabs* are delicious. Luca talks about his relationship with Victor. I will not tarnish this moment of happiness for Luca by telling him what the witch Emma has done to me.

The ones from my Adonis' fan club are coming. They whisper when they pass by us. I have to bite my tongue not to tell them anything. Luca notices.

'Calm down, Dani. Don't even listen to them. They're dead jealous.'

'*Grazie*, Luca. Your words always help me.'

Raúl arrives before we enter the classroom. He grabs me by the waist, kisses me on the cheek and we enter the classroom

'Beautiful, I missed you,' he whispers to me.

I blush.

Today Elizabeth takes the reins of the class and Raúl seems very happy and very proud of his sister.

We started the class. Raúl looks great in that tight T-shirt and those trousers that make him a perfect ass. My heart rate goes up just by watching him.

It bothers me how the harpies on my right look at him. It looks like they're going to eat him up with their eyes. I give them a quick glance and they bow their heads.

Today we go over the dance steps from last week. This time I am the first to dance with the Adonis. I am happy. At this moment nobody can make the smile on my face change. Neither the looks of the harpies nor what happened with Emma or anything else.

Raúl stares at me, his eyes burn with desire. I try to hide, but I am just like him.

'I want to hold you in my arms,' he says in a whisper, and my body trembles in response to his words.

'Technically I am in your arms now.'

'You know what I mean' he says with a half smile.

So far, Raúl has not asked for a change of partner and the class is about to end. It's the first time he's done it and I don't know if it's because of me, but I think it is and that makes my self esteem rise even more.

'Wait for me outside, I'm going to the bathroom for a moment.'

Luca nods his head and leaves the class.

'Shall I wait for you?' Raúl asks me.

'There's no need. You can wait for me outside with Luca. Thank you,' I answer.

I come out of the bathroom and at the door of the class there are still those from Raúl's fan club. I take my bag and leave without a word. One of them trips me up and I fall to the floor without any time to react.

Raúl sees me on the floor from outside and rushes in to help me.

'What happened to you?'

He bends down and lifts me up from the floor. My left hand hurts. I look at the harpies out of the corner of my eye who are laughing silently.

'I stumbled.'

'Are you sure?' He asks suspiciously.

'Yes, yes. I'm a little clumsy.'

'Are you in pain? Are you okay?'

'The left hand.'

Raúl touches my hand and I let out a scream when he moves my little finger.

'You have to go to the doctor. Come on, I'll take you.'

Elizabeth runs to me.

'Are you OK?' I saw what happened.

'Yes, it was nothing. My hand just hurts a little.'

I grimace at her and say no with my head so that she won't say anything to Raúl. I don't want to poison the atmosphere.

Elizabeth resigns herself and doesn't say anything, but out of the corner of her eye I see that she's going towards the girl who tripped me. I don't know what she says, but they gesture too much.

Luca is outside waiting for me. He worries when he sees that Raúl has to help me walk.

'What happened to you?'

'I tripped when I left the class,' I explain to Luca.

'Are you sure?' he asks as he looks at the harpies coming out of the Pavilion in triumph.

'I'm sure.'

'I'm going to take her to the hospital,' says Raúl.

'I'll go with you.'

'Don't worry, Luca. Go home and let Carol know that I'll be there later, but don't tell her the reason so that she doesn't get worried. You have to rest.'

Luca reluctantly agrees.

We went to Raúl's house to get his car, which was in the garage. He activates the GPS in his car and sets off for Saint Vincent's Hospital.

'Let's hope they don't make us wait too long in the ER.'

'I hope so. I'm exhausted and I feel like sleeping.'

If you knew the day I had today... you would understand.

We are in the waiting room. There is no one here. I'll go to the doctor's office right away and have an X-ray taken.

A porter accompanies me to the X-ray room. They take two X-rays in different positions and another porter accompanies me back to the doctor's office where Raúl is also waiting for me.

'As I thought, you have a fissure between the distal phalanx and the middle phalanx of your little finger. This will take at least three weeks to recover.'

It can't be true. I have to keep working. I can't stop doing it. I've only just started!

'Look, doctor. I'm a veterinarian and I have to work. I can't afford to be on sick leave. Will I be able to keep working?' I ask, still puzzled by the diagnosis.

'Well, Miss Duarte. The best thing would be for you to recover at home, but since I see that you are eager to continue working, I will tell you that you can, but with great care. Which is the hand you usually work with or write with?'

'The right hand' I say lifting the safe hand.

'I advise you to be very careful when working. Any movement can make the injury worse.'

'I will.'

The doctor puts a bandage on my finger. He does it by joining the little finger to the ring one. It bothers me a little, but it's all for the sake of recovery. What a day! What a mess.

Raúl takes me home and we say goodbye in the car.

'Rest, beautiful.'

'Have a good rest, my prince.'

He gives me a sweet kiss as he caresses my cheek. He gets out of the car, goes around, opens the door and helps me out.

'Thank you.'

'You're welcome, beautiful. For you, anything.'

I give him a kiss on the cheek.

I go in the house. Luca was waiting for my arrival and he's with Carol. Obviously, he couldn't keep quiet.

'What did they say?' asks Carol with a worried face.

I show her the medical part.

'You'll stay at home, won't you?'

I'm shaking my head.

'You need to rest,' scolds Luca.

'Don't worry. The doctor said I can work as long as I'm careful. Besides, I'm right handed and I don't use my left hand much, and Rose will surely help me with whatever I need.'

'Well, as you wish,' says Carol.

'I'm going to rest. Today was a long day.'

I leave Carol and Luca in the living room and go to sleep. Indeed, today has not been my best day.

I receive a message.

> *Rest, my princess. Tomorrow will be another day and I will make it better than this one.*

Raúl's words encourage me.

> *Thank you for helping me. See you tomorrow. Kisses.*

Raúl says goodbye to me with a smiling emoticon and another with hearts in his eyes. They make me laugh.

I fall asleep thinking about the date I'll have tomorrow with Raúl. I can't wait for tomorrow night to arrive and enjoy an incredible night with my Adonis.

My Raúl…

# Friday, 24th November, 2017

My finger hurts. I take an ibuprofen. As always, the day is excellent. It's sunny, there are no clouds and it's warm. Summer will be here in about a month.

This is the only thing I don't miss about Spain, the cold winter that is about to come with its rains, its frosts and even its snowfalls.

I remember when Hugo and I went skiing. A little tear escapes from my right eye. I dry it right away. I don't want that memory to affect my day.

Today at least I didn't fall asleep despite going to bed late.

We are in the kitchen and both Carol and Luca ask me about my finger. I explain to them the same lie I told Raúl, that I tripped and fell. They will think that I can't even walk, but it's more difficult to tell them that a shrew tripped me.

I get to work early; it's still 15 minutes to seven. I like to have a cup of coffee before I start.

I'm waiting for Darel at the reception to show him the diagnosis the doctor gave me yesterday. He tells me to be careful and if I need a day off, to ask for it without any problem.

I answer him that I prefer to work.

Rose told me that she would help me with anything I needed. She said not to hesitate to call her no matter how small the help is.

Today Henry came. I was worried that Emma and her contaminated vaccines might come back. That reminds me of testing all the fluids in my practice for any contamination.

Rose helps me do that.

'It's all right,' says Rose.

'Thank you.'

'I'm going to go and help Jack for a moment. I'll be right back.'

'Okay.'

'If you need me, please let me know.'

'I will. Thank you very much.'

Rose is a very good partner. I am more and more happy to have Rose always by my side. I feel more protected with her. Jack is also a very good colleague, taking away the little mental derangement of Monday.

Hours and patients are passing by. Nothing can go wrong today. Today is the big day when I will have a formal appointment with the Adonis. It seems like a lie, but I'm nervous. I shouldn't be, I'm not fifteen anymore. I remember when I went to the cinema with my first young boyfriend. We were sixteen. We were so innocent... Sometimes I miss that time, when life seemed to be pink, but then you discover that sometimes it can be black.

I'm having a cup of coffee in the kitchen and I'm checking on the animals in the hospital. There's a cat that was castrated yesterday afternoon and the dog that I operated on. He's much better now. That fills me up as a veterinarian and as a professional.

I receive a message from my mother. How strange! It's still two o'clock in the morning in Madrid and it's very strange that she writes to me at this hour.

I open it impatiently.

> *Daughter, Grandpa has become very ill. The doctor says he doesn't think he will make it to next week. I'm sorry to give you this news, but I think you should come.*

How? It can't be. I knew he was in poor health. When I came here I was afraid that I would never see him again and it seems that my fears have come true.

> *What happened to him?*

> *Last night he got worse. He couldn't breathe properly and we had to call an ambulance.*

> *I'm going to talk to my boss and look for flights and I will try to go this same night.*

> *Okay, honey. Let me know if you can come and what time to pick you up at the airport. I'm sorry you have to come in this condition. I love you, my baby.*

> *Yes, mummy. I'll write to you in a little while. I love you all too. Give a kiss to Grandpa from me.*

I leave the coffee cup on the kitchen table and walk down the stairs so fast that I trip over several steps. I enter Darel's office without knocking. He is not there. I ask Kayla.

She wants to know what's wrong, but I'm not able to explain it to her at the moment. I just want to find Darel. She tells me he's in the office.

I go in without calling again.

He's with a patient and I have to wait in the corridor until he's finished to explain what happened to me.

Darel is leaning on the desk with his arms crossed, while I explain my situation to him. He says nothing. He just listens to me and nods yes.

'Yes. No problem. Take as many days as you need. I hope that your grandfather will recover soon.'

He gives me a hug and a kiss on the cheek.

'Thank you.'

I go back to my office and Rose comes behind me.

'What happened?'

'My grandfather has fallen ill and is in hospital. The doctor doesn't think he'll make it past this week. I have to go.'

'Oh. I'm so sorry,' says Rose as she hugs me.

'Thank you. Do I have any appointments now?'

'No.'

'Okay. I'll see if I can find a flight for today.'

Rose nods, leaves the office and closes the door.

I go on the Internet from my computer at work and look for flights for today. I have to go to Spain as soon as possible.

Well, there's one leaving tonight at a quarter to ten. I look for my bag, which is in my locker, and take the card out of my wallet. I go back to my office and buy the flight, one way. I don't know when I'll be back.

I pay a whopping 801 dollars. Although I don't mind, going to see my grandfather.

I can't wait to get out and pack. I print out the ticket and go to the printer at the reception desk to get it. Everything that is printed comes out there. Kayla gives me the paper and looks at me with bewilderment.

'You're going to Spain?' she asks, frowning.

'Yes. My grandfather is ill.'

'But you will come back, won't you?'

I say yes with my head as I return to my office.

I look at the clock on the wall several times, but time seems to have stopped. I have the feeling that I've become obsessed. When I want time to pass quickly, there is no way the hands can move.

I sigh.

I am at home. Rose has brought me here, which I thank her for, because I wanted to get there early.

Carol and Luca are not here yet and I would love them to be here right now. I need them. I send them a message informing them that I have to go to Spain.

Carol tells me that she will come as soon as she can and Luca has left me an emoticon of a face with his hands on his cheek and his mouth open.

I pack my suitcase. I haven't checked in. I'll take a small suitcase. Besides, at my mother's house I have almost all my winter clothes. I only brought my summer clothes and a jacket just in case, although here, winter is not cold; or so Carol told me.

I'm going to an ATM to get some money. I want to leave the rent for this week and next week. I'm thinking of changing dollars into Euros, but I still have a bank account open in Spain with some money and I have the card here.

Carol arrives and is almost as worried as I am. I give her the money in an envelope.

'Take it' I say giving her the money.

'Why are you giving me next Friday's rent?' she says, counting what's in the envelope.

'In case I don't get there in time for the next payment.'

'But you didn't have to. You'll give it to me when you come back. I don't care if you arrive next Friday or not.'

Carol is so understanding with me, that it makes me cry. She gives me a big hug.

Luca arrives and joins in the hug. I feel good with them. I explain to Luca that the fee for the dance classes is charged directly to my bank account. I want to leave it all here.

Carol has brought some pizzas for lunch. We are sitting on the sofa watching TV, or rather; the TV is watching us, as we are not paying attention to it. We talk about my trip and my grandfather's situation.

I am not hungry, but I make a great effort to eat. Then I have a twenty-six hour trip ahead of me and I need to be well.

I leave Carol and Luca in the living room and go to my room to finish preparing everything. I go to the bathroom, take a shower and wash my hair too. I dry it and straighten it with the irons.

I go back to the room already dressed and combed. My mobile phone is on the bed and has a flashing blue light. It tells me that I have pending messages.

*Beautiful, are you ready for tonight?*

Shit! I forgot about the date with Raúl. I've been busy preparing for the trip and I hadn't remembered the Adonis at all. I have to tell him that I won't be able to go.

*Hi. I can't make it tonight, I'm sorry.*

*Why did you change your mind?*

His question hurts me. It hurts me that he thinks I don't want to meet him. But it is for a major cause.

*It's not that I don't want to. It's that I can't. I really can't.*

*What's wrong with you?*

*I received a message from my mother telling me that my grandfather is very sick and I have to go to Spain. The flight leaves today at 21:45.*

*Oh. I'm so sorry. I'll take you to the airport.*

> *Don't worry about it. Carol has offered to take me away.*

> *Let me take you, please.*

I can't say no to the handsome Adonis. I can imagine the look on his face with what I just said.

I accept.

> *I'll pick you up around eight. Is it OK?*

> *Yes. Perfect. I don't have to check in, so my time comes.*

I close the suitcase and put the laptop in its case and leave everything in the entrance, next to the door. I look for the jacket that is the warmest of all and leave it next to the suitcase.

'What time do you arrive in Madrid?' asks Luca. He's making a cup of coffee in the kitchen. 'Do you want one?'

'Yes, please,' I say as I walk down the corridor. 'I'm going to get the itinerary.'

Back to the kitchen. Luca is sitting at the kitchen bar with his coffee cup in his hand and my cup in front of him.

I sit down.

'Departure time is at 21:45 and I make a stopover in Doha. I arrive in Madrid at five to two in the afternoon. It will be almost midnight here.'

'Even if you arrive at three in the morning. You write to me as soon as you land and keep me informed of everything.'

'Yes. Don't worry.'

He extends his hands over the table and I do the same. He holds them tightly and looks at me with love.

The hours continue to pass slowly.

I look at the clock.

It is 7:03 p.m.

I tell Carol that Raúl is going to take me to the airport.

'Okay, but I would have liked to take you.'

'Thank you, but I haven't been able to say no to Raúl.'

'I hope you have a good trip and let me know when you arrive' she says with resignation.

'Yes.'

Raúl is at the entrance. Luca has opened the door for him. He is very handsome, with a pair of tight jeans and a linen shirt.

He takes my suitcase and laptop case. I say goodbye to Carol and Luca with tears in my eyes, and Raúl and I go out.

'See you soon,' I say.

'We're going to miss you,' answers Luca.

We are on our way to the airport. The GPS says we have ten minutes left to reach our destination. I am very nervous. I want to get to Madrid and give my grandfather a kiss.

I look at my mobile phone every few minutes waiting to receive a message from my family. I decide to write to my mother to let her know the time I will arrive at the terminal.

> *We will be waiting for your arrival.*
> *I love you, my little one.*

I look at my mother's reply and realise that I need her very much. I need her hugs, her words of encouragement and her pampering, and I miss when I was sick and she took my food to bed, or when she combed my hair, even though she knew I hated it.

The darkness of the night floods the car. Raúl looks very focused while driving. I can see his face through the reflect of the odometer lights. He has a perfect profile.

He takes his left hand off the wheel and puts it on top of mine and squeezes it hard.

'I'm going to miss you so much,' he says without looking away from the road.

'And I miss you,' I reply.

'We have a pending date.'

'I won't forget.'

I squeeze his hand tighter.

'How many days will you be gone?'

'I don't know yet,' I say sadly, 'I've only bought a one way ticket.'

'What do you mean?' For a moment Raúl stopped looking at the road to look at me.

'Look at the road!' I laugh at him. 'I just want to stay a few days with my family and I don't know how many days my grandfather will be in the hospital.'

'Ah!' His face muscles have relaxed and his expression is sweeter. 'I understand that,' he adds.

We're in Terminal 1. It's half past eight. It's a little over an hour before my plane leaves. Raúl is next to me, with his arm over my shoulders and my suitcase in the other hand.

I look at the screens in the lounge and look for my flight.

'It's gate 31,' Raúl says. 'Do you want to eat something before you go?'

'No, thanks. I'm not hungry. I ate late.'

We approach passport control. We can't suppress the sadness we feel.

'Have a good trip.' Raúl keeps hugging me and I answer him in the same way.

'Thank you.' Tears flow from my eyes without asking permission.

'Don't cry, Princess.' Raúl wipes my tears with a handkerchief he has taken out of his trouser pocket.

He gently caresses my cheeks and gives me a passionate kiss on my lips. It's a different kiss. More than a kiss, it seems like a farewell. I have the feeling that this is the end for us.

I reciprocate in the same way.

'See you soon' I say winking at my Adonis.

He keeps looking at me while I pass the control. It's easier to get out of the country than to get in.

We look at each other one last time until he disappears in the crowd. I miss him already and I haven't been with him for five minutes. I'm afraid he's going to forget me these days.

I receive a message.

*I'll be waiting for you.*

Raúl's message gives me the strength to make this journey and return as soon as I can.

*I will miss you. I will try to come back as quickly as possible.*

I sit in front of the gate. I wait impatiently for it to open. It means that I will be closer to Madrid. The airport is full of people coming and going and workers in the terminal as well as pilots and hostesses. I almost get dizzy watching.

They open the boarding gate and a very kind stewardess tells us to make two lines. In one are the passengers who have paid for priority boarding and in the other are all the others. The line is very long and I'm almost at the end of it.

I get on the plane and look for my seat. Row 36 seat A. I leave my suitcase in the overhead bin and sit down. I am next to the window.

I get ready to spend more than fifteen hours on the plane. I have brought some sweets and movies on the laptop.

I'll let my family; Raúl, Carol and Luca know that I'm already on the plane and that I'm going to unplug the phone.

I turn it off and make myself comfortable in my seat.

The stewardesses do the safety demonstrations before take off while the pilots do the checks on the motors.

I still have to wait a while before I can turn on my laptop. Until the plane is stable in the air, you can't, so I take advantage of that time to look at the last messages I have on my mobile and some photos.

# Saturday, 25th November, 2017

I look at the clock. I don't know what time it is because my mobile phone hasn't been updated and it has Sydney time on it. I've already watched three films, so I reckon it must have been about five hours since we took off.

I turn off my laptop. I'm going to try and get some sleep. The plane's lights are off and you can't see anything from the window, everything is darkness.

I rest my jacket on the window and use it as a pillow. I fall asleep thinking about Raúl. Suddenly, his face turns into Hugo. *"No!"*, my subconscious screams. I am afraid to see him again. I don't know how I'm going to avoid him in the hospital. I hope he is not working.

I wake up startled and I wake up the man next to me. I ask him to forgive me and I take the opportunity to ask him if he knows how much time is left to land.

The man makes beads with his fingers. He tells me that we will be about four hours from Doha, which means that I have slept for more than six hours.

I am not able to go back to sleep. I turn on the laptop again, plug in the headphones and double click on the next movie in the list. So one after the other until we are informed that we will be landing in twenty minutes.

The stewardess asks me nicely to turn off the laptop and I obey. I am now a little closer to home.

Many flights have arrived almost at the same time. This delays the entry at the airport and there are long queues at passport control.

I'm looking for the airport's Wifi so I can update the time on my mobile phone to know what time it is and if I have new messages.

More than ten messages come in. I answer them one by one. It's almost six o'clock and the next plane leaves at eight.

In Sydney it is two o'clock in the afternoon. I exchange several messages with Luca. He tells me that in the evening he's going out with Victor, Carol and David for dinner and dancing. "Dinner for couples," he tells me.

In Madrid it's two hours less than here. My family will still be sleeping.

It's seven o'clock. I go back through passport control. I go into one of the grocery shops and buy a croissant and a hot chocolate. It's going to be more expensive on the plane.

I look for the boarding gate. This time it's the B3. I go inside through one of the corridors that indicate where my door is going. I sit in front of it and eat what I have bought.

I am nervous. Not hearing from my grandfather makes me desperate. I don't want to go crazy sending messages to my family either. They will be asleep and I don't want to disturb them. I want to get to Madrid now and see him.

I get on the plane and look for my seat again. This time it's almost an eight hour flight. Luckily I have enough films and series to watch and be entertained, although I'll try to sleep for a while.

The flight is taking forever. I get up several times to go to the bathroom. My legs are numb. This time I go to the side of the corridor and don't bother anyone when I have to get up.

I've stayed up for a while, which has helped the hours go by a little faster.

It's not long now. The driver has announced that we will be landing in ten minutes. It seems that many years have passed since I left Madrid, and it's barely been three weeks. I hope that when I return to Sydney my boss will not fire me.

I have my laptop in storage and everything ready for when the doors open. I shuffle around in my seat, nervous.

I bite my nails.

I go through passport control. I'm finally here. In my house. I cross the long corridors to the automatic doors.

They open.

My mother is waving her arms around for me to see her. She's very funny. She makes me laugh alone.

I run towards her and we merge into a big hug. I don't want to leave her. It's a warm hug. She gives me noisy kisses on the cheek, like when I was a child. What memories! My father is waiting impatiently for his turn.

I hug him.

'I am very happy to see you, my daughter,' says my father.

'And I, to you.'

'What happened to your hand?' My mother holds my hand very carefully.

'Two days ago I tripped and fell. I put my hand down wrong. That's all,' I explain, playing down the importance of it. If she knew the truth, she would probably never let me go back.

Let's go to the car park. My father takes the car keys out of his trouser pocket and opens it by pressing the button on the remote control. He puts my suitcase in the boot while I sit on the back seat.

I ask for my siblings.

'Your sister is with your grandfather and your brother has stayed at home waiting for you.'

'And how is Grandma?'

'She's worried, daughter. You know how she is.'

'And Grandpa?' I ask with clear signs of concern. My mother has noticed.

'He's still the same. They don't give us any hope.'

I try to suppress the tears. I play hard to get.

We go through the bustling streets of Madrid. The traffic is very dense and it is almost impossible to move forward normally.

'How was your trip?' asks my father. He looked at me by the central mirror and tries to change the subject.

'Well, but it's been a long time and, although I've slept a bit, I have not rested long enough.'

'You can sleep when you get home. Your room is just like when you left,' says my mother.

My brother comes running down the corridor when he hears the door and gives me such a tight hug so that my bones crunch.

'How I wanted to see you! The house is not the same without you.'

'I wanted to see you too, little brother.'

My brother asks me about my hand just like my mother and I have to explain it again with the same lie I told her. I'm afraid it's going to be the question of the week.

We sit down at the kitchen table. My mother prepares a salad and some beef to eat; meanwhile, I have a cup of hot tea.

Unlike Sydney, it's cold here.

My brother helps to put the dishes on the table. It's the first time I see him helping out at home and I am left with my mouth open.

'What's new?' I ask him, raising an eyebrow.

'Since you've been away, I've been a slave,' he says, laughing and pointing at my mother.

'How exaggerated you are! It's not that bad.'

My mother gives him a glance and we all laugh.

Everything my mother prepares is always very tasty. I missed it. Lately I always eat out or just salad.

'I'm looking forward to going to see Grandpa now' I mean eating in a hurry.

'Don't you want to rest for a bit?' asks my mother.

'No. I'll sleep at night. Now I just want to be with Grandpa.'

I finish eating and go to the bathroom. I take a shower, get dressed and brush my teeth. I straighten my hair a bit and I'm ready to leave the house.

I'm waiting for my parents, who are finishing up, while my brother tells me about his battles at school. He tells me about video games that I don't even know existed. Luckily we have our favourite series in common.

'Have you got a girlfriend yet?'

My brother gets nervous and starts to snort.

'Well... Something is going on,' he says quietly.

I can't help but laugh at the faces he's making.

We are on our way to the hospital. My father avoids the traffic by cutting through small streets. My mother has a free parking pass. My father parks without any problem. It is impossible to find a parking space on the street.

My mother stops to talk to all the people who work at the hospital. My father waits with her. Jonathan and I go up in the lift. My grandfather is on the fifth floor.

My sister, when she sees me, gets up running from the chair next to my grandfather and gives me a hug and many kisses on both cheeks.

My grandmother is sitting on another chair with her eyes full of tears. I go towards her and, without giving her time to get up, I'm already hugging her.

I look towards the bed. My grandfather is sleeping. He has been given an oxygen mask and an IV with saline. He looks very fragile.

I can't suppress the urge to cry. I sit down next to him and talk to him. I hope he can hear me. I talk to him about my work. I know that he is very proud of me, he has told me so many times.

I remember that my grandparents were very sad when I went to visit them the day before I left for Australia.

I hold his hand and he squeezes it lightly as a sign that he is listening to me. He opens his eyes slowly and says my name. Tears start to flow from my eyes again.

I smile.

'Daniela, is that you?'

'Yes, Grandpa. I'm here.'

'I had… a lot… of… seeing… you' he says hesitantly.

His breathing is sharp. He tries to take off his mask, but my mother tells him he can't.

'Calm down, Grandpa. You don't have to say anything.'

He caresses my hand. Seeing him like that is very hard. He has always been a strong man. He has always been my example.

I have to get out of here. I can't see him in this condition anymore. I need a cup of coffee.

My sister is coming with me. We walk down the corridor and I look towards all sides in search for Hugo, without noticing.

'He's not here,' my sister says. She has realised my intentions.

'Huh?'

'Hugo is not here. He has the day off today.'

I sigh of relief. I wouldn't like to have to see him now that I'm starting to get over him.

'Do you miss him?' she asks.

'I used to. Now I miss him less and less.'

'Is there a new Hugo in your life?' After me. My mother, my sister knows me best.

'There is something. But I don't want to get my hopes up.'

I shrug my shoulders.

'What's the lucky man's name?'

'His name is Raúl. He's Cuban and a dance teacher at the school I go to.'

'Oh.'

'He is also a physical education teacher in a school.'

I show her one of the photos from The Cuban Place.

'He is very handsome. He looks like…' My sister keeps quiet.

I know who she means he looks like because I know who he looks like, too.

'Yes, I know, Hugo' I finish the sentence that Amelia has not been able to finish.

We sat down in the hospital cafeteria in the workers' area. Amelia has an employee discount.

'For me, a coffee with milk, please' I say to the waitress.

The waitress greets my sister. Amelia orders tea and the waitress leaves us to prepare what we have ordered.

She comes back a few minutes later. On the tray she brings the tea, the coffee with milk and some sweets to go with it.

'Do you have a date for the wedding?' I ask.

'Not yet.'

'Alicia is getting married by the end of August and it would be good if the date was close to hers because this way I wouldn't have to make two trips.' I suggest.

'It's true. Besides, I'm also invited to Alicia's wedding.'

Amelia and I have almost always had the same friends. Two years separate us and we've always gone everywhere together. We have a very good relationship, apart from some silly fights when we were little, but not important ones.

For many years it was just me and her until the dwarf came along, how many jokes we played on him and how much we laughed at him!

My mother joins us. She orders a cup of coffee and sits next to me. I missed the three of us being alone. I'd like to tell them everything that has happened to me, but I've always been a bit reserved about telling my things.

'The doctor told me that your grandfather's heart is getting weaker every day and it is only a matter of a few days before he leaves us' says my mother with tears in her eyes.

'We have to resign ourselves,' replies my sister.

She is right. My grandfather is nearly ninety years old now, and as much as it hurts, it's the law of life. Every day people die.

'I'm very sorry to see him like that,' I said.

My mother grabs my hand and squeezes it tightly.

'We have to be strong,' she says.

'I'd like to stay with him tonight.'

'I'm staying!' exclaims my sister. 'You have to rest.'

I grudgingly accept because I know that, as my sister, I have a lot to lose. My sister is more stubborn than I am.

We finished and got up from the table. My sister and mother say goodbye to the staff working in the *cafeteria* and to some of their colleagues sitting at other tables.

We go back to the room and take over from my brother, my father and my grandmother, who are still accompanying my grandfather. They leave the room and I sit next to him. He is awake, although a little disoriented.

He doesn't know where he is and he doesn't know who I am. He is different from when I arrived and that disconcerts me. I look at him with great sadness. I nod my head in denial.

My mother gets up from her chair and approaches me to comfort me.

'It's normal, Dani,' my mother says, caressing my cheek.

'It can't be. When I arrived, she said my name' I say unable to resign myself.

'It's because of the medication they're giving you. He is fine.'

'He is not!' I say almost shouting.

A nurse passing in the corridor enters and signals to me to lower my voice.

'Calm down, Dani. That happens to a lot of people.' My sister tries to calm me down, but seeing my grandfather ranting makes me angry.

I take my bag and my jacket and leave the room. I sit down on a chair in the lift area.

I take the phone out of my bag. I have a lot of new messages. They are all from my friends in Sydney. I forgot to write to them when I arrived.

I open Raúl's messages first.

> *Beautiful. Did you get there okay? I haven't heard from you in many hours.*
>
> *I saw on the Internet that your flight has already arrived in Madrid. Please, answer.*
>
> *Hello, Princess. If you don't answer me, I'll have to file a missing persons report.*
>
> *Hellooooo. Answer me, please.*

I feel really bad. I should have sent him a message when I landed, but I completely forgot. I hope he is not too angry, although his messages are more worrying than anything else.

> *Hello, my prince. I completely forgot to write to you. I arrived safely. My parents went to pick me up at the airport and then I went to lunch. Now I'm at the hospital. I am very sorry. I hope you are not angry with me.*

Luca sent me a voice mail.

'*Ciao, Dani. I hope you arrived safely. Carol is with me and we are looking forward to hearing from you. Please write to us as soon as you can.*'

In the background, Carol snorted. How bad I feel.

> *Hi, guys. I got here okay, but I've been busy. In fact, I'm at the hospital now. My grandfather is very sick. I miss you.*

I don't get an answer. It's twenty past four in the morning in Sydney and I remember Luca telling me that they were going out for dinner and then dancing.

Raúl might be sleeping or with... I don't want to think that he might be with another girl. It would hurt me a lot, although it would be quite logical. I dismiss that idea from my head immediately.

I enter into Raúl's conversation hoping that the double tick will turn blue. I don't succeed.

I go in and out of the conversation several times, desperate

Nothing.

My father gets out of the lift together with my brother and my grandmother.

'What are you doing here?' he asks.

'It's very hot in the room' I lie.

Actually, I came out because it hurts me to see my grandfather like this, so fragile, so helpless, and I feel hopeless for not being able to help him.

My father tells my grandmother and my brother to go into the room, and he sits next to me.

'Daughter, I know you well. You haven't gone out because it's hot in the room, or am I wrong?'

I'm in denial. My father knows me better than I thought.

'Seeing Grandpa like this hurts me a lot.'

'I know, Dani. But you have to be strong. You've always been very brave.'

My father's words together with his hug make me feel slightly better, although it doesn't make this pain in my heart go away.

'Come on, daughter. Let's go to the room.'

My father gets up from his chair and holds my hand so that I can get up too. He puts his arm around my shoulders and we walk down the corridor to the room.

It's eight o'clock and the warden tells us that visiting hours are over and that only one person can stay with my grandfather. I'd love to stay, but Amelia has already given herself that position.

I kiss my grandfather on the forehead. He's in a deep sleep. He looks very peaceful. I don't want to wake him up.

My grandmother hugs him with tears in her eyes; she doesn't want to leave him. She argues with my sister, but finally Amelia wins again.

We say goodbye to my sister and leave the room not knowing if tomorrow we will see grandpa alive again, although nobody says anything. I realise this because I think the same thing. I am going to be on the phone all night in case my sister calls to give some news.

We are all at home, including my grandmother, who has stayed with my parents and my brother so as not to be alone in their house. That depresses her even more. There is no problem of space because Amelia's room is free.

I help my mother to prepare dinner. My brother and my father put the dishes on the table.

We have dinner.

'I clear the table,' says my mother when she sees me get up from the chair to pick up the dishes. 'Go and rest.'

'Yes, daughter. You haven't rested at all since you arrived,' says my father.

I kiss my parents and my grandmother. I give my brother a slap on the wrist. It is a custom of ours. And I go to my room. Fatigue takes over my body and my mind.

I'm in bed, looking at the shadows on the wall, with the light coming through the holes in the blind, and I think about my grandfather, my work and Raúl.

It's already daylight in Sydney. I look at my mobile phone hoping that there will be some new messages. I feel selfish, because the only message I want to get is from the Adonis.

I try to sleep quickly. Tomorrow we are all going early to the hospital. I move around several times until I fall into a deep sleep.

## Sunday, 26th November, 2017

My mother has to wake me up almost screaming. My mouth is open and I drool. I was sleeping very soundly. I fell asleep. I didn't hear the alarm.

'Come on, sleepyhead. It's time to get up.'

'Yes, mummy,' I say reluctantly as I toss and turn in bed like a little girl.

'The others are already dressed and eating breakfast.'

'I get dressed right away and go.'

My mother leaves the room and closes the door behind her. I get out of bed, reluctant. Still very sleepy, I take a change of clothes from my suitcase and go to the bathroom to take a shower.

My grandmother and my mother are in the kitchen. I hear them talking about my grandfather and decide to wait in the corridor to listen to the conversation without being seen. I am leaning against the wall next to the door.

'I didn't want to tell Daniela the truth so as not to worry her,' says my mother.

'It's better that way. She would suffer a lot if she knew.'

'That's true. She would never have left and we all know that she needed to leave.'

I can't believe my ears. I can't hear anymore and I open the door with a push that almost makes it turn.

Both of them are left open mouthed.

'What can't I know?' I ask with an angry tone.

'Calm down, daughter.' My mother approaches me and takes my arm so that I can sit on a chair.

'Let go of me!' I exclaim with a shout.

'Sit down, please. I'll explain everything to you. But you have to calm down.'

I regain my composure and sit down on the chair. I take a deep breath to try and calm down. I am angry, not because my grandfather could be worse or better, but because they are hiding information from me like when I was 10 years old.

'Daughter. I didn't want to tell you anything, but Grandpa got worse since you left.'

'Huh?'

'The same day you left, he had a heart failure and had to be admitted. Since then he must have oxygen 24 hours a day.'

'What? You're telling me now that he's like this because of me? Why didn't you tell me? I would have come back on the same plane.'

'Well, that's why we didn't tell you anything,' my grandmother said. 'We knew how excited you were about this trip.'

'I don't care about the trip or work or anything. I would have given everything for Grandpa to be well.'

They keep quiet. My mother is beside me with her elbows on the table and her hands at face level. My grandmother is standing with her arms crossed and her eyes down.

'It's not fair,' I say, banging on the table.

I get up and go back to my room. My hunger has suddenly gone away. I can't help feeling guilty about my grandfather's state of health. I am very angry with my family. I can't believe they kept it from me.

I walk around the room, from the door to the window and back. So again, and again trying to suppress my anger. I would gladly leave at this very moment and never return. If I don't, it's because of my grandfather. I know he needs me by his side.

I take a coat from the wardrobe and the bag. I walk down the corridor avoiding being seen. My mother and grandmother are still in the kitchen. I look in secret and see that they are on their backs, so I pass by without being seen.

My brother had the door to his room closed and he hasn't seen me either.

My father is in the living room, reading the newspaper. He's so absorbed in the news that he doesn't see me.

I open the door with the ability that I have so that no one can hear me and I go out. I close the door with a slight pull. Good! They didn't hear me.

I go outside and head for the hospital.

As I walk through the busy streets of Madrid, I think about the conversation I heard in the kitchen. I deny with my head just thinking that it was my departure that made my grandfather worse. I would like to go back in time and return to that 2nd of November.

I walk for more than half an hour until I reach the hospital. I am determined to ask my sister for an explanation, she knew about it too and didn't tell me anything. We have always told each other everything and now, when I most needed to trust her, is when she betrays me.

On the way to the fifth floor I meet several acquaintances. They are hospital workers, whom I know from my mother and my sister. They greet me and I just wave to them because I am in a hurry to get to the room where my grandfather is.

I go into the room, but there is no one there. My grandfather is still in a deep sleep. My sister must not be far away. Her things are here.

I go up to my grandfather, kiss him on the cheek, sit down next to him and take his immobile hand. I talk to him so that he knows I'm here. I wish by all means that he gets well.

His skin colour has changed. He is very pale.

'Grandpa, I know you have been like this since I left, but I am here now. I promise you that if you recover I will leave everything and stay here with you. I don't care about anything else.'

He doesn't react. He is still. My eyes fill up with tears.

'Please, wake up. We have to go home.'

'Dani, he's not going to wake up,' says Amelia, who heard me from the door.

'How are you so sure of that?' I ask her angrily.

'He's gotten worse last night and the doctor says he doesn't believe that he will make it through today.'

'What do you mean, the doctor doesn't believe it? Who is this doctor who says that? Tell me his name and I'll talk to him. Is that guy a fortune teller?'

'Calm down. I don't think you like to know who the doctor is.'

'What do you mean?' I ask in bewilderment, but in a split second I realise what he meant.

'Is he here?'

My sister nods her head and suddenly I start to get short of breath.

Amelia takes a chair that is free and brings it over to sit next to me. She holds my hand and comforts me, but I put my hand away immediately. I'm still angry about the information she's been hiding from me all this time.

'So you knew that grandpa had been upset by my departure and you haven't told me anything. Who do you think you are to play with something like that?'

Amelia stirs herself in the chair and takes a long time to answer, as if she was thinking through what she was going to say to me.

'First, calm down. Grandfather is here and we don't know if he can hear us or not,' she says in a low tone. 'Mum forbade me to tell you because she knew it would affect you a lot and she didn't want you to give up your dreams for anything in the world.'

I find it difficult to assimilate this information. At the moment I am not able to think or decide.

I look at my poor grandfather carefully.

'Do you think he would have wanted you to come back?' asks my sister.

I nod my head in denial. I hate to say it, but she is right.

'You have to resign yourself to the fact that this was going to happen sooner or later,' she adds. 'By the way, where is the rest of the family?'

'I've come alone. Nobody knows I'm here.'

Amelia takes the phone from inside her bag and calls my mother, who was hysterical because she didn't know where I was. She was looking for me everywhere and my sister says that they have called me several times.

I look at my mobile phone. I have several missed calls.

'Why did you do that?'

'Because I was very angry. I overheard a conversation between Grandma and mum about Grandpa's health.'

'We did everything for you, so that you would have peace of mind.'

'I insist that you should have told me.'

My parents come into the room. They are slightly upset. I look at them as I did when I was a child and did some mischief. In the end, they always forgave me.

'Why did you leave?' My mother's face changes from anger to concern.

'I'm... sorry' I say stuttering.

My mother approaches me and gives me a hug.

One of the machines connected to my grandfather starts to beep. I get up from the chair in anguish. My eyes open wide like plates. My mother approaches the machine and hits several buttons.

She rings the bell that connects the room to the nurse's station so that someone can come right away.

My grandfather's heartbeat has dropped and his breathing is laboured. He starts to convulse. I throw my hands in my face. I can't see him. I think of the worst. No, no, no. This can't be the end.

'Mum, do something, please' I beg her.

'Daughter, calm down.' My father grabs me by the shoulders and carries me out of the room.

I go out with my father and, as I go with my head down looking at the floor, I stumble upon someone who enters at that moment.

I raise my head. No! It's Hugo. I close my eyes in the hope that it was a nightmare and that, when I open them, another doctor will come in.

Nothing. It's him. He's the same as always. He looks at me for a few seconds with those bewitching eyes. I look at him for a few moments and then turn my face away from him.

He greets me with a simple hello and rushes in.

Contradictory feelings are stirred up inside me. Why now? I close my eyes again to think about Raúl. Yes! He will be waiting for me.

My heart has taken a strange turn. A chill has run through my body.

I look at him while he is treating my grandfather. He starts with the resuscitation manoeuvres because he goes into cardiac arrest and my mother stays with him while my grandmother, my siblings, my father and I have to wait in the corridor.

They have closed the door and we are all uncertain what will be happening.

After several minutes of anguish, my mother leaves with Hugo with tears in her eyes and I know that my grandfather will never say my name again or give me advice. Many memories come back to me.

I cry without consolation. Hugo approaches me.

'Not now' I say before I can mediate a word.

He walks away and goes to the nurses' station. He sits down on one of the chairs and types on the computer. He looks at me out of the corner of his eye from time to time, although now that is the least of my worries.

We go into the room so I can be with my grandfather. My mother is in the corridor talking to the undertaker.

The nurses come into the room and ask us nicely to wait in the corridor while they take away all the appliances he was connected to.

Hugo goes from room to room visiting the patients on the floor. I look at him without much interest, like another doctor doing his job. At the moment I have no head to think about anyone other than my grandfather and my family.

The funeral service has arrived and taken my grandfather away to prepare him for the mortuary. On the one hand, I am calm because at least I was able to be with him in his last moments.

'Let's go home and eat,' says my mother.

'I prefer go for a walk' I answer.

'I'm going with you,' says my brother.

While my parents, my grandmother and my sister have left in the car, my brother and I are going home for a walk in the streets of this city. My brother asks me questions about Sydney as I hold on to his arm. We tell each other stories about our grandfather.

We laugh, though with tears in our eyes.

At home they already have the food done. Amelia and Carlos, my parents and my grandmother are at the dining room table.

'It's about time, kids,' my mother replies.

We sit on the chairs that are free. We eat in silence. Nobody says anything. I have barely eaten a bite. My mother scolds me.

'Eat something, daughter. You haven't had breakfast and now you aren't eating.'

'Mum, don't insist. I'm not hungry.'

I get up from the table and pick up my plate.

'I'm going to sit on the sofa,' I say.

My father nods his head in agreement. It has always been the custom in my house to ask permission to leave the table and today will be no exception.

I'm on the sofa looking at old photos from an album my mother has. My grandfather, when he was young, my mother as a child, and her brothers and sisters. My siblings and I on the beach. There are many, many pleasant memories.

I have several messages on my mobile

> *Hi, Dani. I hope you are well and that your grandfather is better.*

Luca sent me the message at three o'clock in the afternoon from Sydney. It was still five o'clock in the morning here, but I hadn't seen my mobile phone until now.

I answer him with tears in my eyes.

> *Hello, Luca. I'm fine, as far as I'm concerned. My grandfather is now in a better place. He has been dead for four hours.*

It's early morning now and he'll be asleep. In a few hours he has to get up to go to the university.

I also have a voice message from Raúl. I'm going to get the headphones that I have in my bag in the room. I sit up in bed and listen to the message.

'*Hello, Princess. I was sleeping when you wrote to me. The time change is a nuisance. I would love to talk to you in real time and not have to wait for you to reply. I hope everything is fine.*'

I reply to him right away.

> *Hello. I would love you to be here now. I need you more than ever. My grandfather has been dead for four hour.*

I know that Raúl will not answer either, because he also gets up early and is already sleeping. I suppose he will read it in six or seven hours.

We are on our way to the mortuary. I've changed my clothes and I'm dressed in the darkest clothes I have, but I don't have anything black. I don't care, though. I don't care what they might say.

A lot of people come to the morgue. My uncles and cousins have been here for a long time on my mother's side. I haven't seen them for a long time. Each one of us has a different life and we didn't even coincide at Christmas, as was the custom when we were small and the family was closer.

I am in the entrance getting some air, alone. Thinking. There are many things that go through my mind. On the one hand, I would like to stay here, but on the other hand I want to go back to Sydney now.

I take my mobile phone out of my bag and look at the social networks.

'Hello.'

Someone is talking to me; it's a man's voice. I turn around to find out who is doing it.

I am frozen. It's Hugo. He's here, in front of me. It's like if time had stopped.

'H... Hello' I say stuttering.

I'd like to run away right now. My heart is beating so hard that it feels like it's going to come out of my mouth.

'How are you? I haven't heard from you. I asked your mother and Amelia, but they wouldn't tell me anything.'

My family has not told him anything because I asked them to, but I'm not going to tell him that. My friends are also forbidden to tell him anything.

'Fine; well, not now.'

'Normal. I'm very sorry about your grandfather. I tried everything, but it was impossible.'

'Yes, I know. Thank you.'

'What happened to your hand?' he asks.

'A minor accident.'

'If you come by the hospital, I can take a look at it.'

'Thank you, but there's no need. My doctor will check it out.'

'Why haven't you come to see your grandfather before?' He's determined to know what I've been doing.

Since we broke up last August, we had been meeting somewhere, or when I went to pick up my sister or mother from the hospital.

'I've had a lot of work,' I reply.

'Where do you work?' he asks.

'In a veterinary clinic on the outskirts.'

Lying, what is said to be lying, I am not doing it. In fact, I work in a clinic on the outskirts, but I haven't indicated how far away it is.

'Oh.'

He has realised that I want to avoid any questions about my private life from him.

'Well, I have to go in.'

I turn around, but I can't go any further. Hugo grabs me by one arm and pulls me towards him so that I don't leave. We stay in front of each other.

'Don't go away. We have to talk.'

'What do you want to talk about?' I ask as I move my arm to let go. 'You still have the little shame to talk to me after playing with my feelings.'

He keeps quiet and bows his head.

'Now, you tell me, why have you been able to fool me for so long?'

I am facing my fears for the first time.

'You know that I tried to leave her, but it was impossible. She's not doing good.'

'Always with the same excuse. I've heard it many times before.'

'But it's true.'

'Certainly you've had me fooled. If we had been honest from the first day, we would have saved ourselves a lot of tears.'

'But I love you.'

Huh? Are you still able to tell me that? This is the very last straw.

'What?' I say with a shout.

People here turn around and look at us.

'Please keep your voice down. Everyone is looking at us.'

'I don't care about that. I'm leaving. I don't want to listen to you anymore.'

I run into the mortuary room where my grandfather is. Everyone turns around and looks at me because I'm panting to get my normal breathing after the race from the street to here.

Hugo enters shortly afterwards. He sends his condolences to my whole family. He passes in front of me, but I twist his face. Seeing him again and hearing the same excuse has made me go back to the past. It was a really unpleasant moment.

I can't wait to get over this bitter trance and get on with my life. I look at the coffin. It is open and my grandfather is with his hands on his chest. He is at peace. He is resting after all the ailments he has suffered.

It's already nine o'clock at night and the workers at the mortuary announce its closure. They tell us that tomorrow the doors will be open from 10 a.m.

I think that my poor grandfather will be alone all night. In this cold place. In the hospital we could be with him.

I'm sitting in the back seat of my parents' car. My father is driving and I am behind him, looking out the window. I watch people walking down the streets. Some are in a hurry, others with the phone in their hands. Others chat quietly on the café terraces.

My mobile phone vibrates inside my bag.

> *Good morning, beautiful. I just got up and saw your message. The fact that your message is the first thing I see makes Monday a better day.*

Raúl just got up. It's a little after seven o'clock on Monday morning there. His message makes him smile.

> *Hi. They just closed the mortuary and I'm in my father's car on my way home.*

> *How are you? Are you better? Although I can imagine how you are. I understand you perfectly. I've been through that a few years ago.*

> *Well, more or less, assimilating it. These are very difficult times. Tomorrow during the afternoon will be the burial.*

> *Now I have to get ready for work, but every time you feel bad you can write to me, and as soon as I see the messages, I answer. I love you, my princess.*

He said the magic word to me. "I love you". I read again the last message. I still don't believe it. He said it to me. My heart is coming out of my mouth. My inner self dances with joy in the midst of so much sadness.

> *Thank you. I wish you could be here, although you already know that. I love you too.*

I press "send" and wait for it to get the blue ticks. Yes, he has read it, but he doesn't answer me. I receive another message. This time the one who has written to me is Charlie. I haven't spoken to him for a long time.

*Hello. How are you? I hope everything is going well.*

*Hello. I'm in Spain.*

*Have you left Sydney?*

*It's only temporary. Family problems.*

*What happened?*

*My grandfather passed away this morning.*

*I am very sorry. I didn't know anything.*

*Thank you.*

While I was exchanging messages, we arrived at the garage and my father parked in his parking space. Carlos parks in the next square. My parents own several parking spaces.

We got out of the car. Sadness is written on our faces and nobody says anything. It's a very empty feeling.

If my grandfather were here, he would be talking about when he went into military service, or about the hunger he experienced in the postwar period. Those were difficult times for many. But he is simply not here. We will never hear his stories again.

We have dinner, talk about tomorrow and organise everything. Amelia and Carlos have dinner and leave because he is working very early tomorrow morning.

I just want to sleep and think that none of that has happened. Today has been a very long day and I'm afraid that tomorrow will be much worse.

I want time to pass as quickly as possible, but since I got here it seems to have stopped. The days are slow and agonizing.

I fall asleep thinking about Raúl's message. It is what keeps me alive at this painful time.

## Monday, 27th November, 2017

We're on our way to the mortuary. I predict that today will be the longest day of my life and the most agonizing. I have hardly slept. I have dark circles under my eyes that are almost bigger than my face. I've had to hide them with makeup.

In Sydney it's almost eight o'clock in the evening. I take advantage of the drive to send a message to Darel, Kayla, Rose and Jack. I explain to them how the situation is here.

Darel answers me almost immediately. He's been on duty this weekend with Henry and he's working today and tomorrow. He has given me some good news, and that is that these days that I am not going to work he will pay me as a holiday.

> *Take as many days as you need and I'm very sorry about the situation you're in. Best regards.*

Darel has behaved very well, although some of his gestures are not to my liking.

Jack is also working with Rose and they are sending me a voice message. Kayla has been working mornings, as always, and sends me greetings and condolences.

Everyone has been very kind to me at this time. I have good colleagues, of that I can be proud.

There are many people coming and going to the mortuary from my grandfather's room. I sit in one of the individual chairs and they give me their condolences, but I don't know many of them. I greet everyone warmly.

The morning is unbearable. My head hurts from the bustle of people talking. They have no respect for anything or anyone. It costs them nothing to go outside and talk.

My mother seems upset for the same reason that I am. We look at each other and tilt our heads from right to left with discretion.

'We're going to eat in turns. Will you go now?' asks my father.

'No, thanks, Dad. I'm not hungry.'

'You haven't eaten since Saturday night. If you go on like this, you'll get dizzy.'

'Take it easy, Dad. I'm fine. If I'm hungry later, I'll go eat.'

My father is going to eat with Jonathan and my paternal grandparents, who have been very happy to see me. I'm staying with my mother, my grandmother and my sister.

Hugo arrives out of the blue and bursts into my thoughts.

'Hello, I invite you to eat.'

'Huh?'

'I invite you to eat. Please, come with me. Just, to talk.'

My mother is behind Hugo and nods her head so I agree.

'Okay, that's fine. I'll go eat with you.'

We left the mortuary and got into the car. Hugo looks in the GPS for a restaurant nearby.

'We can go to the *Islazul* shopping centre, which is close by' he suggests.

'Perfect, with me. There's an Italian restaurant there that I like.'

Hugo sets off for the shopping centre. It takes just ten minutes; there is less traffic in this area.

He puts the car in one of the free parking spaces; we get out of the car and walk towards *La Tagliatella*.

I'm still wondering what made me agree to eat with this traitor. I don't know what I was thinking about. I shouldn't have come. What will Raúl think of all this? I'd better not tell him anything, because I don't want to spoil what we are starting to build.

We go into the restaurant. The waiter accompanies us to one of the few free tables. It's a very cosy restaurant. The tables and chairs are made of wood and the tablecloths that dress the tables are white.

Hugo is sitting in front of me and is watching me without blinking. I cover my face with the menu so that he doesn't see that my cheeks are red.

I look at the menu carefully. Everything offered here is very good, but I'm not hungry. My stomach has closed up since the conversation I heard between my mother and my grandmother, and I'm still thinking about it.

'Good afternoon. What will you have?' asks the waiter.

'A four season pizza and water to drink for me. Thank you' replies Hugo.

'I... A tartar of salmon and water too. Thank you.' I'll make an effort to eat, even a little.

The waiter leaves with our order and returns shortly afterwards with the drink and a tray of bread.

'I really wanted to see you,' says Hugo with a sweet smile.

He is just as seductive as ever.

'Honestly, I didn't.'

His face draws a serious look. But I wasn't going to lie to him. I have only told the truth.

'Well... I'm sorry you feel that way. I just wanted to spend some time with you.'

The waiter comes with our food. He first serves my tartar, which smells great, and then he serves Hugo his pizza.

I take the fork and try a bite. The salmon is exquisite.

'I wanted to apologise to you once again.'

'You don't need to apologise to me. I don't need to listen to them' I answer. I don't want my food to be indigestible. 'I have accepted to eat out of politeness' I continue.

'Don't tell me that. I would like you to say, rather, that you wanted to see me or be alone with me for a while.'

'What do you want?' I ask without mincing my words.

'I don't want anything. I just wanted to be alone with you and to be able to talk without anyone bothering us.'

'And what do you want to talk about? What we had to say to each other we already did at the time.'

'I want to be with you,' he says as he holds my free hand.

'How can you say that to me?' I take back the hand that has held me. 'After all you've done to me...' I keep quiet.

'I've explained to you, both actively and passively, the reason for the situation.'

'But I'm sure you're still with her, or am I wrong?'

Hugo looks down.

'Silence means consent.' I reply.

'Is that...' he pauses to take a breath. 'I love you.'

He looks at me with that penetrating and so seductive look that for a second I forget all the bad things I have lived with him.

'You've been cheating on me for more than a year and now you think that a simple *I love you* will solve everything, but it doesn't. You should have been honest with me from the first day.' I'm angry, so angry that I want to get up and leave.

'Don't go,' he pleads, holding my arm. 'We won't touch that subject again if you don't want to.'

I nod with my head and keep eating reluctantly.

'How are you doing at work?'

'Good. Very happy.' I won't go into detail.

'Have you met someone?' He wants to know.

'That's none of your business.'

'It's a curiosity. I'm sure you've met someone,' he insists.

'If I have met someone or not, it's something you don't have to care about. It belongs to my private life and you've been out of it for a long time.'

'Please don't treat me like this.'

'I treat you as you deserve. Don't play the victim.'

I hate that he wants to play the victim with me. After all he's done to me, he still wants to know if I've met someone or try to be pitiful.

'Well, how's the tartar?' He changes the subject.

'Delicious. And your pizza?'

'Exquisite.'

We finish eating and the waiter comes and collects the dishes.

'Would you like some dessert or coffee?'

'No, thanks' I answer.

'A black coffee for me, please' Hugo answers.

The waiter walks away with the dirty dishes and gives orders to another waiter behind the bar to prepare Hugo's coffee.

'You really don't want a cup of coffee?' asks Hugo.

'No, thanks. I just want to go back to the morgue and be with my family.'

Hugo takes his coffee in a couple of sips. He pays the bill and we leave the restaurant in the direction of the car park.

We arrive at the mortuary and I get out of the car as soon as it is parked.

'Wait for me,' he says.

I don't listen to him and keep walking.

Hugo grabs my arm and pulls me towards him, bringing us very close together, almost so close that I can hear his heartbeat.

His breathing increases and his gaze darkens. My body trembles warning me of his intentions.

I want to run away but, I don't know why, my feet don't move from where they are.

My brain has stopped thinking. My heartbeat has shot up and my breathing is choppy.

Hugo approaches me dangerously and kisses me on the lips in a hurry. His kisses haven't changed. They are the same as always. All the memories of my life come to my mind. Time has stopped and it seems that we have been here for a long time.

I come to my senses, separate myself from him and run away. I enter the mortuary room still panting. Everyone turns around and looks at me.

I enter and sit on one of the sofas that are free. I try to avoid the looks that follow me. Hugo arrives behind me and also hides. I look at him sideways in anger.

Raúl comes to my mind. It is as if I had been unfaithful with that kiss that Hugo stole from me. My mixed feelings return to the surface. Not at this moment, no. Now I can only think about this moment. About my grandfather, who is there, with his eyes closed. And he won't open them again.

Time is not moving forward. We are all exhausted by the situation. My grandmother has not stopped crying since yesterday. My mother is a little stronger, but inside she is just like her. My sister is sitting with her boyfriend and my brother is coming and going every few minutes.

My friends have just arrived. I get up running and hug them one by one. My sister comes and does the same. They give us their condolences and sit with us.

They start asking questions about my life in Sydney. I silence them right away. Hugo has noticed something because his eyes are wide open and he scrutinises me with his gaze.

'Are you crazy?' I say to them in a whisper. 'Can't you see that Hugo is there?' I say by signalling with my eyebrows.

'Sorry' they apologize.

We go out to talk. They ask me a lot of questions and I answer them one by one as best I can. They look like journalists in search for the news of the day. I have to admit that they are a little gossipy. They have asked me thousands of questions about my hand. Alicia is very interested in knowing about my love life. She talks about my wedding plans.

'I already have a wedding date,' she says.

'When?' I ask.

'The 25th of August.'

'Carlos asked me to marry him a few days ago,' Amelia informs.

Carla is the eternal bachelorette. She is very selective with men. We have never met any of her boyfriends, and Marta, as much as she looks for and goes out on the hunt every weekend, there is none that fills her eye.

And I, well, I simply have no luck.

'I still have to discuss it with Carlos, but maybe we could get married a week later so that Daniela can be at both weddings and doesn't have to make two trips.'

We all nod our heads in agreement.

'Do you have any lovers in Sydney?' asks Marta.

'No,' I lie, although it's not very common for me to lie to my friends, but I know that they are going to shout and call attention to themselves and this is neither the time nor the place.

'Well, I've seen on your *Facebook* profile that you're tagged in some photos dancing with a very handsome guy.' Alicia is very up to date with social networks.

I try to hide it as much as I can.

'Well, he's just the dance teacher. Although, I didn't know him then. He just invited me to dance of course.'

My mother comes to tell us that the employees from the funeral home have already come to take my grandfather to church.

We enter the room again and I see my grandfather's face for the last time. Tears start to flow from my eyes. Carla, Alicia and Marta hug me to comfort me. My sister is hugged by Carlos.

We go to the car park.

'Will you come with me?' Hugo asks me.

I nod my head and walk to my parents' car. My friends are in Marta's car.

'We see each other in the church,' I tell them.

We go behind the hearse. Without doubt, the saddest moment I have ever experienced. Nobody says a word. The silence is echoing and the radio in the car is off.

The priest is waiting for us at the door and greets my parents and grandmother. We enter the church behind the coffin.

We sit in the first pews of the church. I look back. Alicia, Marta and Carla are sitting quite far back. They wave to me and I respond in the same way.

Hugo sits next to me.

'What are you doing here?' I ask, puzzled.

'I just want to be with you in these hard moments' he answers.

He tries to hold my hand, but I pull it away immediately.

We stand up and the priest begins the rituals of this sacrament. It's not something I like. I can't stand the priest's words that God called him up to heaven.

I pout.

I look sideways at Hugo who has tried several times to hold my hand or to pass his arm behind my waist.

My mother looks at us with a smile. She would love to see us together because she doesn't know what the reason for our separation was. We are the perfect couple for her.

We give each other peace and Hugo shakes my hand and hugs me.

'I want us to come back' he whispers to me.

'It's not the time to talk about this,' I answer.

He gives me a kiss on the cheek and we separate.

The priest ends the mass and we leave for the cemetery.

My grandmother collapses in the cemetery when she sees the coffin being put in that hole. My tears flow down. I can't help crying heart brokenly as Carla hugs me and says words of comfort.

Hugo is on my right side. From time to time he caresses my back, but that, instead of helping me, makes me uncomfortable.

I go to my grandmother and hug her. It's a comforting hug, even though I know that nothing can comfort her at this moment. It's going to be a long time before she gets used to the loneliness of not having my grandfather.

I pluck a flower from the arrangement of flowers that we have put on it. I give a kiss and throw it into the niche.

'Bye, Grandpa. You don't know how much I'm going to miss you.'

My father hugs me and takes me aside so that the workers can place the tombstone. I can't believe that the first time I come to Spain since I left is for this. I saw myself coming in February, to celebrate my birthday, but it's clear that life is whimsical and not always the way we want it to be.

While our friends and some distant relatives are leaving the cemetery, my uncle, aunt and cousins, as well as my grandmother, parents and siblings, are still looking at my grandfather's gravestone. Immobile. Without a word.

It starts to rain and one by one they move away. I stay under the rain. The hair gets soaked in rain, but I don't care.

I want to be alone to say goodbye to my grandfather. My reference. He has always been my example to follow. And now he's gone. He has left us.

'Daughter, let's go. If you stay here, you're going to get sick.'

'Leave me. I need to be alone. Please.'

'As you wish. We'll wait for you in the car.'

'It's not necessary. I'm going home later.'

My father is trying hard to get me to go with him, to move me from the place where I'm anchored. He doesn't succeed.

I am alone. It's starting to get dark and the rain has started to be more intense. Someone with an umbrella protects me from the tremendous downpour.

Hugo is here. He insists on being with me.

'Go away. I want to be alone.'

'You're soaked. You'll catch a cold. Come with me.' He grabs me by the waist and accompanies me to the exit of the cemetery. 'Come. I'll take you there,' he insists.

I accept.

Hugo takes me on a route that is not that of my parents' house.

'Where are we going?'

'To my house,' he answers with some calm.

'Where are we going?' I ask in a higher tone.

'I want you to see with your own eyes that I'm already free.'

Hugo puts his car in the car park of his building and we go up in the lift to the fourth floor, where he lives. It's the first time I'm here. I had only seen where he lives on the outside. I didn't even know what floor it was.

We went inside.

It's a flat. He gives me a tour so that I can see everything; he even opens the wardrobes so that I can see that there are no clothes other than his inside.

In the bathroom there is only a toothbrush and no feminine products.

I sit down on the sofa and, while waiting for Hugo to bring me a towel to dry my hair, I take my mobile phone out of my bag and turn it on. I have pending messages from Raúl.

> *Hello, beautiful.*
> *I hope the day won't be too long.*
> *I miss you and I look forward to your arrival. I would have liked to have been with you. I love you.*

> *Hello, my prince.*
> *It's getting longer than I expected.*
> *I miss you too. I love you.*

Hugo comes with a towel and a cup of coffee with milk. He tries to watch what I'm doing on my phone, but I'm quicker and turn off the screen and put the phone back in the bag.

He sits down next to me and approaches me. He starts kissing my neck, caresses me over my blouse and starts undoing the buttons one by one. His lips run through mine.

*"No!"* my inner self shouts at me. *"What are you doing? Think about Raúl"*. I immediately stop Hugo's action.

'Take me home, please,' I say as I button my blouse.

'I want you.' His words run through my body and make me shiver.

'I'm leaving.' I get up and Hugo, feeling guilty, agrees to take me back home without mentioning a single word.

There is an annoying silence in the car, so I turn on the radio and look for a station with a variety of music.

Hugo drives away in his car while I quickly enter the portal. I sit down on the stairs. I think about what has been about to happen. I feel very guilty. Doubts invade me.

How could I have lent myself to this? How could I not have been able to say no before he kissed me?

I go inside. Everyone is sitting in the living room, except my mother who is in the kitchen preparing dinner. I say hello and go into the kitchen. I need a hug from my mother.

My mother sees me, and the expression on her face is sweetened and she hugs me tightly.

'Daughter, you are soaked. Go take a shower. You will catch a cold.'

I do what she says. She is always right.

I'm in the shower. The water is running down my hair, my face, my back... I try not to be tormented by what has happened at Hugo's house. I refuse with my head. Nothing has happened. I have been able to say no. When I get to Sydney I have to tell Raúl and get it off my chest. I hope he understands and won't leave me.

He told me that he loved me. Yes. I will only think about that.

At dinner, all we talk about is the inheritance left by my grandfather. My grandmother tells us that he has had some money for the grandchildren. I am surprised because I didn't know anything about it. Nor do I know the amount, nor do I care. I have never been greedy about that.

I work for love, not for what I earn. Although it comes in handy.

My mother tells us that tomorrow we have to go to the notary's office so that he can reveal what my grandfather has arranged for us.

'When are you leaving?' asks my mother.

'I still don't know. When I finished dinner I was planning to look for flights. When I came I bought one way,' I explain.

'Stay,' my brother pleads.

'I'd like to stay with you, dwarf. But I have to go back. If you study, I'll pay you for the trip in the summer so that you can come and see me.'

My brother is very happy and gives me a big hug.

I'm in the room. I turn on my laptop and look for flights for this week.

On Thursday, one leaves from Barajas at 2:25 p.m. I buy it.

I inform my parents, who are still in the living room, about the day and time I'll be leaving.

'We'll take you there,' says my mother.

'I know, mum.'

I give them a kiss and go to bed.

My brother is in bed, watching TV. Tomorrow he won't go to school because we have to go to the notary; besides, he's very sad.

My grandmother went to bed early. She was very tired. My grandfather's departure was very hard for her.

I fall asleep with the frustration of what has happened in Hugo's flat, of his plea for us to come back and of how I am going to tell Raúl.

If he had asked me four weeks ago...

## Thursday, 30th November, 2017

Today is the day of farewells. Today I have to go back to Sydney. I have to talk to Raúl and explain to him what happened with Hugo. I haven't been able to sleep thinking about that moment.

On Tuesday morning I went with my parents, my siblings, my uncles, my cousins and my grandmother to the reading of the will. My grandfather left us speechless even after his death because of his extraordinary generosity.

He left my mother and my uncle fifty thousand Euros and a house for each of them.

My grandmother will continue living in the house that will be my mother's and she also enjoys the money they had in a joint account, although I think my grandmother will stay with my mother.

He has left twenty thousand Euros each to my two cousins, my siblings and me. That's something we didn't expect.

My father is going to take care of investing our money well in his bank to make a profit in the medium and long term. Now I don't need it and I prefer to invest it.

My brother wanted to buy a motorbike, but as he is underage he can't and it will be my parents who will take care of safeguarding his money.

In the afternoon I was enjoying a good cup of coffee made by my mother, talking to her and my sister, sitting in the kitchen, like in the old days.

My sister and I spent the morning together, shopping. Then we had lunch with my parents and my brother in a restaurant near my father's work.

In the evening, Amelia and I had dinner with Carla, Marta and Alicia. We took pictures, laughed and even cried with some memories.

These days have made me think about staying and enjoying doing what I like with my family and my friends, but I miss Raúl and I want to see him, hug him and kiss him.

I'm afraid to go back and that my Adonis has forgotten me. He hasn't sent me a message since Monday. Could it be that he has already found someone better than me? Could it be that he senses what I have done here? That's impossible.

*"Daniela, stop thinking about silly things"*, my subconscious scolds me. I'd better just think about going back and then we'll see what's there when we get there.

I'm just finishing packing my suitcase. I put my laptop in the case and check every corner of the room and the bathroom so I don't forget anything.

'Daniela, shall I make you something to eat?' says my mother from the bedroom door.

'No, mum. Thanks. I'll eat something at the airport. It's still early,' I answer.

The clock reads twelve and four minutes in the afternoon.

My father is leaving the bank early to take me to the airport. He said he would be there around one o'clock. I sit down on the sofa. My brother is playing PlayStation. He hasn't been to school all these days because of the funeral of my grandfather and me. He wanted to be with me. I watch him play and help him in the missions.

My mother is nervous, I know, because she keeps cleaning up on top of it. My grandmother is sitting on the other sofa criticizing the aggressive games my brother plays and giving me advice. For her I am still a child and she treats me as such.

Although it makes me a little tense, it also consoles me. She does it from the affection she has for me. She still does it with my sister and even with my mother.

While I nod my head so that my grandmother thinks I'm listening to what she says, I take my mobile phone out of my pocket and send a message to Raúl to pick me up at the airport.

> *Good afternoon, my prince. I say good afternoon because it is half past twelve in the afternoon here. My flight leaves Madrid today at twenty-five past two. I arrive in Sydney tomorrow at half past ten in the evening. Kisses.*

It is half past ten in the evening in Sydney. It takes me a little more than ten minutes to get an answer.

> *Good night, beautiful. I just finished class. It hasn't been the same without you. I'll be waiting for you at the airport, wanting to kiss and hug you. How are you?*

> *A little better.*

> *I'll be here to comfort you, I love you.*

And again he wrote "I love you". I love to read it. I get schoolgirl eyes and a silly smile invades my face.

> *I love you too.*

We are on our way to the airport. My grandmother has stayed at home, crying. My brother gave me a hug and stayed to be with my grandmother so she wouldn't be left alone. I said goodbye to my sister and her boyfriend yesterday, as well as to my friends.

I haven't seen Hugo since Monday, so it was better that way. I was afraid that I would end up faltering and succumbing to the sin that was dragging me down. I realised that I am weak.

I take one last look at the city where I was born and my father drives into the airport car park. There are few free spaces and he has trouble finding one.

Finally, after making several detours, he parks.

We enter terminal T4. There are a lot of people. I have one hour to go through passport control and find the boarding gate.

'Daniela, we are going to miss you very much.' My mother is crying uncontrollably.

'I'm going to miss you very much, too.'

'Have a good trip, my daughter,' says my father.

'I'll let you know when I land in Dubai.'

'Yes, Daniela. Keep us informed at all times. By the way, eat something. You haven't eaten since yesterday.' My mother, as always, so protective.

'Yes, mum. I'll buy something inside. I have to go through passport control.'

'Yes, Dani. Your door is S41,' says my father, pointing at the board size information.

I take my passport out of my bag and my boarding pass and put it in my trouser pocket. My father gives me the bag and I say goodbye to them with a big hug.

'Take care, Daniela,' insists my mother.

'Yes, mum. I will.'

I put my bag and my jacket on one of the trays and my suitcase on another, and I put them on the tape to be checked at the X-ray machine.

I go through the metal detector, go to the other side of the tape and pick up my belongings. I thought it would take longer to do this because there are quite a few people, but they have a lot of workers and everything is very well organized.

I can still see my mother in the distance waving to me with one hand and wiping her tears with a handkerchief she is holding with the other.

My father wraps his arm around her waist and says goodbye to me with his free hand.

I kiss them, say goodbye with my hand and walk away towards the flight information area.

I go through the information screen once more and enter the aisle that indicates the gates from S20 to S45. My gate is S41.

A few days ago I was like this, sitting in front of a gate, eating and thinking. Today I do the same, but with a difference, there is one less person in the family. I leave with a great sorrow.

I eat the sandwich I bought in one of the shops. I look at the pictures my friends, my sister and I took last night. Carla posted them on *Facebook* and tagged me in all of them.

I finish the sandwich and take advantage of the fact that I'm in line at the gate to send a message to Darel.

> *Good afternoon. I am at the airport in Madrid I will arrive tomorrow night in Sydney. I can go back to work on Monday. I hope it was not a problem my sudden departure. Regards.*

His answer is not long in coming.

> *Good evening. I was about to go to sleep. We managed very well. We expect you on Monday. Best regards.*

> *Thank you. Same to you.*

I get on the plane and sit by the window in my assigned seat. The stewardesses give the instructions while the pilots check the engines and, when the demonstration is over, they sit down and prepare for take off.

I send the last messages before putting the phone in flight mode and I receive the messages from my family and friends immediately.

I don't get an answer from Luca or Carol or Raúl. It is midnight in Sydney and they are already asleep.

The plane stabilizes in the air. It's been a bit of a rough take off because of the wind.

The hostesses start to walk with the trolleys offering drinks and food of all kinds. They have a great variety.

'Do you want something?' asks the hostess.

'A coffee with milk, please.'

'A coffee for me,' says the young man sitting next to me.

The stewardess prepares the coffees very skilfully and gives them to us. I leave it on the tray. I take the card out of my wallet and pay for it.

I still have six hours of flying time ahead of me. I am tired and my eyes close. I put my coat on the window and rest my head on it.

I plunge into a deep and relaxing sleep.


I wake up startled by turbulence. I look through the window, it's night. The boy next to me holds my laptop because it almost fell down with one of the blows from the turbulence.

'Thank you' I say grateful.

'You're welcome,' he answers.

'What's going on?' I ask, still rubbing my eyes.

'We are going through a turbulent area,' he explains.

The hostess comes up to me and kindly asks me to turn off the laptop and close the tray. The seatbelt indicator is on.

I do as the kind hostess tells me and place the laptop inside its case, under the front seat.

I look at the clock. It's eight o'clock in the evening in Spain. It's three more in Dubai.

The turbulence doesn't stop. The cabin lights go out and there are people who scream. I hold on to the armrest and close my eyes.

'Calm down, it's normal in this area.' The boy sitting next to me tries to calm me down.

Images of my life, of my family, of my grandfather's funeral, of Hugo and Raúl, especially of him, pass through my mind. I want this nightmare to pass now. I want to see him.

The plane plummets for a few seconds and people's screams become louder, but I am simply mute. I am unable to make a sound. I close my eyes tighter and feel my seat mate's hand caressing mine.

The tranquillity it emits relaxes me.

The pilot speaks through the speakers. He says that the situation is controlled and deactivates the seat belt indicator. I open my eyes slowly.

'Are you OK?' says the boy next to me, looking at me with bewilderment.

I nod with my head still dazed.

All the people on the plane, including the flight attendants, sigh for relief. And no wonder. I've had the shock of my life. I thought I would never see the people I love again.

There is one hour left to land. I ask the stewardess for a lime tree tea to calm my nerves.

I sigh.

## Friday, 1st December, 2017

The plane touches the ground. The faces of everyone on board are of relief. Some sigh with relief and, as soon as the plane stops, we start clapping.

We are half an hour late.

It is almost one in the morning. I have an hour to get through passport control to get into the airport and back to the next gate to Sydney.

Despite having slept for a few hours, I am tired. The weariness of not knowing what was going to happen has left me very exhausted. I hope that the next flight will be quieter.

The passport control area is almost empty. I show my passport to the policeman and walk to the terminal.

The guy who was next to me on the plane is behind me.

'My name is Steve,' he says as he holds out his hand to me.

'My name is Daniela,' I answer.

'Where are you going now?' he asks.

'To Sydney,' I say. 'I only have forty minutes. And you?'

'I'm staying here. I have to visit another hotel in Dubai. I'll stay three days and then go to Japan.'

'Thank you for encouraging me on the plane. It was a tense moment and I'm not used to it.'

'You're welcome. I've already noticed.' The boy laughs. We pass the passport control and I say goodbye to him while I run so as not to miss the next plane.

I head for gate B15. I run. They are about to close it. I get in line, trying to recover my normal breathing and get on the plane.

I send a voice note to the *WhatsApp* family group and another to the group I have with my friends. I leave out the problem of turbulence. I'll tell them about it when I'm home. I don't want them to be nervous knowing that I have to fly again now.

I have unread messages from Carol and Raúl. Carol's is a voice message. I listen to it with my headphones.

'Hello, Dani. We are waiting for you with open arms. I'm going to pick you up at the airport. Kiss.'

From behind I could hear Luca excited about my arrival.

'Hello, Carol. I am making a stopover in Dubai. In about fourteen hours I'll be in Sydney. You don't have to pick me up. Raúl is picking me up. A kiss for you too.'

I open Raúl's message.

> *Hello, beautiful. I look forward to your arrival. I am counting the hours. I am going to work. I love you.*

Raúl's message was sent to me at 7:30 a.m.

> *Hello, my prince. I'm on the second plane. See you in fourteen hours. I love you too.*

I put the phone back on flight mode and settle down in my seat. It's going to be many hours and I need to be as comfortable as possible. I've bought some snacks. It's in my bag and I have more films on my laptop.

It's past two in the morning and the plane still hasn't taken off. They warn us that they have to make some checks first. Fear takes hold of me.

I want to get to Sydney safe and sound.

It's half past two and for the umpteenth time I listen to the instructions of the stewardesses again. Again I experience a take off. This time more relaxed. And again the food and drink cart passes in front of me.

I ask for a coffee with milk while I turn on my laptop again and plug in the headphones.

The stewardess comes with a tray and serves me what I have ordered. As the seat on my right is free, I put the tray the hostess gave me with the coffee on it.

The coffee suits me fine. It's hot and I take small sips while laughing to myself with my favourite series.

The image of Hugo and me in his house comes to mind again. Kissing each other, and him unbuttoning my blouse. I don't know yet how I'm going to tell Raúl. I don't want it to affect the relationship that we are starting to consolidate.

I snort.

It's something I need to resolve and move on. Hopefully I won't see Hugo again. Or so I think. The further I am from the hospital where he works, the better.

I'll try to avoid him when I get back to Madrid.

I move around in my seat again and again with the intention of looking for the best comfort to rest, but I don't manage to do so. I get up and go to the bathroom several times and, while I'm at it, I stretch my legs.

It's been four hours since the take off. I go back to my seat, close my laptop and settle down with my jacket on the window as a sleeping pillow.

I have to buy an anatomical pillow to be placed on my neck. Many people use it and it looks comfortable.

The longer I sleep, the faster the hours go by and the closer I get to my Adonis. I look forward to seeing him. I can imagine what that reunion will be like. And I fall asleep thinking about him.

There are three and a half hours left to land and I've already seen all the films I have on my laptop and also the series. I connect the headphones to the mobile and listen to music.

The flight is taking forever. I can't even sleep for hours. I call the stewardess and ask her for another coffee with milk. I'm a bit cold because the air conditioning on planes is always too strong.

*Ed Sheeran* and his *Perfect* wrap me up in his beautiful lyrics. One by one, they play the songs on my list. *Romeo Santos*, *Pablo Alborán*, *Fito y Fitipaldis*, *Luis Fonsi* or *Maluma*, among others, accompany me on this journey with their songs, some more romantic and others more sensual.

I enjoy each one of them. My inner self has a microphone and is humming them.

The hostesses walk up and down the corridor with the dinner. With the time change it must be a little after eight in the evening in Sydney. I ask for pasta and a *Coke*.

The food service is really good. The food, despite being precooked, tastes good.

Slowly, the arrival time is approaching and I can't wait to get off this plane and run into Raúl's arms. I hope he's still as handsome as before.

Finally, the pilot announces that we will be landing in twenty minutes. I thought this moment would never come. I'm preparing for the landing. I put on my seat belt and close the tray.

The nerves bloom under my skin. The time is coming to see my Adonis and get the courage to tell him what happened. That's all I think about. My mind is not able to think about anything else.

The plane touches the ground gently and stops in front of the terminal. It takes a while until the plane's doors open and I slowly walk down the stairs to the landing strip.

I walk to passport control. Again the long queues. Again the form declaring that I am not carrying anything strange. I'm already looking forward to going through this procedure.

I walk, exhausted, to the entrance. There he is! Raúl has a bouquet of flowers in his hand. I suppose for me, although I don't want to be disappointed. What? Next to him is Carol, and Luca, as always, drawing attention to himself. He jumps for joy and the people around him watch him laugh.

My plan to tell Raúl what happened in Spain will have to wait.

I run to them. Luca comes towards me and gives me a big hug. Carol and Raúl arrive behind. I have to separate Luca from me if I want to greet the others.

Carol gives me a kiss on the cheek. Raúl fixes his eyes on mine. I feel that time has stopped and that it is only us at the airport.

He gives me the flowers. With a touching smile. I can't hold back my tears. There are too many sensations together.

Raúl takes the flowers away and gives me a kiss on the lips, sweet and passionate. It could be like this for a lifetime.

Our lips separate.

'I've missed you so much' he says as he wipes the tears from my cheeks.

'I missed you, too. I missed you so much.'

'What about me?' complains Luca.

'You too,' I answer with a kiss on the cheek. 'I missed you all very much.'

We are going to the car park. Raúl has brought his car.

'You have deceived me' I grumble.

Luca and Carol laugh.

'It was Luca's idea. He thought it would be a good idea for you to see us all together,' explains Carol.

'That's right. I really wanted to see you.'

'How is everything in Spain?' Raúl puts his arm behind my waist.

'More or less. What happened to my grandfather was very sad. When I arrived he said my name.'

Carol and Luca look at me with affection.

'It must have been very hard,' Carol says. I nod my head.

Luca goes into the copilot's seat. Carol and I are sitting in the back. They talk about this week's dance classes. I just hope the harpies didn't take advantage of the moment to hit on my new boyfriend.

Carol tells me all about the week she's had at work. From what she tells me, she's been very busy with a lot of trials.

'How is your family?' she asks.

'Everyone is fine. My sister's boyfriend asked her to marry him and she said yes. If all goes well, they will be married by the end of August. My grandmother is now living with my parents and my brother so that she is not alone. She is devastated.'

'I understand you very well. I went through the same thing a couple of years ago.'

'My grandfather has left me twenty thousand Euros in inheritance' I'm downplaying the importance of that.

Luca turns around and looks at me with his eyes wide open. Carol is speechless and Raúl looks at me through the central mirror.

'And what are you going to do with the money?' asks Luca.

'My father is a director in a bank and he will be in charge of investing it well. At the moment, what I earn at the clinic is enough.'

'I would travel, buy a car or...' Luca has started to wander.

We laugh.

It's half past eleven and Raúl parks in front of Carol's house.

'We go inside,' says Carol, winking at me.

'We'll take your things to your room.' Luca has a big smile on his face.

They did it to leave Raúl and me alone.

'Well. The princess has arrived safely to her house.'

'Thank you. The trip took forever.'

'The days have been long for me too.' Raúl hugs me.

We merge in another sweet and passionate kiss. The unfortunate moment with Hugo comes to mind and, without realizing it, I push my Adonis away.

'What's wrong with you?' he asks. I'm surprised.

'I'm sorry. I didn't do it on purpose. It was unconscious.'

'It's okay, honey.'

Raúl caresses my cheek with his hand and looks at me with bewilderment. I smile trying to hide it.

'Tomorrow I come to pick you up and we can spend the weekend quietly at my house. I want to spoil you.'

'I don't know. I have to think about it.'

Alone for two days with my Adonis. In his house.

'Don't tell me no. I feel like having you all to myself.'

His words make my whole body tremble and my mind starts to wander.

'Tomorrow I will give you an answer.'

He walks me to the door of the house and says goodbye to me with a kiss on my forehead.

'Please don't say no to me,' he whispers in my ear.

My body temperature suddenly rises four or five degrees.

'Good night,' I say goodbye as I enter the house.

I watch Raúl from the kitchen window. He's still as handsome and as sexy as ever. I look at him with little eyes as he gets into the car. He says a final goodbye with his hand. I respond in the same way. And he gets lost in the dark.

Luca and Carol are in the living room waiting for me to tell them in detail about each and every one of my days in Madrid.

'I don't feel like talking. I am very sleepy.'

They don't say anything; they just follow me with their eyes.

I go into the room. Luca has brought all my things. I look for my mobile phone in my bag. I still have it in flight mode. I turn it on.

More than ten messages come in.

*Good night, princess. I will sleep thinking you'll say yes to me.*

Raúl's message makes me stir up in bed. I haven't been with anyone since Hugo and I'm afraid to take that step.

> *Good night, my prince, I'll sleep on it.*

I open the pending messages from the family group. I have a voice message from my mother.

'*Daughter, we are nervously awaiting your arrival. We hope you had a good journey. We love you and we miss you.*'

My mother as endearing as ever.

> *Hello, family. I have arrived safely. I'm home now. The first flight was a bit difficult, but from Dubai to Sydney everything went very well. I love you.*

> *Sis, I'm glad you've arrived safe. What happened in the first flight?*

> *I was sleeping and I woke up because of some turbulence. Then the plane plummeted for several seconds and the landing was quite rough. But fortunately nothing serious happened.*

I hope they won't be alarmed. My father writes almost immediately.

> *Well, daughter. The worst is over. Now, rest, that's already very late. Kiss.*

My father is always so formal.

> *That's for sure. Now I just want to rest. I love you.*

My friends have written me all kinds of messages and sent photos. I'm writing to tell them that I've arrived safely and that I'm going to rest.

I yawn. What I slept on the plane didn't do me any good. I put on the pyjamas I have under my pillow. I go to the bathroom to brush my teeth and go back to my room. I get into bed and try to sleep.

I shuffle off thinking about each and every thing that has happened to me this week. The last thing, Raúl's proposal to spend the weekend together at his house.

I laugh alone, in the darkness of the room, like a little girl. I am excited and nervous at the same time.

## Saturday, 2nd December, 2017

I open my eyes. The sun enters through the window, as always, without asking permission. I missed this, the sun, the smell of the sea, my bed... I don't feel like getting up. I have hardly slept at all thinking about Raúl's indecent proposal.

Today I have to give him an answer. I don't know if I'm ready to take that step. Two days with my Adonis. Just the two of us. I shudder at the thought of all that we could do in his house.

Today is the first month since I arrived here. I could not have imagined all that would happen.

In one month I started a new job. I've had an unpleasant time with Charlie. I've made an enemy, Emma. I've had to live through the worst moment of my life, the death of my grandfather. And it seems that finally I have turned the page on Hugo.

Well, to really move on, I have to be honest with Raúl and tell him about the very uncomfortable time I had with Hugo at his house. I'm still thinking about it. I don't know how I could have been so foolish and let myself be fooled by his charms.

Today is the day. I'm going to say yes to Raúl. I hope that after I tell him what has happened in Spain, he won't change his mind and take me out of his life forever.

I'm looking for my mobile phone. It's on the little table, next to the bed. The clock reads twenty three past ten in the morning and I have a message from Raúl.

> *Good morning, beautiful. I hope you slept well. I'm also looking forward to your reply.*

He sent me the message more than an hour ago. He is up early. Could it be that he was waiting for my answer? I still can't believe that a boy like Raúl would wake up early waiting for an answer from a girl like me.

Just by snapping his fingers he could have any girl he wanted.

Luca knocks on the door.

'Can I come in?' he asks as he opens the door and nods cautiously.

'Yes. Come in.'

He sits down on the bed. I don't know what he wants. The expression on his face is strange. A mixture between funny and enigmatic.

'How did you sleep?'

'You're the second one to ask me that today.'

'Really?' I'm nodding with my head. 'So?'

'Not very well,' I answer by raising my eyebrows.

'*Perché?*'

'I have a worry that keeps me awake.'

'Is it because of your grandfather? Or because of Raúl's proposal?'

'Huh?' I am surprised by his question. 'How do you know about the proposal?' When I came home last night I didn't tell him anything. I ask him directly.

'*Buono...* It's just that...' he hesitates. 'Raúl asked me for advice on whether or not he should ask you to spend the weekend with him.'

'Ah.' He left me speechless.

'And what are you going to tell him?'

I sigh.

'Well, after much thought, I've decided to say yes.'

Luca doesn't believe what I've just said and cheers with joy.

'And that's what worried you?'

I take a deep breath and count to three. There he goes!

'Well... When my grandfather was in the hospital, I saw Hugo. The one I told you about.' Luca nods his head and I go on. 'I don't know how, but I ended up at his house after my grandfather's funeral. I was in a very bad state, I was very sad about the loss.'

'And?' asks Luca, intrigued. 'Did you sleep with him?'

'No!' I exclaim.

'So? What's the problem?'

I'm getting my breath back.

'He kissed me and I let myself go, and he started to unbutton my blouse. But I knew how to stop in time.'

Luca puts his arm around my shoulders.

'It's all right, Dani. Think about how strong you've been. You knew how to fight your feelings.'

'Yes, but...'

'But, nothing. Don't give it anymore thought.'

'I have to tell Raúl and that's what scares me.'

A tear falls down my cheek.

'I'm sure he'll understand. Just be honest. That's the most important thing.'

Luca holds me tightly and his words make me feel more secure.

'Well, I'm going to send a message to Raúl to set the time and take a shower.'

Luca leaves me alone and I take my mobile phone. I open Raúl's *WhatsApp* conversation. I answer the message he sent me.

> *Good morning. I didn't sleep much. After checking with my pillow, my answer is yes.*

His answer is not long in coming.

> *Did I read it right? Did you say yes? You don't know how happy you make me. I hope you didn't sleep too little because of me.*

If he only knew... I hope he won't change his mind when I explain what happened.

> *No. It was the journey. We'll talk about it later. I'll be ready in two hours.*

> *I'll be there. I love you.*

> *I love you too.*

I get out of bed, go to the wardrobe and prepare a small backpack with clothes. I also take out some leggings, a T-shirt, some panties and a bra from the wardrobe, and I go to the shower.

The water falls warmly on my head and body. I shampoo my hand and rub my hair from the roots to the ends.

I rinse my hair. I take the sponge, I put some gel on it and I rub all the body.

I finish and get dressed. As I don't feel like drying and straightening my hair with the irons, I take the pot of hair foam that is on top of the bathroom cabinet. I put a good amount of it in my hand and spread it all over my hair, and I shape my hair with my fingers.

I'm ready and anxious as well as nervous about Raúl's arrival. There are still ten minutes to go.

I walk around the room. I think about how I can tell my Adonis what happened. I can tell him on the way home or when we are eating, I don't know.

I scratch my head.

Last time I was alone with a man was with Hugo, although never at his home, or at the beach, or when we went to some country house. With Raúl I will be at his house, in his territory.

It scares me a little.

Every time I think of all the excuses Hugo gave me for not going to his house, my blood boils. It bothers me that he took me for a fool. Inevitably, I'm afraid the same thing will happen to me.

*"It's your entire fault,"* my inner self shouts at the bastard.

I go to the kitchen. Luca and Carol are preparing pizza for lunch. They smile at me maliciously. I feel that Luca has gone off his tongue and told Carol about the proposal Raúl made to me and my answer.

'Luca, you're a gossip' I laugh at him, but with a smile.

He knows that I don't mind him telling Carol these things. What's more, I like that between the three of us there is this confidence.

'What time will you meet Raúl?' Carol asks me.

'In five minutes,' I answer with a wide smile.

I see Raúl arrive through the kitchen window and I run to the door. I open it before he has time to ring the bell.

'Hello,' I exclaim, excited.

'Hello, beautiful. How did you know I was coming?'

'I saw you through the kitchen window.' I let out a smile.

I let him in to say hello to Carol and Luca. He enters and gives me a chaste kiss on the lips.

'Mmm...That smells good!' says Raúl as he greets them.

'Would you like to eat with us?' asks Luca. Raúl looks at me.

'Do you want to?' he asks.

'I have no problem with that.'

Luca takes a tablecloth from one of the kitchen drawers and places it on the dining table. Carol carries the dishes, and Raúl and I help with the glasses and cutlery.

The doorbell rings.

'Were you expecting someone?' I ask a strange question.

Carol runs to the door. I look at Luca, who has a mischievous smile.

'You know who it is,' I say.

Luca nods his head, but says nothing to me. Carol comes to the table with David. She introduced me to him the time we ate together in the restaurant. She introduces him to Raúl and they shake hands firmly.

The pizzas are delicious, they have an extraordinary flavour. They look like they were made by professionals.

'They are delicious' I say.

'Thank you', Carol and Luca answer in unison.

'Well, Luca did most of it, I just helped him,' Carol says humbly.

'That's not true. We both did it,' Luca claims.

'Well, we're not going to fight here over who did more or less. The truth is that they are better off than in any pizza restaurant.' Raúl puts the house in order.

'What about Madrid?' asks David. Carol must have told him I was there.

'More or less. The trip wasn't for pleasure, but because major force.'

'I am very sorry.'

'Thank you, David.'

'Well, I'm not going to let you get anymore depressed.' Raúl puts his arm behind my back and hugs me.

We finish eating and Carol brings the coffee pot full of coffee, four cups, spoons, sugar and hot milk in a jug.

We each take a cup and prepare the coffee as we like it best.

We finish drinking the coffee and between the four of us pick up all the pots and pans from the table. It's getting close to the time to be alone with my Adonis and to face that fear that runs through my whole body.

We say goodbye to Carol and Luca. I take the rucksack with the clothes and the bag and we go out.

Raúl has come on foot because he lives nearby and we go for a walk holding hands like two lovers. It is hot. The streets are empty. Most people are on the beach or gone during the week.

'What shift do you have next week?' Raúl asks me.

'I work the morning shift and I also have to work the weekend.'

'That means you won't have time for me.' Raúl makes a sad face.

I laugh out loud.

'What are you laughing at?' he asks, offended.

'The look on your face,' I reply.

Raúl opens the door of his house and steps aside so that I can go in first.

I look at the house carefully. The living room is large, with two sofas. One for three people, and another for two. There is also a dining table for six people.

At the end there is a corridor. We go inside. There are four doors; one of them has a translucent glass top.

There are two doors on the left. One is a very well decorated room and the other is a complete bathroom with a bathtub at least one and a six feet long.

The door with translucent glass on the right is the one in the kitchen. It is large. The furniture is black with a white worktop and the appliances are made of steel. It also has a table with four chairs in white.

Raúl opens the last door, at the end of the corridor.

'This is my room.'

'Oh.'

'What do you think of my room?' Raúl is in front of me and he is holding me by the waist.

'It's very cosy. I have seen that the other room is very well decorated. It does not look like an empty room, like a guest room.'

'It's my sister's.'

'Does Elizabeth live with you?' I ask, puzzled.

'Yes, but she's not going to be here this weekend. She has left the whole house to us.' Raúl winks at me with malice.

Raúl's room is big. He has a bed that I think is bigger than mine, flanked by two little tables on each side. The wardrobe is built in with two sliding doors and there is also a desk with a computer and an office chair.

On the left there is another door. It is another bathroom, smaller than the one in the corridor. It has a toilet, sink and a shower with a screen.

'What do you think of my house?' he asks nervously.

'Mmm... Awful.' I lie

'What do you mean?'

I'm so serious that he believed it, but I can't take it anymore and I start laughing.

'How mean you are to me!' he exclaims.

I laugh so much that my tummy starts to hurt.

'It's very pretty and I'm surprised that it's so clean.'

'Why?' he asks, raising his shoulders.

'Normally a man alone doesn't have such a clean house. But I've already discovered why it's so clean' I laugh.

'When I lived alone my house was always clean.' He sticks out his tongue at me.

We go back to the living room.

'Do you want to go to the beach or do you prefer to do something else? We can go to the cinema' he suggests.

'I am very tired, I'd rather we stay here. If you don't mind.'

Raúl looks at me sweetly and passes his arm over my shoulders as we go to the sofa.

'How will it bother me? On the contrary. We can watch a film and then order food for dinner' I like the plan, actually. Between the week I've had, the trip and not getting any sleep last night, I'm exhausted. 'Make yourself comfortable,'' he says.

Raúl has put on a pair of shorts and a T-shirt and is walking barefoot.

I go to my room, take out of my backpack a black dress with short sleeves and a v-neck with pockets.

I take off my T-shirt, my leggings and go barefoot. I take the dress and I put it on.

I go back to the living room where Raúl is with a bowl of popcorn and a film prepared on the DVD.

'Do you like action films?' he asks.

'Yes, very much,' I answer, sitting next to him.

The film he has chosen is The Fast and The Furious. I've watched it about a thousand times, more or less, but I'm not bored with it. Besides, Paul Walker is beautiful in all of them.

'I have them all. We can do a marathon and watch them all between now and tomorrow.'

I'm nodding with my head in agreement with the idea.

We finish the first film and take a break to go to the bathroom. Raúl prepares some nachos with cheese sauce and puts them on the living room table.

We finish watching the third film and Raúl suggests ordering something at home for dinner. It's nine o'clock at night. My Adonis profile looks stunning. He's on the phone; I think he's calling a restaurant called *Coco Cubano*. The light from the streetlights coming through the window of the lounge makes him look enigmatic and very attractive.

Dinner arrives forty-five minutes later. Raúl puts what he has ordered on the table. It is a tasting of various typical Cuban dishes.

'I hope you like it,' he says.

'I'm sure I will.'

I try each and every one of the different dishes. It is exquisite, especially the ham roll with pineapple. The mixture of sweet and salty makes it delicious. It looks like the Hawaiian pizza.

We take the leftovers to the kitchen. There is not even a trace of the food left. I am full. I have eaten more than I am used to.

'Would you like a cocktail?' Raúl asks me, taking the shaker out of one of the kitchen furniture.

'Yes, please.'

Raúl looks like an expert making cocktails. He shakes the cocktail shaker with total security. I watch him gawking. I was not wrong to call him Adonis. The more I look at him, the more handsome he seems to me.

The Daiquiri has a sweet taste. We drink a couple of them and Raúl makes more. We talk about work, about childhood, about the past and the future.

'I've had a serious relationship for four years, but he left me for another, more than a year ago, and since then I've only had sporadic relationships.'

'I have been with a doctor at the hospital where my family works. My mother and my sister are nurses.'

'And what happened?'

'He cheated on me,' I said angrily. 'For no less than fifteen long months. He's the one I told you about who had a girlfriend. But since August when I left him I haven't seen him again' I lie shamelessly.

I'm still not ready to tell him anything. Everything is going very well between us and I don't want it to be spoiled by anything in the world.

I keep quiet and let Raúl keep talking.

'I have a younger brother and two younger sisters.'

'How old are you?' I ask with curiosity.

I don't think he's more than thirty, but you never know. There are people which are very well preserved.

'Last 6th of September I turned twenty-seven. My brother is twenty-two. My sister Elizabeth is twenty and the little girl is fourteen, she's the only one who was born here.'

'I have an older sister who is twenty-six years old and a younger brother who is sixteen. I will be twenty-five on February 14th.'

'What a coincidence! You were born on Valentine's Day.'

'Yes,' I say with a face of resignation.

'Don't you like that day?'

'Not really. Every time I write my birthday on a form I get told that.'

Raúl caresses my cheek and smiles sweetly.

'Should we put on the next film?'

'Yes.'

The Adonis takes the CD out of the box and puts it in the DVD. We continue drinking daiquiris and watching the film.

I place my head on Raúl's chest and he runs his arm behind my back.

We snuggle up and cover ourselves with a small blanket.

The film ends. I fall asleep. In the end, the tiredness was stronger than me.

'If you want, we can go to sleep.'

'Together?'

Did I say that out loud? I think I've screwed up. Raúl looks at me and I don't know what the expression on his face means.

'Of course,' he answers, laughing.

Fortunately, he took it as a joke.

I sigh.

We walk down the corridor towards the room and the nerves start to appear from inside me. Raúl opens the door and steps aside so that I can go in first.

I take the toilet bag out of my rucksack and go straight to the bathroom. I take out the makeup remover, the toothbrush and the night cream.

First I remove my makeup with the wipes. Then I brush my teeth, one by one. Finally, I uncover the jar of cream, take some with my fingers and spread it all over my face and neck with gentle circular movements.

I make time in the bathroom. I'm nervous about what might happen as soon as I get out. I don't know why. I'm not fifteen years old. It's not the first time I've been alone with a man. But Raúl imposes a lot. That face, that body…

He has me totally hypnotized. Raúl knocks on the door.

'Can I?' he asks.

'Yes. Come in.'

Raúl kisses me on the forehead, takes his toothbrush and brushes them.

I'm ashamed to be seen with cream on my face. I finish and go back to the room.

I look at the bed. I don't know which side I should be on.

I feel Raúl's hands on my shoulders. He is behind me.

'What are you looking at?'

'I don't know where I should sleep.'

'Wherever you want. If you don't want to sleep here, you can sleep in the other room.'

'I don't mean that. I mean the right side or on the left side' I clarify.

'Oh. Wherever you want, princess. Get into bed without fear, I won't eat you.'

That phrase reminds me of the night we had dinner at the beach. That day he told me the same thing when Luca was leaving.

I obey him and get on the left side, under the sheets.

Raúl gets into bed and turns off the light. He curls up next to me. I have my back to him and I feel his body attached to mine.

He embraces me.

'Sleep, princess. I will watch over your sleep.' He gives me a kiss on my cheek.

Those are the last words I hear and keep in my mind. I fall deeply asleep thinking of his kisses and caresses.

# Sunday, 3rd December, 2017

*Where am I?* I sit on the bed and look around. For a moment I don't know where I am. This is not my bed. The same thing happened to me when I woke up for the first time in my room at Carol's.

Raúl is not here, but I can hear noises in the kitchen. It smells like toast and coffee.

I slept well.

My Adonis enters the room. He brings a tray in his hands and puts it on top of my legs. There are four pieces of toast, two glasses of juice, butter, jam, two cups of coffee with milk and two knives to spread the toast.

I look at him impressed. No one has ever brought me breakfast in bed before. Not even the one who said he loved me so much. I put that thought out of my mind. The bastard has no place in my life or in my thoughts.

'Good morning, princess.'

Raúl approaches me and gives me a sweet kiss on the lips.

'Good morning,' I smile.

'Do you like breakfast or do you prefer something else?'

'It's perfect,' I answer as I sip the juice. 'Is it natural juice?' I ask, pointing at the glass.

'Yes. With these hands,' he answers by raising his hands.

Raúl sits down next to me. He takes the knife and the butter. He smears the toast with the butter and then with the strawberry jam.

'Open your mouth' he orders.

I do as he says and he brings the toast to me for a bite.

He gives me the rest of the toast and he makes himself another one.

We have a quiet breakfast between laughs. I feel as if I've been here forever. Without a doubt, it is Raúl who makes me feel this way. I forget about my problems when I'm with him.

I finish the last toast and drink the last sip of coffee. My Adonis gets out of bed and takes the tray to the kitchen.

'Would you like anything else?' he asks from the bedroom door.

'No, thanks. Usually I just have a coffee for breakfast,' I explain.

'Well, you have to have more' he scolds me as he leaves the room and walks away.

Raúl returns and sits down again next to me. A chill runs through my body. His look is very seductive and I think he wants something else. I want him as much as he does.

He approaches me until I can feel his breath. He pounces on me and kisses me on the lips. With his sudden action he has made me lie down on the bed.

He's stood on top of me.

His hands go all over my body. His kisses are more and more intense, they are full of desire. His hands go down to where my dress ends and she slowly lifts it up, until he takes it off.

I'm almost naked in front of this Adonis. I thought this moment would never come.

He stops kissing me and starts making a tour of kisses through my body. First, my breasts; then, my belly, until he reaches the elastic of my panties and, with a soft movement that makes me shiver, he takes them off. First, one leg, and then the other.

I look at him without blinking. This seems like a sweet dream from some romantic Hollywood film.

He ceases his torturing kissing action and sits on the bed to take off his shirt. My body temperature is rising like foam and my heartbeat has accelerated to the point that I can feel it in my head. That body…

He removes his underwear with extreme skill and exposes his entire Caribbean anatomy. It is better than I had dreamed. I can't stop looking at him. I don't think I've ever seen anything that size in my life.

He starts his torturous kissing tour of my body again. I squirm in bed. I want him more and more.

He reaches my deepest parts and starts kissing them. I can't take it anymore. I want him to make love to me now.

I pull him towards me with my legs and start kissing him on his neck. He moans with pleasure. I put myself on top of him and do the same. I go over his naked chest with my lips until I reach his erect member. I lick it with my tongue and lips. I look sideways at Raúl, who is staring at me with his mouth open.

He pulls me up and stands on top of me. He looks for my vagina with his member and penetrates me gently. I am on a cloud.

I embrace him and let myself be carried away by his rhythmic movement.

With a quick shake I'm the one who is now on top of him, riding. I can see him better from above. I feel his limb reaching deep into me. It is pleasant.

I can't take it anymore and I explode in an orgasm like I've never had before. I moan with pleasure and Raúl groans almost at the same time as me.

He gives me a kiss on my forehead and lies down next to me still trying to catch his breath. I am exhausted.

We look at each other and smile.

'Did you like it?'

I nod my head because I am not able to articulate a single word at this moment.

He embraces me and kisses me on the lips and we fall into a deep sleep.

I wake up. Raúl is still sleeping. I look at him for a few seconds. He is handsome even sleeping.

I don't know what time it is, so I get up very slowly so as not to wake up the handsome man in bed and look for the mobile phone.

I need to take a shower. I go to the bathroom. While the water runs through my body, I think that his kisses have done the same almost two hours ago.

I shudder.

I feel someone's hands caressing my body and I get scared for a second.

Raúl has entered without asking and without making any noise, and has got into the shower.

'You scared me' I scold him.

'Who else would it be? It's just you and me.'

That's true.

'I know, but you were so asleep that I didn't count on you breaking into the shower while I was using it.'

'Well, technically I'm not breaking in because it's my shower.'

And he's right again.

He starts kissing me like he did before. I feel his erect limb against my belly. He takes me in his arms and penetrates me. My back is stuck to the cold tiles, but I don't care.

That rhythmic movement comes back again. I moan with pleasure. The onslaught is strong and makes me want to reach orgasm immediately.

Shortly after, the orgasm comes and I abandon myself in his arms.

Raúl holds me with one hand so that I don't fall because my legs are shaking, and with the free one he rubs my body with the sponge. When he finishes I do the same to him.

I finish combing my hair and leave the bathroom with a towel around my body. Raúl has already made the bed and tidied up the room.

'We can go to the beach and then eat at Bondi' he suggests.

'I think it's a good idea.'

Raúl looks for a swimming costume in the wardrobe and puts it on. I look for a bikini and clean clothes in the rucksack and sit on the bed to get dressed.

The beach is crowded. There are people everywhere. I am fascinated by the people who are surfing. I wouldn't be able to keep my balance on top of that, not even as a joke.

Raúl comes with some soft drinks he has gone to buy. He draws the attention of all the girls on the beach. I'm feeling jealous. I don't like the way they undress him with their eyes. I frown.

I am lying face down. Raúl undoes my bikini bra, takes the sun screen from my rucksack, pours some on his hands and rubs it on my back with a gentle massage.

Slowly, his hands reach the bottom of my back. She pours more cream on his hands and continues with his gentle massage on my buttocks and then down my legs. It's very sensual.

'Do you like it?' he asks, whispering in my ear.

His question sends a chill down my spine.

'Much' I answer.

'Turn around and I'll pour cream on you too.'

That sounds very tempting.

Raúl buttons up my bikini and I turn around as he instructed. Although for me it's not an order, it's a suggestive idea.

He's back in action with his massage skills and rubs my top of the breasts, belly and legs.

He ends up with his sensual friction and I draw on my wits to do the same with him. I massage his back, shoulders, arms and legs. He turns around and I take the opportunity to slowly massage his chest.

I enjoy the moment.

'We can go and eat now if you want.'

'Yes. I'm hungry' I answer.

The heat is becoming unbearable.

We pick up the towels from the floor and put them in the backpacks. We go straight to Bondi Pavilion, holding hands in front of the envious faces of many women, who look at us sideways.

We find a free table on the terrace of The Bucket List. The sea is in front of us. Raúl pulls out one of the chairs and I sit on it. He sits next to me.

The parasols are unfolded and we are in the shade. The water mist on top of the parasol disperses cold water vapour every little time.

A young and handsome waiter approaches our table.

'Good afternoon. I am going to be your waiter. Here is the menu.'

He gives us a menu for each of us.

'What will you have to drink?'

'I'll have a *Coke*. Thank you,' I reply.

'Well, I'll have another one. Thank you.'

The waiter retires to get our drinks and we take a look at the menu. There is meat, fish, salads and a great variety of starters.

'What would you like to eat?' Raúl asks.

I think for a few seconds while I check the menu for the last time.

'I feel like eating fish.'

'The salmon here is exquisite,' he suggests.

'Salmon, then. And what are you going to have?'

'I'm going to have half a grilled chicken today.'

Raúl puts his hand on my cheek and takes a tuft of hair in front of my face.

The young waiter returns with the drink. He places the two cans of *Coke* and two shot glasses with two pieces of ice.

'Have you already chosen what you are going to eat?'

'Yes. Half a grilled chicken for me, and salmon for my girlfriend. Thank you,' says Raúl as he hands him the menus.

Did he say girlfriend? How nice that sounds from his lips. My inner self dances salsa with a big smile. I mentally review again and again that wonderful word: girlfriend!, girlfriend!, girlfriend! Now letter by letter: g-i-r-l-f-r-i-e-n-d.

I sigh.

'Are you all right?'

Raúl makes me go back to where I was with that question.

'Yes. I was thinking.'

'What about? If I may ask.'

'About work' I lie again.

'Oh.'

Since I've been living here I've lied more than in my whole life. I also think that I should tell Raúl what happened in Spain.

I look at him.

I am afraid. I'm afraid that he won't want to know anything else about me. No, I'm not ready to tell him yet. I don't want to spoil this day, everything is going perfectly.

The waiter arrives with the food. It smells delicious. The salmon is presented on a rectangular white plate and comes with rice noodles, avocado, cucumber, carrot, soya and sesame. All mixed together like a salad.

The half grilled chicken that Raúl has ordered is served on a large round white plate. As a side dish he brings a salad of lettuce, green papaya, cherry tomatoes and jalapeños, all seasoned with a coconut dressing.

I take a piece of salmon with my fork and put it in my mouth. I taste it slowly to appreciate the different flavours. It is seasoned with salt and spices.

Raúl takes a piece of chicken with his fork and puts it in my mouth.

'Taste this,' he says.

I open my mouth and Raúl introduces the piece of chicken. I taste it. It tastes very good. The taste of barbecue reminds me of those summers in the village. My father, with an apron on which you could read *"El cocinillas"*, in front of the grill, and I, in the hammock, swinging.

I give my Adonis a piece of salmon to try. It's very erotic to see him chewing on the piece I've given him to try.

He is a very sexy man.

'Will you like dessert?' I ask.
'If I'm honest, I don't remember what's in it.'
I laugh.
'What are you laughing at?' he asks, raising one of his eyebrows.
'I don't remember either.'
We look at each other and laugh out loud.

The waiter arrives a few minutes later and, after asking if he can pick up the dishes and inform us about the desserts they have, he clears up everything from the table.

'I want a glass of ice cream with chocolate and vanilla, please.' I ask the young waiter

'Same for me. Thank you,' says Raúl.

The waiter leaves with the dirty dishes and returns a few minutes later with our ice creams.

The ice cream is cold and refreshes my body. I love chocolate. There is nothing better. Well, the Adonis is like a big chocolate.

I can't stop looking at him.

'When we finish the ice cream we can go to my house, take a shower and change clothes, and then I have a surprise.'

'A surprise? For me?' I'm surprised.

'Yes. Come on.'

Raúl takes me by the hand, pulls me gently and helps me to get up from the chair.


We are going around a small roundabout from where you can see the Sydney Harbour Bridge and the Opera House. I hadn't seen it up close yet. I haven't had the chance to visit this beautiful building. It's amazing!

'I hope to visit the Opera House soon.'

Raúl clears his throat and I can see a slight smile on his lips out of the corner of my eye. I don't quite understand why. I frown. We enter an underground parking and park in one of the free spaces. We hold hands and go to the emblematic place.

'I hope you like the surprise,' he says, showing me the pictures.

I jump for joy and give him a kiss on the cheek.

'Thank you very much. I'm looking forward to it. I had it on my to-do list.'

'Well, I think you're going to be able to cross this task off.' He passes his arm over my shoulders.

'Wow! It's huge.'

The large window at the entrance is spectacular and the oval shapes make it unique. I am amazed to admire this great work of architecture.

'You'll see it inside,' Raúl whispers to me.

As we queue up to go in, I take the phone out of my bag to put it in silence and I see that I have an unread message.

It's from Charlie.

> *Hi. I don't know anything about you. Are you already here or still in Spain? Please, when you read this, answer me. Greetings.*

I will answer him tomorrow. I don't want anything to tarnish this moment and this happiness I feel.

'Good afternoon,' says the tourist guide. 'Follow me this way.'

We access the entrance of the building. I can't help but admire so much beauty.

'The Sydney Opera House is a fabulous building located in the city of the same name. Its construction was designed under the inspiration of the abstract art and it is a huge construction dedicated to the performance of events of opera, theatre, piano, symphonies, among other works of artistic character. The work was inaugurated on October 20th, 1973 by Queen Elizabeth II, and during this ceremony spectacular fireworks were launched while the ninth symphony by Beethoven was being performed.'

I walk behind the guide with the rest of the tourists taking thousands of pictures. I only think about bringing my family so they can see this beauty.

'Do you like it?' Raúl asks me.

I nod with my head while I listen carefully to the explanations of the young guide.

'The Sydney Opera House contains five theatres, five rehearsal studios, two main halls, four restaurants, six bars and numerous souvenir shops. This way, please.'

We enter the concert hall. It has 2679 seats. I sit in one and admire every detail of the hall. There is a large organ which, according to the guide, is the largest mechanical organ in the world, with about 10 000 pipes. Some kind of rings hang from the ceiling. We move to the next room and enter the Opera House, which has 1547 seats. It is the main space of the Australian Opera Company and is also used by the Australian Ballet Company. We see the rest of the rooms and finish the tour. I would see everything again. It was fascinating and it was very short.

'There is still another surprise.'

'More?' I'm impressed.

We go down the immense stairs and head towards the Opera Bar and sit at a table that has a sign that reads "Reserved. Mr. Raúl Rodríguez". The views of the sea and the bridge are incredible. Night falls and the front of the Opera House is lit up. The colours change slowly. It seems like a dream. There are many people taking pictures. The waiter brings us the tasting menu that is included with the ticket to the building. It contains seafood and salads in small proportions.

'Do you know something?'

'Tell me.'

Raúl has a different look. And for a moment I think that maybe he doesn't want to know anything more about me.

No, no, no. I have to start being more positive and more sure of myself. Why would I want to change my mind? I am fine with him and I think he is fine with me too.

'I don't want this day to end.'

Raúl hugs me tightly and gives me a passionate kiss on the lips. I reciprocate in the same way.

'You know what?' I ask still hugging this monument.

He looks at me.

'I don't want this day to end either. It's being perfect.' I say.

Raúl smiles.

'What would you like to visit next time?' he asks.

'I would love to see kangaroos and koalas.'

'There is a perfect place for that, Kangaroo Island.'

'Kangaroo Island? Where is it?'

'It's a little far away, near Adelaide. You have to go by plane because it takes about eighteen hours by car,' he explains. 'We can go whenever you want.'

'I have to look at the work schedule, but maybe a weekend. There are some where I finish on a Friday at two o'clock in the afternoon and I don't have to go back until Monday afternoon.'

I love making plans. This is going well.

We take several photos with the bridge and the Opera in the background, smiling, happy, as if there were no tomorrow. It's been a perfect day. The best in a long time.

We get into my perfect boyfriend's BMW and leave the car park at full speed.

'Are you angry?' I ask.

'No. Why?' he answers.

'You are very quiet and it scares me.'

'I'm a little sad,' he answers.

'Why?' I ask puzzled.

'The day is over and it has been perfect, at least for me' he explains with his hand on his chest.

'It was perfect for me too.' I put my hand on his hand, which is on the gear lever.

Raúl parks and I get out of the car before he has time to open the door for me.

He accompanies me to the entrance.

'I'm going to miss you,' he says, caressing my cheek.

'And I will miss you.' I can't take it anymore and I kiss him.

I don't want this kiss to end. Raúl grabs me by the waist and pulls me towards him until I'm stuck.

I feel his heart beating faster.

I separate myself from the sculptural Adonis with difficulty.

'Good night, prince.' I run my hand through his curly hair.

'Night, my princess.'

He gives me a sweet kiss on my forehead and walks away.

Luca and Carol are in their rooms, but Luca comes out when he hears the door.

'How did it go?' Luca is very curious.

'Good,' I say with a smile from ear to ear.

'I would say more than fine. You are radiant.'

'What have you done? Tell me everything with hair and signs.'

We went into my room and sat down on the bed.

'Well, yesterday we stayed at his house and watched films. He ordered Cuban food for dinner.'

'Didn't you go to bed?' Luca interrupts me.

'Don't be impatient,' I scold him. 'Not on Saturday. On Sunday he brought me breakfast in bed and then what happened, happened.'

Luca gets excited. It seems that he the one who has spent a weekend with the Adonis.

'And how is he in bed?'

'You can't imagine. It's better than I could have ever imagined. He has exceeded all expectations. Now I understand what they say about if you try a Cuban, the rest is a zero on the left.'

'I'm very happy for you, Dani.' Luca hugs me and gives me a kiss.

'We also went to the beach. We ate in one of the Bondi's restaurants. Then we went to the Opera House, I hadn't seen it yet. And we ended up having dinner at the Opera Bar.'

'I'm jealous of everything you say.'

I know Luca says it with all the love he has for me.

'Well, now I need to rest.'

'Yes, I'm going to sleep too. Tomorrow I have to present a project.'

'Get some rest.'

'*Buona notte, signorina.*' Luca gives me a kiss on the cheek and comes out from my room.

I put on my pyjama. I go to the bathroom, brush my teeth and I take off my makeup.

I sigh, thinking of the magnificent weekend that I have had the privilege of enjoying with the monument. I will never forget it in my whole life. I will not forget his kisses, his caresses and his way of making love to me.

I get into bed. Empty. I could have slept with him, but I still don't think it was a good idea. Better to go slowly. In the end, I didn't tell him anything about what happened with Hugo. I couldn't find the time. Nor did I have the courage to do so.

# Tuesday, 5th December, 2017

Yesterday was a strange day. Going back to work was like starting all over again. I felt the same sensation as when I arrived more than a month ago.

Darel is becoming more and more affectionate with me. He looks for any excuse to touch me. His attitude is starting to make me uncomfortable.

Rose has asked me a thousand questions about the trip, asked me about the family and even about the funeral. She has left my head spinning.

Jack has distanced himself a little from us, I have noticed that he is different. Rose says he was already like that last week. I felt him very different.

I asked him, but he wouldn't tell me anything.

Kayla is the same kind and attentive woman as always. She is a very nice, polite and hard working person.

The work has been hard. I had many patients. Many came to get their pets vaccinated. I only had to do an emergency surgery on a dog because it had a glass inserted and infected in one of its paws. But, fortunately, it was just a scare.

I didn't see Raúl yesterday. I can't wait for tonight so I can enjoy a night of dancing with him.

Today I am walking to work with Romeo Santos in my ears. It's a great day. The sun is shining brightly and it always smells of the sea.

I feel like having my family come to visit me, but for that I need to be independent first, and a two room flat here costs between 2000 and 2700 dollars a month.

Now Darel has raised my salary and I can afford it, but I want to save first. I can also use the money that my grandfather left me, but my father has invested it and I don't want to spend it.

Every day I thank my grandfather for that show of affection he has given us all.

He has always been like that.

I get to work on time. I greet Kayla, who is already at her work station, typing on her computer, and I go up to the kitchen to get a coffee. I also prepare another one for Kayla and go down with the two cups.

'Here.' I leave Kayla's coffee cup on the counter.

'Thank you,' she says in surprise.

She didn't expect it.

'Do I have many consultations today?' I ask.

'Today is going to be a quiet day,' she answers.

'I hope so.'

Kayla gives me the sheet with the appointments I have today and I go to my office. I leave the coffee and the sheet on the desk, and go to my locker to leave my bag and my jacket; I dress in my work coat.

When I go back to my office, Darel is waiting for me. What does he want now? He's always looking for some excuse to get close to me.

'Good morning, Darel,' I say as I button up my dressing gown.

'Good morning. I've come to invite you to lunch today.'

'Thank you. I don't know it's still too early to decide. Then later I'll look for you and give you an answer.'

Darel leaves the office with an unfriendly look on his face. He invited me yesterday and I had to find an excuse. Let's see what I can come up with today so that it doesn't look like I don't want to meet him.

Maybe I'll accept his invitation and that way I'll make him happy. I don't want him to look for any reason not to renew my contract.

Rose is with me. It's already habitual. I love that she is my assistant. The hours fly by when I'm with her. She always has new stories to tell.

We are in the kitchen having a coffee.

'You know what?' I say.

'What?'

Rose is intrigued.

'Darel has invited me to lunch again and I don't know what to do. Yesterday I made up an excuse, but today I don't know what to say.'

Rose thinks of an answer for a few seconds.

'Well, tell him you have a doctor's appointment.'

'I'm afraid that if I refuse his invitations, he won't renew my contract.'

'You can meet him today and he will leave you alone for a while.'

'You could come with me. It's just that lately he's looking for any time to get close to me. I don't want him to be confused with me.'

'No, no, no. I don't want to have any trouble with Darel.'

'Please,' I beg.

'Well, only because it's you.' Rose gives me a hug.

Jack arrives. He looks very down. I give Rose a little nudge in the sack and beckon her with my eyes to have a look at him.

Rose looks at me and lifts her shoulders.

'Are you all right?' I dare to ask.

Yesterday he didn't want to tell me anything, but maybe today he will change his mind. Jack takes a deep breath and sits on the sofa between Rose and me.

'Well, my wife has left me. She has left home.'

Huh? How? I can't believe my ears just heard that. I lie down on the sofa and look at Rose, who has just done the same thing as me, as if we had telepathy. While I raise an eyebrow, Rose has made a surprised face.

'But what did she say?' asks Rose.

'Nothing. She left a letter in my letterbox. She won't answer the phone and her parents won't tell me where she is.'

'Maybe he's with someone else.'

Rose doesn't mince her words.

'I think so, but I can't say for sure.'

I put my hand behind his back and move it in circles to comfort him.

'Calm down. Give her a few days. You'll see how he'll get in touch with you.'

'Dani, do you remember that day when he was strange?'

'Yes,' I said, nodding my head.

'Well, it was because my relationship with my wife was bad and I paid for it with you. I'm really sorry.'

'Everything is forgotten,' I answer, and give him a hug to comfort him.

We finish our coffee and return to our consultations. I still have to give two dogs and a cat three vaccinations, cut the nails of two Siamese twins and check the wound of yesterday's dog.

Darel returns to my surgery with clear signs of looking for an answer.

'Yes, I'll go with you to lunch.'

'Perfect, I'll make the reservation.'

Shit! If you make the reservation I won't be able to take Rose with me. What do I do now? Well, I'm going to eat. I'm going to keep my distance and control the situation.

Darel leaves the office by making a phone call and Rose automatically enters.

'So?' she asks, sitting at her desk.

'He has made a reservation for two. I'm afraid you won't be able to come with me.'

'Well, you take it easy. It's going to be all right. I'll have the phone with me at all times in case you need to escape. You just have to send me a message and I'll call you as if it was something important so you have an excuse to run away.'

'Good idea.'

Rose is an expert in recurring ideas.


Darel is at the entrance waiting for me while I leave my dressing gown in the locker and take my jacket and bag.

We go down the stairs and Darel has had the audacity to put his hand on my waist. Emma comes up and sees us together. She looks at us with suspicion. I don't like that look. I know that after this the reprisals will come.

We walk to the car, get in and Darel puts the address of the restaurant in the GPS.

'I will take you to lunch at a Spanish restaurant.'

'Ah. I didn't know there were Spanish restaurants here.'

'Yes, there are a few.'

Darel drives very skilfully through the dense traffic. Downtown Sydney is full of cars and people.

He parks inside one of the many car parks in the centre and we walk out to the restaurant. Again, Darel puts his arm around my waist.

*Alegrías Spanish Tapas* is overflowing. Now I understand why we had to book.

'Is it like this every day?' I ask.

Darel nods his head.

The place is very welcoming. The tables are made of walnut wood and the chairs are upholstered in black leather. The floating wooden floor is light coloured and the ceiling is dark coloured, which gives it a rustic touch.

There is a half floor with stairs and a wooden floor. The tables and chairs are the same as on the ground floor.

The windows have some curtains that go from the ceiling to the floor, with a white corner curtain and two other curtains on the smaller sides in red colour.

The lamps are pendant, with five candle shaped bulbs in each one.

Darel, when he made the reservation, already ordered the menu as well.

'I hope you don't mind. It's a closed menu so we can taste all the dishes.'

'That's fine with me.'

The waiter comes with the *Gran Reserva Rioja* wine that Darel has ordered. He uncorks the bottle and pours a little wine into each glass.

We give it a try. It has an exquisite taste.

The appetizers include *Serrano* ham, *Manchego* cheese, *chorizo* from Salamanca, olives and *pâté* served with rustic bread and extra virgin olive oil.

I enjoy the flavours of my land. Darel is delighted. He loves *Serrano* ham.

'Are you happy at work?'

'Yes. I've adapted very well. I'm glad to have Rose as my assistant' I'm not mentioning Emma's unpleasant one.

'Yes, Rose is very efficient.'

The waiter brings the starters. Spicy potatoes, Andalusian style squid, sausage in cider, and mushrooms in garlic served on clay dishes.

I spike a few squid with my fork and leave them on my plate. I cut them with the knife and take a piece to my mouth. It's delicious! I missed these flavours.

The cider *chorizos* are spectacular. I have never tasted them like this before.

'The *chorizos* are sublime' says Darel.

'It's the first time I've tasted them this way. My father makes them with white wine.'

'I love coming here to eat, and with such a beautiful girl, even more so.'

Darel puts his hand on top of mine. I put it aside in a concealed way.

'All the food reminds me of my country' Darel orders another bottle of wine. 'I won't be able to drink anymore, and I don't even know what I'm doing.'

'Don't worry, woman. I'm driving.'

The waiter removes the clay dishes and comes back with a salad bowl and a *paella*.

'I'm full. I can't eat anymore,' I inform.

'You have to try the *paella*.'

Darel serves me some *paella*. It has chicken, shredded pork, *chorizo* and vegetables. It's majestic. The mixture of all the ingredients makes it extraordinary. Besides, the rice is just right.

The salad is made of lettuce with caramelised nuts, semi-dried tomatoes, prunes infused with sweet wine and *Manchego* cheese. A somewhat peculiar mix of flavours.

'It's all excellent.' I congratulate the waiter.

The food is being quite pleasant.' For the moment, Darel, apart from the compliment and the hand moment, he is being very polite. I thought it would be worse.

The wine has gone to my head a bit and I feel hot in the cheeks.

My mobile phone rings.

'Sorry, I'm going to answer it.'

Darel nods his head. I take my mobile phone out of my bag and leave the restaurant to answer the call. It's Raúl.

'Good afternoon, princess. How was your morning?'

'Good afternoon. The morning was very quiet. And you?'

'Good, the children are the same as always. I'm looking forward to seeing you tonight.'

'I'm looking forward to it too.'

'Where are you? I can hear a lot of noise' I don't know if I should tell him the truth or not. I think for a few seconds. 'Are you there?' Raúl asks.

'Hey, yes, sorry. I'm with my boss, who invited me for lunch.'

Raúl remains silent.

'Why didn't you tell me?'

'Well... I don't know. It just came up. Rose was going to come, but she couldn't' I'm lying.

I've known for more than three hours and Rose hasn't come, no because he couldn't, but because I told him not to.

'You could have warned me and I would have gone with you.'

Raúl's tone of voice has hardened and he seems angry.

'I'm sorry, you're right. I'll be done soon and I'm going home.'

'Where are you? I can come and get you.'

'No, don't worry. Darel's taking me away.'

'Well, as you want.'

'See you later. I love you.' I hope he's not too angry.

'I love you too, sweetheart.'

I'm hanging up the phone and going back to the table. Dessert has arrived. Chocolate *fondue* with Spanish sweet fritters.

I delight in the sweet chocolate and taste every piece I eat.

'Who called you?' asks Darel.

'He was my boyfriend.'

Darel's smiling expression automatically turns into a big, serious face. I ignore it and continue to enjoy the delicious dessert.

'Can we go now? I want to rest.'

'I'll take you, don't worry. What are you doing tonight?' he asks.

'Tonight I have dance classes.'

I hope he doesn't want to sign up.

'Well, we can meet up one of these nights for dinner.'

'You're very kind, Darel, but I have a boyfriend and I don't want to make him uncomfortable.'

'It's nothing like that. We can have dinner as a boss and employee.'

'Thanks, but I'll have to think about it.'


Darel parks in front of my house.

'Thanks for the food.'

I go over to give him a kiss on the cheek, but Darel turns and I give him the kiss on the lips.

I run out of the car and enter the house almost breathless.

Why did Darel do that? It wasn't right. My head is spinning because of the wine. I lie down on the bed and think. The image of the kiss comes to mind. If I tell Raúl, he'll be furious. He's capable of looking for Darel to attack him and I don't want to lose my job.

Tomorrow I'll go to work and pretend nothing happened. Although, perhaps, it would be better to tell Darel to keep his distance from me. I don't know. I have to think and talk to someone.

Luca's not here and this is when I need him most.

I lie in bed and mentally go over everything I've experienced in the last month. I haven't got off to a good start with Raúl. I have not been one hundred percent sincere. I have kept things from him which, in the end, can have consequences.

Luca has sent me a message to meet him directly at the entrance of Bondi Pavilion at nine o'clock so that we can talk before the class.

I leave home early. I call Luca and propose to buy some kebabs for dinner. Luca accepts and I go straight to the same restaurant where we went with Raúl the first time he invited us to dinner.

The gentleman behind the counter takes care of me and immediately gives me my order in a bag and gives me two cans of *Coke*.

Luca is sitting on one of the benches in front of the entrance to Bondi.

'Good evening, handsome' I kiss him on the cheek and I sit down by his side.

I give him our dinner bag.

'How nice it smells!'

I unwrap the *kebab* and take a bite. Its taste reminds me of that night on the beach and the first kiss Raúl gave me. They are very good memories.

'How was your day?' asks Luca.

'Good. My boss invited me to lunch.'

'I thought you were with Raúl.'

'Darel invited me to lunch yesterday and I gave him an excuse; today he did it again and I didn't know what excuse to give him anymore,' I explain.

'Be careful about accepting invitations. Your boss can be confused.'

I raise an eyebrow.

'I think he's a little confused already, but I don't want to look bad for him either.'

'And, changing the subject, did you finally talk to Raúl about the kiss you gave Hugo?'

'I haven't been able to.'

I take a deep breath.

'The longer you take to tell him, the worse it's going to be.'

'I know, it is' I move 'I don't know how to tell him that I ended up at my ex-boyfriend's house and that we almost ended up making love.'

'Well, like you told me. With a little more tact.'

'Anyway, he got angry when he found out that I was eating with my boss.'

Luca takes a last bite of his kebab.

'Who am I?'

Raúl has covered my eyes, but that voice and that smell are unmistakable.

'It is you.' I put my hands away and turn around.

He approaches me and gives me a kiss on the lips.

'I'll go inside to prepare the class.'

The harpies who were sitting on the next bench get up and run in behind him.

Luca and I finish eating and drinking and throw the wrappers away. We enter the class.

I approach Raúl to give him a kiss before starting, but he twists my face. How could he have changed so much in ten minutes?

'What's wrong with you?' I ask.

He doesn't answer me, he just prepares the music. I don't know what I've done now. Everything was fine a moment ago.

I walk away and stand next to Luca.

'What happened?' he asks me.

'I don't know. I went to give him a kiss and he turned away. I asked him if anything was wrong and he didn't answer.'

'How strange!' he exclaims.

The class starts. Everything is as cold as the first day. Raúl just gives us instructions on how to warm up our muscles. Afterwards, we get into pairs and start dancing the steps we already know.

Today Raúl does not ask for a change of partner, so I do not have the opportunity to ask him for an explanation. He is dancing with one of the harpies. She looks very happy. She's in her element, never better.

She looks at me and laughs.

I'm eating my anger up inside. I can't see how that harpy is touching him and he doesn't do anything about it either. I hold back my tears. Luca notices and turns to me so that I don't see them.

I am disconcerted by Raúl's attitude.

'You'll see how everything will be fine' whispers Luca to me.

I dance without wanting to, although Luca does everything in his power to cheer me up, without success.

Raúl gives us the last instructions before finishing the class. He picks up his things and leaves saying a simple goodbye. Usually he's the last to leave. It's all very strange.

The harpies come out behind, look at me and laugh out loud. I'm afraid that they have something to do with what is happening between Raúl and me.

*"Can there be such bad people in the world,"* I ask my inner self, which nods in approval. Or is it simply because I have gone to lunch with my boss? My head is going to explode.

I walk around holding on to Luca's arm. I'm devastated. Raúl has not given me any explanation about his attitude. Sometimes I think that love is not for me.

I go to bed and call Raúl on the phone. He doesn't answer me. I send him a message. He's on line. I hope he at least replies to the message. He's seen it, I know because the double tick has turned blue. He is no longer on line and my concern increases.

I fall asleep thinking about him and the laughter of the harpies in the dance class. I'm almost sure they had something to do with it.

# Friday, 8th December, 2017

The week has been very long and exhausting. Yesterday I had a checkup at the hospital and, after having an X-ray, I was told that my finger must still be immobilized for two more weeks. Today is going to be an even longer day. Apart from working the morning shift, I have to go back at night to do the weekend duty with Jack.

I will be locked up in the clinic until Monday morning. It makes me lazy, but it will also help me to disconnect a little from real life.

Raúl is still not talking to me. He doesn't answer my calls or messages. I am very frustrated. I need him to tell me why he is like this with me. He was very cold to me in *bachata* class yesterday.

His indifference is hurting me.

Luca has tried to talk to him and get some information out of him, but it has been impossible. He has shut himself off and there is no way for him to say anything.

Today the work is being very heavy. Besides, there is Emma, who has changed Henry's shift again.

I have to be very careful because with this witch you never know what might happen. She is capable of poisoning me or worse. And after seeing me, leaves the clinic the other day with Darel, she may do something crazy against me.

Today Darel is being very respectful towards me, he hasn't tried to approach or touch me. Perhaps the fact of telling him that I have, or rather, had a boyfriend, has made him see reason. It may also be that Emma's presence has slowed down his intentions towards me a little.

Deep down I think that Darel knows Emma well and knows how far he can go.

It's time for a break. Finally! I was already in need of a good coffee. I go up to the kitchen. Emma is preparing a coffee. I say hello, but, as usual, she doesn't answer me.

I hope she ends up, while I sit on the sofa looking at my phone. I have a new message.

> *Hi, how are you? It's been a while and I'd like to invite you to lunch or dinner. Greetings.*

Charlie's message is very sincere. I think it's time to move on from what happened between the two of us and start from scratch.

> *I think it's a very good idea, but we'll have to leave it for next week. I'm working now and this weekend I'm on duty and I don't rest until Wednesday. Another greeting for you too.*

> *Perfect! Whenever you want. I will be waiting for your call.*

Emma leaves and I make the coffee I so badly needed. As usual, I take a cup from the shelf, heat the milk in the microwave and add the coffee and sugar.

I sit on the sofa again and think about Raúl while I stir the coffee.

Rose and Jack arrive shortly after and set out to do the same thing I did a moment ago.

They sit with me on the sofa.

'Emma was here a moment ago and didn't even say hello to me' I say.

'Well, she really hit hard with you,' Rose replies with a laugh.

'I don't like the way she looks at me.'

'Don't listen to her,' adds Jack.

I take a sip of the coffee and spit it out immediately in front of Jack and Rose's eyes.

'What's wrong with you?' asks Rose, without leaving her amazement.

'Don't drink the coffee. What was in the sugar bowl was not sugar, but salt' I warn them.

Rose, even with my warning, takes a small spoonful of coffee and tries it out.

'It's true!' she exclaims.

It's clear to me that Emma's evil has no limits. She must have switched from sugar to salt when I was distracted by the phone. I open all the doors of the kitchen cupboards and find a sugar bowl just like the one that contained the salt.

'This time Darel will know.'

'I'm going with you,' says Rose.

'There's no need, Rose. I can manage on my own. I'll be right back.'

I take the two sugar bowls and go straight down to Darel's office. I go in without knocking. Darel is on the phone and beckons me to sit down.

'Is there a problem, Daniela?'

Darel hangs up the phone, lies down on his chair and crosses his arms to listen to me.

'Look!' I exclaim. 'They are two sugar bowls that are exactly the same, right?' Darel nods his head. 'In one there's sugar and in the other, salt' I continue.

I give Darel the two sugar bowls and he checks inside.

'It was Emma,' he says with complete certainty. 'It's not the time she does it.'

'And it's not the first time he's tried to do something against me.'

Darel frowns. He doesn't understand what I just told him.

'What do you mean? 'He puts his elbows on the table.

'First was the discussion we had the day we shared Rose and, before I left for Spain, she changed my vaccines for bleach and I almost injected it into one of the dogs.'

Darel is speechless.

'I'm going to talk to her right now. One thing is to change sugar for salt or a simple discussion, and another very serious thing is to sabotage the vaccines.'

He snorts.

'I don't know if I can continue working under these conditions. I love this job, but I don't want to have anymore problems with Emma.'

'Don't worry. Go upstairs and enjoy your free time, I am going to put this clinic in order.'

Kayla comes up to tell us that Darel has called an urgent meeting in his office. Rose, Jack and I look at each other; we know perfectly well the reason for that meeting: the change of sugar bowl.

'A storm is brewing.'

Rose is always so creative.

'Well, let's go to the slaughterhouse,' adds Jack.

We are all in Darel's office. He is sitting in his chair and the rest of us are standing. I'm leaning against one of the walls.

'Good afternoon. I have called you because there has been some friction between some colleagues lately and in my clinic I want us all to get along, to be a team. I'm going to ask a question and I hope that the guilty party faces up to it. Here I have two identical sugar bowls. Good. Who had the absurd idea of bringing one of the sugar bowls with salt?'

Nobody answers. We look at each other. I'm almost sure it was Emma. I look at her. She's looking down at the floor.

'I see that it was nobody. I am not stupid and I know well who it was. I just want the person who did it to be able to take the blame. I also know that someone has changed the vaccines in Daniela's surgery for bleach. I know it was the same person both times. I'm going to give you a warning: at the slightest problem, I'll throw you all out.'

Kayla and Sarah are protesting against Darel's drastic measure. They are angry. Almost all of us are the same as them. It is clear that it is not because they are very upset and do not want to lose their jobs.

'Well, go to work. I'll call you one by one and talk in private.'

I'm about to leave Darel's office.

'Wait, Daniela. Close the door and sit down, please.'

Rose, Jack and Kayla are staring at me.

'I thought Emma would confess, but she didn't. I'm sorry. I'll talk to her later.'

'Thank you, Darel, and I'm sorry if I cause you too much trouble. If you wish, I can resign and we can avoid problems.'

'Not at all. It's not your fault. Relax and go back to work.'

I go back to the office where Rose and Jack's gossip is waiting for me, eager to know what I've talked to Darel about alone.

'So?' Rose is sitting at the desk.

'Darel tells me not to worry about work; that he knows it was Emma and that he'll talk to her later. I told him that, to avoid problems, it would be better to quit the job.'

'How?' Jack lets out a shout.

'As you heard, but Darel said no.'

'Well, I'm going to my office. There are patients waiting.'

Rose comes out after Jack and brings my patient and another patient into Jack's office. I feel like going out and getting home so I can rest.

There is still an hour to go and it seems that the minute hand has stopped. I deal with all the appointments I have for today and I relax sitting at my desk.

I finish writing some details of the patients on the computer.

I take my mobile phone out of my dressing gown pocket and look for Raúl's conversation. He's seen all the messages I've sent him all these days, because the double tick is blue, but he hasn't wanted to answer me.

I send him another message.

> *Please write to me. Tell me why you won't talk to me. What have I done to you? I miss you and I love you very much.*

I wait a few moments hoping that he will get on line and read my message. Nothing. He must be teaching.

Rose is taking me home.

'Have you finally entered the website I sent you to validate your driver's license and be able to buy a car?'

'No. I haven't had time. Maybe after Christmas.'

'Sounds good to me. There's no way you can have your own car and move around Sydney without having to depend on anyone.'

'You're right. In Madrid it was more comfortable to go by underground than by car. There is never a place to park in the centre and there are always traffic jams.'


I walk into my house. I thought that this moment would never come. I lie down on the bed and leave my bag and jacket on the floor. I'm exhausted. I'm not hungry. Between the problem at work and Raúl's problem, my stomach has closed.

I get out of bed and go to the shower. When the water falls warm on my body it helps me relax and think.

Luca knocks on the bathroom door.

'Come in' I say rolling up in a towel.

'How was your morning? Did you hear from Raúl?' he asks.

'Removing a small problem with the witch of Emma, who changed my sugar for salt, everything was fine. I don't know anything about Raúl. He doesn't answer my messages.'

'*Mamma mia*!' Luca's mouth is open. He looks at me in disbelief. I nod my head.

'You must be careful with that companion of yours,' he warns.

'I'm thinking of going back to Spain.'

'Why?'

'Because I am burdened with so many problems and I feel lonely.'

Luca is offended.

'And me?' he asks.

'Yes, I know I can count on you. But between the harpies of the dance classes, the senseless indifference of Raúl and Emma, the witch, I can't take it anymore.'

I feel like crying, but I hold back.

'You have to be strong. The harpies; don't pay attention to them. Raúl's thing will surely have a solution. And the witch in your job, you'll see how your boss will put her in her place.' Luca comforts me.

'Maybe you're right.'

I sigh.

'Well, shall I order something to eat?'

'Yes, although I'm not very hungry.'

Luca steps out of the bathroom and makes a phone call. I come out of the bathroom. I go to my room and put on a tank top with thin straps and a pair of shorts.


We are sitting on the sofa, eating the barbecue pizza Luca has ordered. Carol arrives pissed off. She sits down on the individual sofa and does nothing but complain about men.

'What happened to you?' asks Luca.

Carol looks at him.

'David didn't come to work today. He told me that he had a setback yesterday. I know what his problem was.'

'Maybe it's true what he told you.'

'He's with a girl from his school.'

'Don't get the wrong idea. Talk to him first.'

I just listen to the conversation between Luca and Carol while I eat the pizza.

'Lately he's been getting a lot of messages and he goes to the bathroom to talk on the phone. I am not here to waste time with a child.'

'Do what you think is best, but if you are wrong, don't come then crying.'

Carol gets up to eat and grabs a slice of pizza.

'Well, guys. I'm going to get some sleep; I have to be back at the clinic at nine at night.'

'Have a good rest,' says Luca.

'Rest, and I'll take you to work later.'

Carol is always so kind to me.

I get up from the sofa and go to the bedroom. I look at my mobile again. I still have no news from my Adonis. I am more and more worried. Our relationship has gone from passionate to cold.

A message from my mobile wakes me up. I take it from the table and look at it quickly in the hope that it will be Raúl's.

*Hello, daughter. How are you? I'm looking forward to seeing you. Kisses.*

*Hello, mum. I'm fine, with lots of work. This weekend I have duty and do not rest until Wednesday. How are you? Kiss.*

*All well. Your brother is stressed out about the exams. Your sister is already planning her wedding. Your grandmother is fine and your father, as always.*

> *I'm glad. Give my brother luck with his exams. Give my grandmother a big kiss. Tell my sister to be calm, she still has a lot of time left, and for you and dad, a big kiss and a big hug.*

> *A big kiss and hug to you from all of us.*

I wake up still dazed by the dream I have. I'm lazy to have to go back to work tonight. I would like to go out for a few drinks and forget about this terrible week for a while.

Why doesn't Raúl write to me? What have I done wrong? He used the word "girlfriend" when we ate together last Sunday. Everything was going well, even on Tuesday when he saw me, he was so affectionate. What must have happened inside the classroom to make him change his mind? I'm going to have to gather my courage and face the harpies.

They had something to do with it. I'm becoming more and more sure of that theory. On Tuesday they walked in behind Raúl and in the classroom they were very strange, more so than usual, and they left laughing out loud.

It's not my fault that Raúl chose me over one of them. It's not my fault, I didn't try to make him like me, he approached me. He approached me even before I knew it. The night of The Cuban Place I was not aware.

I have to move on, but not without solving this problem first. I have to face both the harpies and Raúl, even if it's in the next class, in front of all the students. I don't care.

I remember last weekend with tears in my eyes. I don't think it's fair that what was beginning to be a stable and formal relationship has ended overnight. I don't accept that.

Luca has gone out because he went to the beach with Victor, and Carol is still on the sofa lying down with the TV remote in her hand, changing the channel.

'Hello,' I say.

'Hello,' Carol answers in a broken voice.

As far as I can see she is still in a state between depressed and angry.

'Are you all right? Do you need anything?'

'I'm fine, Daniela. Thanks.'

'Well, I'm going to make some coffee.'

I go to the kitchen and prepare two cups, two teaspoons, the sugar bowl, a small jug of cold milk and the coffee maker on a tray.

I take everything very carefully and leave it on the small table in the living room in front of the sofa where Carol is.

'It smells good,' she says.

'Do you want some?' I ask.

Before she answers, I have already poured coffee and milk into the cup. Carol raises her head and looks at me.

'How many spoons do you want?'

'Two, thank you,' she answers.

She sits down and we drink the coffee together.

'Things with David are not going well' she confesses.

'I thought so, but I didn't want to bother you.'

'I think he's with another girl.'

'If you want some advice, you should talk to him before making any decisions.'

She nods her head and takes another sip of her coffee.

'I'll make dinner today,' she says.

'And what are you going to make?' I'm curious.

'A salad and grilled chicken. What do you think?'

'I think it's great. I'll help you.'

We get up from the sofa and take the tray to the kitchen. I wash the cups while Carol takes out everything we need to prepare our dinner.

'Luca isn't coming,' says Carol, looking at a message on her mobile. 'It will be you and me. Then I'll take you to work like I told you.'

'I wish I didn't have to work so I could stay with you and keep you company.'

'Don't worry. Maybe Luca is right and, before judging David, I should talk to him. I'll call him later, when I drop you off at the clinic.'

'Sounds great to me. You, who are a lawyer, will know better than anyone else that everyone is innocent until proven guilty.'

'That is true.'

We had dinner sitting at the kitchen table. I taste the grilled chicken that Carol has prepared. She has seasoned it with some sauces I don't know and they give it an exquisite touch.

She has dressed the salad with Greek sauce.

Carol leaves me in front of the clinic. I take the jacket, the bag and the rucksack with my personal belongings. I say goodbye to Carol and get out of the car. Jack comes walking on the pavement, I wait for him and we go up together.

'Good night, Daniela.'

'Night, Jack.'

Beth is getting ready to go out like the rest of the colleagues.

Jack and I wait in the entrance for everyone to come out and close the door.

'Coffee?' suggests Jack.

I nod my head.

We are sitting on the kitchen sofa quietly drinking the coffee. The truth is that being like this is not bad at all. There is no hustle and bustle of appointments and no annoying companions.

I can't stop thinking about Raúl. I look at my mobile phone every few minutes. I still hope that he will want to talk to me, that he will give me an explanation as to why he has decided to stay away from me.

'What are you thinking about?'

Jack is in front of me waving. I had not seen him.

'I'm sorry. I was thinking about a problem I had.'

'Emma?' he asks.

I deny with my head. I don't want to talk about it.

'Have you heard from your wife?' I change the subject.

'No. I hope that she thinks about it and comes back home or at least gives me an explanation as to why she has left.'

In the end, Jack and I are not that different. We have a fairly similar problem. His wife has left without explanation and Raúl has walked away from me, also without explanation.

In observation we have a shepherdess who had an emergency Caesarean yesterday and was very weak. I check on her. She is asleep. I look at the file. Henry gave her the last dose of acepromazine two hours ago. At two o'clock in the morning it's her turn for the next dose.

I add an alarm on my mobile phone.

I hope we have a good night. I'm exhausted from all the thinking and I haven't been getting much sleep these days.

*We have to talk.*

Raúl's message feeds my hope, but the words he used and how short it is, scare me.

*I am working.*

I don't want him to think that I'm desperate either, although, judging by the previous messages I've sent him, that's probably what he's thinking.

*I know. When can we meet?*

He wants to see me and my inner self jumps for joy. *"Don't get your hopes up"*, I tell her. Maybe he just wants to see me to make the breakup real. Well, I'll try to be positive.

> *I leave on Monday morning, but I have to come back in the afternoon. It will be best to meet after the Tuesday class.*

> *Perfect.*

I send a message to Carol and give her the news. She's happy for me. I'll tell Luca tomorrow, he's very busy today with his boyfriend and I don't want to spoil his evening.

'That smile?' asks Jack.

'A message I received.'

'I hope to hear from my wife soon,' he says, devastated.

'Surely.'

I give Jack a hug. At this moment it is what he needs most.

'I'm going to make some more coffee.'

I get up and take other cups out of the cupboard.

'I go to get the folding bed so we can get comfortable and we can watch some film. I brought some popcorn.'

I fall asleep on the folding bed while listening to Jack's film in the background. I think about Raúl's messages and I have the doubt if he wants to talk to fix what we have. I hope he will give me an explanation or tell me the reason for the indifference I have suffered on his part these days.

I sigh.

I am terrified that it might be to break up with me definitely. I don't want to.

I hope it's the first choice.

## Sunday, 10th December, 2017

Yesterday was a quiet day. There was no emergency. Jack and I spent the whole day talking about our problems and comforting each other.

We ordered Japanese food for lunch, which I invited it, and Jack ordered Italian food for dinner and he invited it.

Rose came in the afternoon; she had nothing to do and brought some chocolate cakes that we ate with tea. We laughed a lot with her and her stories in the supermarket.

Today we got up early because a mastiff arrived with a snake bite and we barely saved it, although we left it for observation until tomorrow to rule out any damage to the organism.

'Thank goodness the mastiff arrived on time,' I say.

'If they had arrived ten minutes later, the animal wouldn't be here now.' says Jack.

He's right.

'Coming to breakfast? I'm hungry.'

'I'm hungry too' he replies.

We sat down to eat the chocolate cereals that Jack brought. I brought *Cola Cao*. Jack has never tried it and I want him to know the typical things we have in Spain.

Jack was delighted with the *Cola Cao*. I bought it on the Internet. I paid eight dollars for only 400 grams, it's not great, but every now and then I feel like having things from my country and *Cola Cao* is one of them. I love it.

A ringing of the doorbell interrupts our delicious and peaceful moment. We leave breakfast halfway through and go down immediately.

There is a man at the door. He's holding a Yorkshire in his arms. Jack rushes to open the door. I accompany the man and the dog to the first examination room while Jack closes the door.

The dog is convulsing.

I try to keep the dog's neck as extended as possible, holding its head so that it can breathe.

Jack takes the data from the dog and the owner into the computer.

'Is this the first time this has happened to him?' asks Jack.

'Yes.'

'Have you been to this clinic before?'

'No, this is the first time. We moved to this neighbourhood only two months ago.'

Jack finishes filling in all the details about the animal and takes the phenobarbital out of the medicine cabinet. He injects it.

'We are going to keep him under observation for 24 hours to prevent this from happening again. We are also going to carry out several tests to rule out infection.'

'Whatever it takes,' says the man with great concern.

Jack checks on the vaccination card to make sure that the dog has all the necessary vaccinations.

'I see here that he has all his vaccinations up to date.'

'Yes, I have always had him vaccinated when I have been told to. He is also well dewormed,' adds the man.

'Well, don't worry. You can go in peace; we'll take good care of him here. If there is any news, we will call you.'

'Thank you very much.'

The man kisses the dog and shakes our hands. I walk the man to the door and go back to help Jack with the tests.

We test him and I take it to the lab. I look for the results of the test, while Jack takes the dog's temperature.

'His temperature is high. How did the tests come out?'

'Watch it yourself' I answer.

Jack looks closely at the results.

'Thank goodness the man brought the animal in on time. He has pyroplasmosis. I will call to report it.'

We supply the Yorkshire with the necessary medication and we'll put him up for observation.

'Breakfast is cold,' I say.

I drink the milk and wash the cup.

There's a knock at the door again. And again, we run down to the entrance.

A girl with a mongrel dog is at the door. She has a bite from another dog on her right rear leg. The mongrel is already a patient of this clinic.

The girl keeps looking at Jack, I think she likes him.

I go into the history and write down the injury she came for today and the treatment to be given.

Jack cleans the area of the bite and disinfects it. I take out the shaving machine, needle and thread and help him heal the wound. It is not too deep, but we had to give him four stitches.

The girl leaves very grateful for our work. We had to put an Elizabethan collar on the animal so that it would not lick its wound.

We went up to the kitchen; Jack heated his cup in the microwave and drank the milk with *Cola Cao*, which was more than cold.

'That girl with the mongrel dog I think she likes you. Jack turns red.'

'You think so?'

I nod.

'I think you should give yourself a chance. You can't be thinking about your wife all the time. If she's gone, you have to try and rebuild your life.'

'What if she shows up again?' he asks.

'If she comes back, tell her you want a divorce and move on.'

Jack gets sad and changes the subject.

'We've already had two emergencies in a row.'

'Yes, yesterday nothing and today two in less than two hours.' He asks.

'I hope that the afternoon will be quieter, that I will not rest until Wednesday.'

I sigh.

'It's true. It's my turn to rest tomorrow and Tuesday, and yours on Wednesday and Thursday,' he explains.

'Yes!' I exclaim.

'If you want, I can change your shift,' he suggests.

'Thank you, but no. I prefer to get used to the different breaks. It is not fair that you do not rest when it is your turn.'

'Relax. I'm used to it.'

'Thank you again.'

The animals under observation are calm thanks to the sedation that keeps them relaxed. Jack reports the hours at which they are given medication for the companions who will come tomorrow. The morning has passed quickly with the emergencies we have had.

'I will order fish and chips, which is very typical here for eating. It's my treat, what do you think?'

'I think it's very good. I'm already hungry' I answer.

While Jack calls on the phone, I take the opportunity to check that there is everything in the cabinets of the four consultations and the operating room. I replace gauze, bandages and disinfectants. I go back to the room where the animals are, they are still the same.

I take a look at my mobile phone, which has a blue light, letting me know that I have pending messages

I have a message from Charlie.

> *Hello, Daniela. I know you're working now. I propose to pick you up tomorrow morning and take you home. I'm sure you'll be tired and I'd like to take advantage of that time to talk and see you. Kiss.*

> *Hello. I'm indeed on duty. Thanks for the offer, but my partner Jack is taking me home tomorrow.*

I'm lying; Jack and I haven't talked about taking me home tomorrow. I think it's better to avoid Charlie for the time being. I'm afraid it's just a pretext to abuse me like he tried the last time we were together.

> *I would like to see you.*

> *I have two days off: Wednesday and Thursday. We can see each other on one of those days. What do you think?*

> *Okay, perfect. I'll call you on Wednesday.*

> *Okay.*

I put my mobile phone back in my dressing pocket. The doorbell rings. This time it's the delivery man, who arrives with the food.

'I hope you like it. I don't know if that's typical in Spain.'

'No, it's more typical in England. In Spain we are more of a potato omelette.'

'I ordered the typical fish from here, I don't know if you know it. It's called Barramundi. It's a bit more expensive, but it's worth it.'

'Yes, I know it. Carol, the owner of the house where I live, baked it once. It was very good.'

We eat the delicious fish sitting on the kitchen sofa watching a comedy show on TV.

I take the potatoes in my hand, one by one, and dip them in ketchup.

'I'll have to go to the gym. With so much food I'm going to get as fat as a seal.'

'You'd look pretty anyway.'

'You're a liar.' I recriminate.

I make some coffee and we have it lying down on the sofa, watching the film that has just started.

They ring the bell again. And again we have to run down the stairs. I am going to stumble and fall down one of those stairs. It's not the first time I've tripped and fallen on a staircase. It happened to me several times in my maternal grandparents' village house.

We have a dog with clear signs of poisoning on the table in the consulting room.

'We are going to induce vomiting,' I inform.

All attempts to make the dog vomit are failed.

'We're going to insert a probe.'

To do this, we first anaesthetise the animal. Jack brings in an endotracheal tube and I carefully insert it under the watchful eye of Jack and the dog's owner. I then insert the gastric tube.

Jack places some pillows on the animal's bottom so that its head is lower than the rest of its body and so that the liquid comes out of its stomach more easily.

I introduce saline solution through the tube and retrieve it, several times until the liquid from the stomach shows toxic presence.

'Well, I think that's about it' I say with satisfaction.

'Congratulations, Daniela.' Jack puts his hand behind my back.

'Thank you very much.'

The dog's owner is calmer.

'You're welcome. It's our job,' I reply.

There's nothing better in the world than having your work recognized. Helping animals is my vocation and I don't think I could do anything else in life.

'Let's wait a little while for her to wake up from the anaesthesia and you can go home.'

The owner nods.

I take advantage of this and ask him a few questions to find out how the dog was poisoned and leave it written in his record. I see that he is a regular patient of Emma's.

After an hour we say goodbye to the man and his dog from the entrance and return to the kitchen. Jack makes more coffee. The film we were watching is over and they are showing 6 Below: Miracle on the Mountain, a film I cry with every time I watch it.

Carol calls me on the phone.

'Good afternoon, Dani. How are you?'

'Good, now I'm resting a bit.'

'A lot of emergencies?'

'None yesterday, we seemed to be at home. Today we have already had a few.'

It's weird that Carol calls me at work. I think it's the first time she's done it. What will she want?

'How are you? Everything OK at home?'

'Yes.'

That short answer makes me suspicious.

'Seriously?'

I'm trying to get information out of her.

'Well... Someone came asking for you this morning.'

'Who? Raúl?'

'No, it wasn't Raúl.'

'So?' I'm starting to worry.

'I don't know, Luca took care of him. I didn't want to tell you anything so as not to worry you. I was going to tell you tomorrow. Don't tell him that I told you,' she explains.

'Did you see his face?'

'No. I was in the kitchen and only heard them talking.'

I'm getting more and more nervous. Maybe Emma is trying to find out where I live; or maybe the harpies. At least I know it wasn't Charlie, because Carol would recognise him straight away.

'What did they talk about?'

'Well, I think you'd better discuss it tomorrow with Luca.'

I guess she tells me that because she doesn't want to talk about it anymore. Maybe she's afraid of screwing up.

'Okay, Carol. See you tomorrow. Kiss.'

Carol hangs up the phone and I'm left with a bad feeling in my body. I don't think that man who asked for me comes with good intentions. Tonight I don't think I can sleep.

I doubt whether or not to call Luca and have him clear up these doubts that are eating me up inside. I can't. Carol told me that she told me about the mystery man without him knowing. I can't betray her like this.

I will have to wait until tomorrow to find out. I think the hours will go on forever.

'Is there something wrong with you?'

Jack has noticed my concern. It's because I can't stop wandering around the kitchen from one side to the other.

'Carol called me and said that someone came to the house asking for me.'

'What's the problem?'

'Carol told me that it was a stranger. She doesn't know who asked for me. I'm afraid Emma is trying to figure out where I live.'

I hear myself talking and I don't believe what I'm saying. This is not a mystery film or a murder film. This is real life.

Jack laughs.

'She may have traded you the sugar for the salt or the vaccines, but I don't think she hired a bully, really.'

What Jack says makes a lot of sense.

'You're right.'

Another patient arrives and, during the time we take to attend to the cat in labour, I forget the call I received from Carol. The poor cat is having a difficult labour. We do an ultrasound to see that everything is fine.

I go into her history to see how the pregnancy has gone during this time.

Everything has been fine.

She does not dilate and Jack decides to induce labour. We put an IV in her leg and wait for the medication she has been given to take effect.

Little by little the kittens are born. It's wonderful to help a living being to be born, in this case three. Some tears of emotion come out of my eyes without asking permission.

Jack and I left the operating room and left the cat's owners alone. They love her as if she was their own family. I think that, if everyone was like that, there would be no abandoned animals. I pray every time I see news of abuse and abandonment.

We check that both the cat and her kittens are in good health and we discharge them to go and rest. It has been a difficult time.

'Good job, Daniela.' Jack congratulates me.

'Thank you. It's all thanks to you, who are a good teacher.'

'You're a great student.'

Jack makes my cheeks red.

I go up to the observation room and check the animals. I give them the medication they need and write it down in their records. I am sorry to see them locked up in the cages, but it is for their own good.

'Another coffee?' asks Jack.

'Yes, thank you.'

While he is making coffee, I send a message to Luca.

> *Hi, Luca. How are you?*

He answers a few minutes later.

> Bene. *And you? How's that duty going?*

> *Yesterday better than today. How are you doing with your boyfriend? How was dinner?*

I try not to let him think that I'm writing to him about whom he's gone to ask about me.

> Molto bene. *He took me to dinner and then to dance.*

> *I'm so happy for you.*

> *I don't have any classes tomorrow morning. If you want, I can get up early and have breakfast together.*

I suppose Luca's suggestion has something to do with the mystery man.

> *Okay. I'm fine with that.*

> *Kisses, Dani. See you in a few hours.*

> *Kisses.*

Just over 10 hours left to finish the shift. I take the coffee that Jack has prepared.

'What would you like for dinner?' I ask. 'Do you want to try Spanish food?' I add.

'Yes. I've never tried it.'

'I'm going to call a restaurant where I went to eat the other day with Darel.'

'Did I hear right? With Darel?' Jack looks at me with his eyes wide open.

'He asked me two days in a row. The first day I made up an excuse, but the next day I didn't know what to make up anymore and I accepted his invitation.'

'And how did it go?'

'Well, better than I thought. He has been very kind and respectful to me. I hope Emma doesn't find out. She can scream at the top of her lungs.'

'What?' Jack lets out a scream.

I nod my head in concern.

'Now do you understand why I thought the man who came to my house was coming from her?'

'Yes, now I understand. Be very careful. I think she needs psychiatric care.'

'I'm going to call the restaurant.'

I get up from the sofa and take my mobile out of my pocket. I have a message to be read.

> *Hello, Daniela. We can eat together on Wednesday. If it suits you.*

I don't like Raúl's formal message at all. He used to call me "princess" or "beautiful" and say goodbye with "I love you".

> *Sounds good to me. Where shall we meet?*

> *How about I pick you up at your house around 1:30?*

> *Yes, I'll be ready at that time.*

I call the restaurant and order dinner. They tell me it will take thirty to forty-five minutes to get here.

There is a knock at the door. It's not dinner. It's another patient.

'What an emergency day we have had today,' I say.

Jack looks at me and raises his eyebrows.

We attend to the snake bite of the Dalmatian. Luckily, the dog's owners managed to take a photo of the snake. Jack is an expert in reptiles and recognised immediately what antidote the animal needed.

When we are saying goodbye to the owners at the entrance of the clinic, the delivery man arrives with the food. He is Spanish. We talk a little bit in front of Jack who doesn't understand us.

I pay the delivery man and go up to the kitchen, prepare the table with the necessary cutlery for dinner. Jack has stayed downstairs to cover today's urgency in the Dalmatian's history.

For dinner I've ordered a table of assorted hors d'oeuvres. I prepare everything at the table.

When Jack arrives he is surprised.

'I hope you like it.'

'I'm sure I will' he answers with a big smile.

Jack tastes the Iberian ham.

'It's delicious!' he exclaims.

'It's a delicacy.'

I also ordered a small *paella* for two.

'In the Mediterranean, this is the best known.'

I serve him two spoons. He tests it.

'*Paella*! I'd seen it, but I'd never tasted it,' he explains.

'I hope it's not the last one.'

'You can be sure of that. You've convinced me.'

'Of what?' I wonder.

'That my next holiday will be in Spain.'

'You're going to love it.'

'I'm sure I will, but you have to promise me one thing.'

Jack has a mischievous smile.

'What is it?' I ask frowning.

'That you will be my guide.'

Jack extends his arm and offers me a handshake to close our deal.

'I accept.'

We finish dinner. My stomach is full. I lie down on the sofa. I am tired.

'I'll bring the folding bed so you can rest.'

'Thank you.'

Jack comes and opens the bed, and puts the sheets and the duvet on it.

I lie down on the bed. I think about who will be the mystery man. I hope that tomorrow Luca will tell me who he is or what he looks like. Maybe he's left a phone number so I can call him. Who will he be? What will he want?

My inner self is pensive, sitting on a chair. *"Maybe, Emma does have something to do with it,"* she says. I'm nodding in agreement.

'Let's hope tonight is a quiet night,' Jack says.

It takes me out of my dark thoughts.

'Yes, I hope so. I am very tired.'

'I'm going to put on a film. I hope you don't mind.'

'No, not at all. The TV doesn't bother me to sleep.'

I take a last look at my mobile phone and the messages. Oh, Raúl! You're in my thoughts and in my heart. You don't know the damage you're doing to me with your indifference and with your insulting messages.

I am plunged into a deep and agonizing sleep in which everything I have experienced this week is mixed into my thoughts as a slide show.

## Monday, 11th December, 2017

Jack wakes me up.

'They're ringing the bell.'

I rub my eyes with my hands and blink too much trying to wake up.

I yawn.

'Come on, lazy.'

Jack goes down to open. I wash my face in the kitchen sink and go downstairs.

I look at the clock.

It's a quarter to two in the morning.

The dog has an internal fracture in its right hind leg. We take him to the X-ray room and take several X-rays in different positions.

We had to put a muzzle on him because he tried to bite us a couple of times out of pain.

The X-rays show that there is a very oblique fracture of tibia.

'Look, depending on the condition of the fracture, we have to operate urgently,' says Jack to the animal's owner as he shows him the X-rays.

'I'm going to prepare the operating theatre.'

I leave the surgery and prepare all the surgical instruments that we will need during the procedure.

Jack and the owner of the animal enter the operating theatre with the dog. I accompany the owner to the waiting room and return to the operating theatre.

'Have you checked the dog's history? Any allergies, or problems with anaesthesia before?' I ask.

Jack shakes his head while wearing his sterile gown, cap and gloves.

First, I place the mask on his muzzle so that he is relaxed and, after shaving the right front leg, I place an IV and slowly give him general anaesthesia.

During the surgery, after reducing the fracture, we use two compression screws between the two fragments to provide more stability and rigidity to the implant system. We then apply a 2.4-2.7 mm screw locking plate to fix the bone. This plate helps us in this case, as, in the area closest to the fracture line, Jack uses extra fine screws so as not to damage the bone, and in the areas further away from the fracture, more robust screws.

The result has been very satisfactory. It has been an hour and a half since we started working. I am sweating. I need a shower.

I leave the operating theatre and go to the waiting room. The gentleman gets up immediately from the sofa.

'Everything OK?' asks the nervous man.

'Yes, fortunately everything went very well. We had to place a plate along the tibia and fix it with some screws to ensure that the bone welds well.'

'Thank you, doctor.'

'There is nothing to thank for. We have done it with pleasure. We are going to leave the dog for observation and on Tuesday morning you can come and pick it up.'

'Whatever it takes,' said the man.

'Tomorrow you will be told what care you will need until you have to come for a checkup.'

After dismissing the man and taking the dog to the observation room, Jack throws himself on the sofa.

'I am not sleepy. I'm going to make some coffee,' he says.

'Well, I'm going to take a shower, I need it urgently.'

'Will you like some coffee?'

Jack has got up from the sofa and is in the kitchen preparing a coffee machine.

'Yes, thanks. I won't be long.'

I go down the stairs and go to my locker where I have my rucksack. I take it and go upstairs again and go to the shower.

I look at the clock on the wall. The hands tell me that it is past four o'clock in the morning.

'I'm going to try to sleep for a while' I say lying on the folding bed.

'Me too,' answers Jack.


The bell wakes us up with a start. I have the sound of that bell stuck in my head. I'm starting to hate it. The morning companions are at the door.

Jack and I pick up the folding bed and the blankets and put them away. We take a last look at the animals admitted and leave the time of the checkup written on their charts.

'I'm taking you home,' says Jack.

'I thank you. I'm exhausted.'

'Yes, this weekend has been exhausting. What we haven't worked on Saturday, we did on Sunday.'

'Yes.'

I breathe.

Jack parks in front of my house.

'Rest.'

'I'll try.'

'Do you want me to work today?' he asks.

No, thank you. I can do it.'

I get out of the car. I say goodbye to Jack with my hand and go inside. It smells good, like toast and coffee.

'Good morning.'

Luca is in the kitchen and has a mega breakfast on the counter. There's everything. Toast, butter, jam, coffee, orange juice, bacon, scrambled eggs and fruit.

'You've made a point with breakfast.'

'Yes,' he answers with a broad smile.

'Is Carol gone?'

'No. She's in the room finishing getting dressed.'

I sit down on the stool and start eating breakfast. Luca sits down in front of me. Carol leaves the room and quickly makes herself some toast.

She's dressed in a tube skirt suit and black jacket, and a white shirt. She's wearing black low heeled shoes. She has made a ponytail that makes her taller and thinner. She is always radiant.

'Don't you sit down with us for breakfast?' I ask.

'I can't, I'm in a hurry. I have a trial at nine o'clock and I'm meeting my client at eight o'clock in the office to discuss the details.'

'Have a good day.'

'I hope so,' she answers from the door.

I feel Luca nervous, as if he was trying to tell me something and didn't dare. I can sense what he's thinking, because Carol told me everything yesterday, but I have to hide it because I don't want to look like a tinker.

'Are you OK?' I ask.

'Yes... Well...' he stammers. I frown and Luca stops eating and interlaces his fingers, nervous. 'Well... I just have something to tell you.'

I look at him pretending that I already know what it is.

'Tell me.'

'Well, yesterday afternoon a man came looking for you.'

'A man? Charlie?'

'No, not Charlie. A dark man, tall and very handsome.'

'Raúl?' I ask with excitement.

'If it was Raúl I would have told you. No, I don't know him.'

I scratch my head and put my elbow on the table and my hand on my chin.

'Well... I don't know who that could be.'

'I've never seen him before. He said he'd be back today and asked me where you work.'

'Did you tell him?' I ask, upset.

'No, of course not.'

'That rules out Emma as a suspect,' I say.

'Emma? The nutcase from your job? What's she got to do with this?'

Luca stirs in the chair without understanding why I have named the witch of work.

'The other day, when I went to lunch with Darel, she saw us leave together and, given the history she has, I thought she might have been the one who sent someone to find out where I live' I explain.

'Ah.'

'But if she asked you where I work, it can't be her.'

I think about it and discard all the suspects on my list as I go to bed. I need to sleep and rest. And, above all, to stop thinking for a few hours about the man who has come to fetch me.

I set an alarm on my mobile phone for 12:45. It tells me that it will ring in four hours and fifty minutes.


The alarm tells me that I have to get up. I hate it. I don't feel like getting up. I'm starting to regret not accepting Jack's offer; if I had, I'd be in bed all day.

I hurry to take a quick shower, get dressed and go to the kitchen to make a sandwich.

Bus number 379 runs at 13:24 from the O'Brien Street stop.

I'm sitting in the seats at the end of the bus listening to *Pablo Alborán* and his *No vaya a ser*. How right their lyrics are. They make me feel identified on many occasions.

I can't stop thinking about what Carol and Luca have told me. I feel afraid that someone might be following me to hurt me, although I don't really know why. So far I haven't hurt anyone, although I have made a few enemies without looking for it.

It's 13:45 when I enter the clinic door. Kayla is the first thing I see, always with a smile that lights up the whole reception.

I greet her and go straight to my locker. I leave my bag and put on my dressing coat. I put the phone in my right pocket.

I go up to the kitchen where Darel, Henry and Sarah are having coffee and chatting about what they have done on the weekend. When they see me, they stop talking and ask me how our duty has been.

I tell them all the details we've had. For a moment they don't believe the emergencies we had yesterday, they think I'm playing a joke on them. *"I wish it had been a joke,"* protests my inner self.

Rose arrives with the sheet for today's scheduled appointments.

'We're going to have a relaxed day today,' she says, showing me the sheet.

'Thank goodness. Yesterday we had a terrible day and I hardly slept at all.'

'You know that there are appointments that I can attend to without any problem, in case you feel very tired at any time.'

'Thank you, Rose. You are always so kind.'

We go down the stairs and enter the examination room. The first patient is already in the waiting room. Rose brings him in.

It is an easy appointment. I just have to give a cat a vaccination. Rose gives me the needle and I give it to the cat without any problem. I leave it written on the vaccination card of the Siamese as well as on the history.

In between appointments, Rose tells me what she did yesterday.

'I went to the beach with a friend and we had lunch at the Pavilion.'

'I'm so jealous!' I exclaim jokingly.

'Was yesterday that bad?'

'You can't imagine. The convulsion of a Yorkshire, which was the first time he came, and we had to do a history. We kept him under observation until this morning. He had pyroplasmosis. Then another dog came in with a bite from another dog. And we still hadn't finished our breakfast. Later another poisoned dog arrived. We had to probe him because we tried to induce vomiting, without success. A cat about to give birth also came; we had to induce her labour. And, as if that wasn't enough, a Dalmatian with a snake bite arrived. Luckily, the owners were able to take a photo of it, and Jack, who i didn't know he was a reptile expert, recognised it right away and injected it with the antidote.'

'Well, you've had quite a day.'

'Wait, it doesn't end there.'

'Huh?' Rose raised an eyebrow.

'In the early hours of the morning we had to operate on another dog because of a closed and oblique fracture of the tibia. I suppose he will continue to be under observation. We told the owner to come tomorrow to pick him up.'

Rose is speechless and I nod my head raising my eyebrows.

The afternoon passes slowly. I am very tired. Rose does half my work for me. That helps me and I can finally go up to the kitchen and prepare a well loaded black coffee. The patients have noticed my tiredness and that doesn't look good.

The mobile phone vibrates a couple of times. I take it out of my dressing coat pocket and look at what new things it has to offer, without any hope that my Adonis will write to me to tell me that he loves me.

> *Hello, Dani. That strange man has come here again. Carol opened the door and asked her if she could give him your work address.*

Luca's message worries me. I also have a message from Carol.

> *Hello, Daniela. The same man from yesterday came back.*

First, I'm going to answer Luca, and then Carol.

> *Hello, Luca. I hope Carol didn't say anything to him. I don't know if she's with you now or not, because she just sent me a message also telling me the same thing as you.*

*Carol went out right after that man went out and I'm home.*

> *I'm starting to get scared.*

*I think it's someone who wants to see you. He didn't seem like a psychopath or a rapist.*

> *But I am uneasy anyway.*

*I understand you. Well, I won't keep you any longer. See you later. A kiss. Ciao.*

I say goodbye to Luca and open Carol's conversation.

> *Hello, beautiful. Luca wrote to me almost at the same time as you to tell me the same.*

*Ah. Well, he must have told you that he asked me where you work. Of course, I told him I couldn't give him that information. He seemed like a man who was worried about finding you.*

> *As I told Luca, I'm scared.*

> *Do you want me to go and get you?*

> *Thank you. Rose will take me. Don't worry about it.*

> *Well, Dani. I'm going into an emergency meeting at the firm. We'll talk in the evening.*

> *Kisses.*

I drink the coffee in one sip and prepare another well loaded one to take to the office and a coffee with milk for Rose. For helping me, she has not been able to rest all afternoon.

I pleasantly surprise Rose when I bring her the cup of coffee I have prepared for her. She deserves it for being a good companion and, above all, a good person.

'Thank you.' She gives me a hug.

'They don't deserve it. You deserve this cup and many other things.' Rose can't stop smiling.

'What about you? You're worried about something.'

I'm sitting in my desk chair.

'A stranger came to my house yesterday and today asking for me and I don't know who it is.'

'I'm sure it's someone unimportant.' Rose tries to soften the situation.

'Maybe.'

I sigh.

'You'll see.'

'You know, I thought Emma had sent someone to my house to find out where I live, but when the mystery man asked for my work address, I immediately dismissed her.'

Rose looks at me in puzzlement.

'Emma is a bit strange, but I don't see her coming to that, really.'

'Even so, I'm afraid.'

'I'm still scared. I'll take you home and wait for you to come in to make sure no one is waiting for you.'

'Thank you.'

I hold out my hands and squeeze hers tightly. Now more than ever I need to know who my real friends are and who are not. And even though I know little about Rose, I know that she is one of those people who give everything to others.

I look at the clock. There are two hours left in this long working day. It is overwhelming. I want to get home now and relax on the sofa while I have a light dinner and stop thinking about absurd things.

I think I'm starting to get a little paranoid.

Rose is cutting the nails of a cat and I, meanwhile, am writing down in the histories of previous patients the reason for today's consultation and the solution to it.

'It's almost nine o'clock,' Rose says.

'Finally' I answer with a sigh.

'I'll take you home, as I promised.'

'Thank you, Rose.'

I turn off the computer, close the office and take the cups to the kitchen; I scrub them and put them in the cupboard.

I go down and take my bag from my locker and leave my dressing coat.

We say goodbye to our colleagues and go downstairs.

'Daniela!'

I hear my name. I look around in fear that this mystery man has discovered where I work.

It's Charlie! He's walking up the pavement.

'Hi, Charlie. What are you doing here?'

'I couldn't wait until Wednesday.'

'I see, but I'm going home now.'

'I'll take you there.'

'Thank you. My friend Rose is taking me.'

'Please,' he begs.

I look at Rose. She nods her head.

'Well, okay' I accept.

I say goodbye to Rose and from a distance she gestures for me to call her when I get home. I say yes with my lips.

'Thank you for agreeing. I really wanted to see you.'

You're welcome. I think it was convenient to wait for a while after what happened.'

'Yes, you are right.'

We walked to his car. I am on the alert in case he tries to overreach like last time, although I see him very changed.

'Please, get in.'

Charlie opens the car door to let me in.

'Thank you.'

I sit down and fasten my seat belt. Charlie goes around the front of the car and gets in.

'Can I invite you to dinner?'

'No, maybe some other time. I'm looking forward to getting home.'

'Please' he insists. 'We have a lot to talk about.'

'I just want to get home. Another day, better.'

Charlie changes the expression on his face.

'Well, I won't insist anymore. I don't want you to be angry with me again.'

He seems to have understood.

'Good.'

At this time of day there is never too much traffic, which helps the car ride to be brief.

'Well, here we are' he announces.

'Thank you, but there was no need. My friend lives near here.'

'Thank you for not running away and letting me drive you to your house.'

Deep down I feel sorry for Charlie. He has always been good to me except for that day. I think he deserves a second chance.

Charlie gets out of the car and walks over to my side and opens the door.

'By the way, how did it go in Spain?'

'Not too well. Going to bury someone is not pleasant.'

'I understand.'

'Well, I'll call you on Wednesday and we'll schedule a meeting, but as friends.'

'Yes, yes. I don't want to lose you again. I had to go to the psychologist.'

'Why?' I'm surprised.

'I'll be honest with you,' we sat down on the kerb of the door. I look at the sky. The moon is waning and you can only see half of it. It looks like my relationship with Raúl. I feel that it is waning and that one day only the shadow of the little we have lived together will remain. 'I fell in love with you from the very moment I met you' he confesses.

'I don't know what to say.'

'Don't say anything. I understand that it was crazy, but I haven't been able to sleep since the day I tried to hit on you. The people around me realised that something was not right and suggested that I go to a psychologist. Since then I understood that you can't force things. That if something is about to happen, it will.'

'I'm glad you understood that.'

'I was very jealous of the boy who danced with you at The Cuban Place.'

Another one who remembers what happened that night, except for me.

'I'm the only one who doesn't remember that moment.'

'Seriously?'

'I promise. I don't know how you can be jealous of someone that even I don't remember.'

I omit the fact that he is my dance teacher with whom I had a torrid affair that was frustrated by something I still don't know.

'Because I'm a fool, now I understand.'

'Well, don't worry. Now you are in the hands of experts and that will help you.'

'This has never happened to me before. But I saw those blue eyes through the rear view mirror and I became obsessed.'

'Well. Let's leave that topic. I'm going to go and rest now. I've slept a little over four hours.'

'Okay.'

I say goodbye to him with a kiss on the cheek. I get up, take the keys to my bag and go into the house.

Seeing him in that state broke my heart. He looked defeated. He was badly groomed and his hair was dishevelled. Nothing like when I met him at the airport.

I take out my mobile phone and send a message to Rose, just as I promised.

> *Rose, I've arrived safely. See you tomorrow.*

*Okay, have a nice rest.*

Carol and Luca are lying on the sofa.

'Good night' I say.

'Night, Dani. Did you have dinner?' asks Carol.

'No, and I'm not hungry.'

'I made *cannelloni*. They're in the oven,' says Luca.

'Thank you, but I'm not hungry.'

Carol gets up from the sofa and comes towards me.

'Are you okay?'

'No, I'm not. I'm worried.'

Luca comes towards us and we sit down at the kitchen bar. Carol makes coffee.

'Are you worried about the man who came?' asks Luca.

'Yes, I have a bad feeling.'

'Don't worry, Dani. You'll see that it's nothing important.'
There's a knock at the door.
'I'm coming.'

I get up from my stool and go to the entrance. Maybe Charlie forgot to tell me something or I forgot something in his car.

I open the door with my head down. I look up and there he is. My breathing has accelerated and my heart is racing.

I stay petrify, and my mouth is open. I can't believe my eyes. I am not able to blink or articulate a word.

This must be a mirage or a nightmare because of the lack of sleep. It... may... not. My inner self is standing with its eyes wide open and its mouth reaching to its feet, reflecting perfectly my state.

He is here.
At my door.
In my house.
In my life.

*to be continued...*

# Acknowledgements

I want to first of all thank the Olivo Ramos family, who have been with me since the beginning, it is something that I will never forget. Raquel, Ángel, Helena and Alex, I always carry you in my thoughts and in my heart.

Ramos de Olivo Ediciones extended his hand to me and helped me in the publication process when I was lost and did not know what to do. Step by step, I have grown thanks to you.

Raquel, you are always on the other end of the phone when I need you. To talk about corrections or simply to have a friend listen to me in the most difficult moments.

I want to thank Nere Pérez for her patience with the covers, they are always perfect and also that beautiful layout that leaves no one indifferent. THANK YOU!

Thanks to Emma Sheridan for the translation. Although an ocean separates us and several hours apart, we always find that moment to chat for a while and answer questions. I hope to continue counting on you for that adventure and many more. THANK YOU SO MUCH!

Printed in Great Britain
by Amazon